ANGELS IN THE CITY

GARRETT LEIGH

Cover Art: Garrett Leigh @ Black Jazz Design

Editing: Sue Laybourn @ No Stone Unturned

Proofing: Annabelle Jacobs. Con Riley

PRAISE FOR GARRETT LEIGH

FOREWORD

Many thanks to Nikolai for the Russian sensitivity read. I so enjoyed learning about the *yolkas* of your childhood and what they meant to you.

1

The start of the festive season had always been the bane of Jonah Gray's life. Or at least for as long as he'd been old enough to attend the annual winter ball his parents hosted for the charity foundation attached to their city law firm. He didn't even work for Gray & Gray anymore, hadn't done since he'd quit his postgraduate internship four years ago, and yet here he was, flapping around at the last minute, carrying the same disquiet and anxiety he had at sixteen.

Calm down. If they try and pair you off with Edward again, just tell them you've changed your mind about being gay. Tell them you're sleeping with Lily.

The thought made Jonah laugh as much as it would Lily Dawson, his long-time BFF and partner-in-crime, but his amusement did nothing to make the prospect of the long evening ahead of him any less daunting. He loved his parents...mostly, and he was proud of the charity they'd created with their ridiculous wealth, but Christ, no one had warned him being single and gay would be no less pressured than if he'd been straight. *"You can't cavort around the city forever, Jonah. It's time to grow up."*

Nice. As if founding his own advertising agency and working eighteen-hour days to get it off the ground hadn't been enough. Now he had to attach himself to one of the three queer bachelors his parents had deemed a suitable match and make a happy gay family just to satisfy other people.

Jonah fiddled with his bow tie one last time and stepped out of his glass office. As usual, he was the last to leave. Only a solitary member of the cleaning crew was there to wish him goodnight.

"Have a good evening, Mr. Gray," he said.

Jonah nodded. "You too, Curtis. There are leftover cupcakes in the lounge, and coffee in the pot. Please help yourself. Take the cupcakes home if you wish."

"Thank you, Mr. Gray."

"You're welcome." Jonah left his company offices behind and headed for the lifts that would take him to his waiting car. His legs felt heavy and he'd have given anything to bypass the limo and take a cab home. Even a night alone with his left hand was preferable to the corporate bullshit he was about to endure. Add in the matchmaking he was fairly sure his mother had already started weeks ago, and he was pretty much ready to throw himself in front of the next London bus.

Drama queen.

Without doubt. And it was out of character for Jonah. On a normal day, he prided himself on his cool composure. Of his ability to steer any ship in any crisis and guide it safely to dry land, but the annual G&G ball unsettled him like nothing else ever could.

"...come on," the older man crooned. *"It's just a quick fuck. I won't tell anyone, not even your mother."*

Jonah shuddered. Nine years had passed since he'd wrestled those groping hands out of his trousers, but every time this night came around on his calendar, he was right back there, pressed against a wall, choking on the scent of fear and expensive cologne.

So stop thinking about it. Maybe he won't be there this year and you can quaff champagne and canapés in peace. And in any case, he was just fucking handsy. Lily's had worse taking the Tube.

That wasn't entirely accurate, but the lift arrived, and the muted *ding* broke into the thoughts Jonah usually kept under control. He squared his shoulders and stepped into the empty elevator. His reflection distracted him and he couldn't deny he looked good in his Armani tux. Black and white suited his auburn hair and green eyes, but *Christ,* wasn't cataloguing his features in a mirror the worst kind of cliché?

Jonah turned away from himself and refocused on Curtis, tracking the old man as he moved the vacuum cleaner around the offices of Flash Gray, navigating his way past the vomit of festive decorations Jonah had allowed his staff to put up that afternoon. There wasn't a bauble out of place in the red and gold colour scheme—the benefit of keeping his creative team close. Jonah wasn't sure he could've handled the chaos of tinsel the app development firm in the offices next door had gone with. It was enough to make his eyeballs twitch as the lift doors began to close.

Hurried footsteps startled him. Jonah blinked, gaze still fixed on Curtis. He was in Jonah's office, pushing the vacuum cleaner around. The footsteps belonged to someone else—someone with an expensive wristwatch, and elegant fingers that forced the lift doors open.

A tall figure stepped inside, almost shoulder-barging Jonah out of the way. Jonah stepped back and caught a lungful of clean cotton and musk. And then his vision filled with a long, lean streak of a man who was the epitome of every fantasy Jonah had ever had. Broad-shouldered, with a dark, unshaven jaw, and gold-flecked eyes that swam with wry amusement.

"Apologies," the man said with the barest hint of an accent Jonah couldn't place. "I did not mean to make you stumble."

"You didn't, but call out next time and I'll hold it for you. There's no need to run like a crazy person."

The man's lips twitched. Jonah stared at them, his blood heating in ways he was sorely unprepared for, especially tonight. He forced himself to look away and press the button for the ground floor again. "This good for you? Or are you getting off somewhere else?"

"It is good."

Jonah nodded and fixed his gaze straight ahead again, trying to ignore the presence of the sinfully attractive man beside him. He had to have come from the app company next door, but Jonah was one hundred percent certain he was either a visitor, or brand new. He wasn't a regular employee—he couldn't be. The app company kept odd hours sometimes, but so did Jonah, and there was *no way* this man had been coming and going from the top floor of this building without Jonah noticing.

In fact, without *everyone* noticing and talking about it, because whoever the man was, there was no red-blooded human alive who wouldn't agree he was hot enough to stop traffic.

Jonah snuck another glance at him, taking in his sharp

features and unshaven jaw. His rich, brown hair was unstyled, and had a slight wave to it, the kind of tousle that made him look as though he'd just got out of bed after a long night of—

The lift jolted. Jonah sucked in a sharp breath and darted a quick glance down, checking the warmth blooming in his gut hadn't travelled too far south, then zeroed in on the control panel of the lift. It was frozen between floors and the lift wasn't moving. "Damn. Are we stuck?"

"Maybe." The handsome stranger reached across Jonah and pressed a few buttons. Nothing happened. "Has this happened before?"

"In this building? Never. You don't work here then?"

Smooth. As if that's relevant right now.

"I started today," the man replied absently, his attention still trained on the control panel. "No one warned me that you had Soviet technology here too."

Soviet. Russian. The man's accent solidified and more inappropriate heat pulsed through Jonah. He tempered it with a heavy dose of their reality. They were trapped in a lift of a building where everyone had gone home. Only a single security officer remained, and Jonah was fairly sure he'd be asleep by now, dozing in front of his console by the front door, like he always was when Jonah left in the evenings. "I doubt these lifts are Soviet-made. This building is twenty years old."

"I was joking, no?"

"Oh."

"It's okay. I am not often funny."

The glint in the Russian man's eyes made it hard to tell if he was still being humorous. A grin warmed Jonah's face, but he kept it small. "I'm not known for my hilarity either. Is there a call button we can press?"

"There's an alarm button, and a phone number. The alarm seems a little…"

"Unnecessary?"

"Yes. Unnecessary."

"And there's no one here to hear it. Samson won't wake up unless a bomb goes off."

"Samson?"

"The security officer," Jonah supplied. "He'll be asleep by now."

"Diligent."

"Oh, he is. But he's sixty-nine and he just had a triple-heart bypass, so I give him some slack. I'd rather he was awake at midnight when there's no one around."

"You sound important."

"Do I?"

The Russian man leaned close enough for Jonah to get another whiff of his natural scent. "Yes. Does the security officer work for you?"

"In a roundabout way. My family owns this building."

"Ah, old money."

Jonah laughed. "Something like that. I'm going to call that number. I don't know about you, but I have somewhere I'm supposed to be."

The man didn't answer. He stepped back to give Jonah room and retreated to his own corner of the cramped elevator. He was carrying a laptop case and an overcoat. He set both down and leaned against the wall, the picture of smooth relaxation.

Jonah allowed himself another quick glance at him, saturating himself in his unshaven jaw and cut cheekbones, then forced himself to focus on the automated voice at the end of the line.

Five minutes later, a friendly woman in Oxfordshire told him help was at least thirty minutes away. "Apologies, Mr. Gray. Our team is already out on a job in Knightsbridge."

"You have only one team?"

"Tonight, sir. Yes."

"Oh well. I suppose we'll survive."

"Can I take the name of your companions, Mr. Gray?"

"Of course. There is only one. A Mr...?"

The Russian man held up a security lanyard Jonah had failed to notice hanging around his elegant neck. It was brand new and the grainy photograph didn't begin to do his chiselled face justice. His name was Sacha.

Sacha Ivanov.

Jonah repeated the name into the phone. Sacha Ivanov smirked as Jonah tripped over his surname and turned his gold-flecked eyes to the ceiling.

Wincing, Jonah ended the call. "Sorry, did I say it wrong?"

"No. It's just amusing to hear an English boy speak my name."

"Boy?"

"Man. Whatever. Are we going to grow old in here together?"

Jonah licked his lips, a subconscious run of his tongue where he would prefer Sacha Ivanov's. *Wow. Where did that come from?*

A dry spell of three months, probably. Jonah didn't have time for romance, and heavy work hours, and then building anxiety about tonight, had put him off hooking up for a while. "We're not going to die unless you expire within the next thirty minutes. Think you can survive that long?"

"That depends on your company, I suppose, Mr. Gray."

"And that's how a Russian boy says *my* name, eh?"

"You think I am a boy?"

Jonah shrugged. "Maybe not. But my name sounds far more interesting when you say it."

"You are very interesting to me, Jonah. Can I call you that?"

"Might as well. We're going to be here a while. Would you like me to call you Sacha? Or Mr. Ivanov?"

"Sacha is fine in these circumstances. Mr. Ivanov is for… other things."

Jonah's pulse quickened. The sensation that the Russian was toying with him was overwhelming. And thrilling, which was ridiculous, as it was far more likely that he was taking the royal piss rather than flirting. But still. Heat rose in Jonah and he couldn't fight it. Sacha Ivanov was gorgeous. Literally, the stuff of his every fantasy. "Sacha it is, then."

"Indeed."

Sacha was still leaning against the wall. His expensive suit hung off him like sorcery, letting Jonah know a rocking body lurked beneath—long legs, a strong chest, perfect abs. Jonah wondered if the dark hair on his head dusted other places and had to look away, though he found nothing in particular to focus on. The lift interior was rather dull, unless he wanted another stare down with his own face.

He settled for folding himself into a seated position on the floor, thankful the elevator had been cleaned already that evening. He stretched his legs out in front of him and scowled at his shiny dress shoes. Though he wore suits to work every day, he paired them with boots, a formality mismatch that left him less vulnerable to wet British winters. Functionality versus Saville Row. It also made him less like the toff penguin some of his younger employees took him to be. He was twenty-six for God's sake, not fifty, and his current footwear made him feel like his dad.

"You do not like your shoes?"

Jonah darted his gaze up to find Sacha had mirrored his pose to sit opposite him, his legs stretching out beside Jonah's. *He* wore boots, scuffed and dark brown. Jonah wanted to unlace them and ghost his hands up Sacha's legs, and—

Stop it. Jesus Christ, what's the matter with you?

Nothing that anyone else wouldn't likely feel when trapped in a confined space with someone as gorgeous as Sacha Ivanov, but Sacha's gaze was so penetrating it seemed he might see Jonah's every thought before he computed them himself, and that would be far more embarrassing than the shiny shoes on his feet. "I have a function tonight. I don't usually wear get-up like this."

"Get-up?"

"Clothing. Attire. These shoes aren't my thing."

"They are nice."

"You think?"

"Yes, but if they are not...your thing, why wear them?"

"My parents are hosting a ball at the Dorchester. I am going to irritate them enough by attending alone, so it won't do to draw attention to my sartorial choices too."

"Ah, I see." Sacha nodded as though it made perfect sense to him. Perhaps it did. His wristwatch and overcoat gave him away as a man who knew the finer things in life. "You could not get a date?"

Jonah snorted. "Oh, I could have. Just not one that I wanted."

"No girlfriend?"

"No."

"Boyfriend?"

Jonah shook his head. "Unfortunately no. My parents would've liked that, though. It bothers them that I don't bring men home like I did girls when I was younger—" He cut himself off with a shake of his head. "Sorry. That was more revealing than I intended it to be."

Sacha shrugged. "It makes sense to me."

"It does? How so?"

"They probably think you have some internalised homophobia. You should not be shy about bringing your men home, Jonah Gray, if they are nice men, no?"

Jonah snorted, his mind tracking back to the last date he'd had, if you could call it that. The man had been well-dressed and rich, but closeted and engaged to a girl whose father played bridge with Jonah's at the exclusive member's club in Mayfair Jonah had spent his entire adult life avoiding. The man had fucked Jonah seven ways from Sunday, but with the prerequisite that Jonah never told a soul. "I don't meet many nice men."

"That is a shame."

"Isn't it?" Jonah turned his gaze to the ceiling, studying the panels as though they were the most interesting thing in the world. The night was ticking away. With any luck, by the time they were rescued, the limo waiting for him outside would've moved on, leaving him no choice but to hope every cab in the city was booked and unavailable. Maybe he could go home, take this ridiculous tux off and spend the night alone in his apartment. The prospect of a lonely night in private was only marginally more appealing than one in public, though, and a heavy sigh bloomed in Jonah's chest.

He swallowed it down and cast his attention back to Sacha, curious about why he wasn't doing what the rest of the world did when it had a split second to itself and poking at his phone. "What grand plans are you being kept from? Is there someone waiting for you tonight?"

Sacha shook his head. "No one is waiting to take me to a ball at the Dorchester, or anywhere else. I was going nowhere but home for the night."

"I'm jealous."

"You don't like parties?"

Jonah shrugged. "Not this kind."

"Shame. I like champagne and those tiny foods...what are they called?"

"Canapés?"

"Yes. Canapés. I like those."

"You'd like my mother then. She's obsessed with getting them just right."

"Is there a wrong type of canapé?"

Again, it was hard to tell if Sacha was being serious. He had the kind of eyes that gleamed with whatever mood he might be in, but that didn't make said mood any easier to decipher. And, of course, Jonah didn't know him. Beneath his dry smile, there was every chance he was raging about the half hour he'd lost to Jonah and the broken lift.

Angry men don't make small talk about canapés. Then again, Jonah hadn't been expecting to either in any conversation that didn't involve Eleanor Gray. Like, ever. "Tell you what, if you like them so much you can take my car to the Dorchester when we get out of here and eat all the canapés you desire."

"You say it like it is a joke." Sacha's rakish grin widened. "Like you would not come with me."

Jonah laughed. "I could do worse for a date, I suppose."

"You could do much worse, Jonah Gray."

"You don't have to address me by my whole name every time."

"Twice. Be accurate if you're going to chastise me."

"Okay. Twice. Whatever. You can just call me Jonah."

"I like your whole name."

"I like yours too."

Sacha licked his lips—a tiny dart of his tongue, barely visible had Jonah's gaze not been so intense. But it was snowballing, fixed and deep. He couldn't look away, and inexplicably, the flutters of heat rippling through him were beginning to coalesce in his groin. *Do not get wood. Do not get wood. Do not get wood.*

He bent his knees to hide his predicament.

Sacha smirked, but the lift groaned before he could speak, lurching into action and knocking them both off balance.

The elevator descended, lights flickering like a horror film. Sacha stood and held out his hand to Jonah.

Lacking any brighter ideas, Jonah took it and rose, with the blaze of Sacha's touch scorching a path from his palm to the place he was trying to ignore. "Thank you."

"You're welcome. And it was not thirty minutes. Perhaps you will make your party after all."

"There's still time for you to accompany me." The words left Jonah's mouth before he could catch them, spilling freely into the world beyond his control. "I mean, if you'd like to. You said you were headed nowhere but home."

"And you said you were jealous. *You* could leave your party and accompany me."

"Are you asking me to come home with you, Sacha Ivanov?"

The lift stilled and the doors opened. Sacha took a breath

before he stepped out. "Another time, perhaps. I do not wish to be the reason your mother is upset."

Jonah followed him out and past Samson and the gaggle of apologetic engineers. He waved them away and trailed Sacha to the revolving doors that led out onto the street. Cold air hit him as he stepped outside, and seemed to take with it the remnants of the banter they'd shared in the lift. This was the real world. Of course Sacha Ivanov wasn't going to climb into the waiting limo with him. Nor was Jonah going to school his features into a serious expression and ask.

And in any case, Sacha was no longer looking at him. He was finally engrossed in his phone, his expression nothing like the easy amusement he'd so casually thrown Jonah's way.

Go. It's not like you won't see him again if he's working in the same building. But Jonah's shiny-shoed feet didn't move. They stayed rooted in place while Sacha scowled at whatever was irritating him on his phone.

The limo idled on the pavement like a shiny elephant. Jonah nodded to the driver, signalling that he'd seen them. Then he touched Sacha's arm, lightly enough that he could still walk away if Sacha didn't respond.

Sacha's glittering gaze flickered from his phone screen. A ghost of a frown darkened his features, then it was gone, as if it had never been there. "You are still here."

"So are you."

Sacha smirked. "Perhaps I'm waiting for you to make good on your promise of canapés."

A laugh burst free from Jonah's chest. "Seriously? We're back to canapés already?"

"Is a serious matter, no?"

"Okay, okay. I can take them seriously, but only if you

really do come with me. It would be a shame to waste your killer suit on a day at the office."

"My killer suit?"

"It's nice," Jonah clarified. "It looks good on you."

For a long moment, Sacha said nothing. The pause stretched out to the edge of discomfort and Jonah began to wonder if he'd made a horrible, embarrassing mistake. Then Sacha rolled his elegant shoulders and offered Jonah his arm. "All right then, Jonah Gray. We will go to the ball."

2

Climbing into a limo with a virtual stranger to attend high society's glitziest event of the year wasn't anywhere close to the oddest turn Sacha's life had ever taken. Much crazier things happened in Moscow. But there was something undeniably thrilling about stepping into the famous Dorchester hotel with Jonah Gray on his arm.

Camera flashes had blinded them at the Park Lane entrance outside. Paparazzi shouted Jonah's name. Jonah had ignored them, and so had Sacha, but he was curious nonetheless. "You are famous," he remarked as staff whisked their coats away in the grand entrance hall. "I have never heard of you, though."

Jonah's grin turned crooked. Boyish, even. With his auburn hair and bright green eyes, he was a new level of beautiful. Entrancing, in fact, which went some way to explaining why Sacha was glued to his side like a long-lost lover. "I'm only famous at events like this. Most days no one has a clue who I am, but you better keep it quiet that you don't either," Jonah said with his smooth, English accent. "I'm not about to tell my mother I just picked you up in an elevator."

"So we must pretend we have done this before?"

"Done what? Dated? Yes, I suppose. Hmm. Maybe. I didn't really think it through."

"Then don't think. Let it happen."

"You don't know my mother. I told her I was coming alone. She's going to be hopping mad that I kept you a secret."

"Maybe you didn't know I would come. Perhaps I surprised you after telling you I would not be free tonight."

"That could work. But she's going to ask a thousand questions."

"So we answer them." Sacha glanced around the entrance hall, taking in the glamour, breathing the scent of inherited money. "A truth can be stretched."

Jonah inhaled a breath that was shakier than his cool exterior.

Sacha didn't care. He didn't know this man—only intrigue had lured him this far—but he put his hands on Jonah Gray all the same. One hand, at least, at the base of his spine. "Do not worry. If the questions are too much, I will pretend I don't understand."

"Your English is flawless."

Sacha snorted. "You are too kind. My words flow only when I'm in a good mood. My accent thickens when I'm not. I drop words and make myself sound stupid, which irritates me as it is stupid people who put me in bad moods."

"So now I know your tells if you're upset. Noted."

"You think you could upset me?"

Jonah appraised Sacha with his wide, emerald gaze. "I don't think so. You have hard edges."

"Do I?"

"Yes. I can't tell what you're thinking."

"We just met."

"Shh."

"Oh yes, I forget." Sacha guided Jonah closer to him and brought his lips low enough to barely brush Jonah's ear. "How well are we supposed to know each other? How long?"

"To bring you here?" Jonah murmured. "More than twenty minutes. And they'll expect us to be more than friends. I have plenty of those I could've brought tonight."

"You have no friends with benefits?"

"No."

Sacha smiled to himself, though he couldn't say why. "You promised me champagne."

"I did. We have a gauntlet to run first, though, unless you've changed your mind. The fire escape is to your left."

"I haven't changed my mind. Where is this gauntlet?"

"Heading straight for us."

Sacha glanced up in time to see a regal couple fast approaching them. The man was as tall as Jonah, but with sandy hair, not red. He had the same wide eyes, though, and strong jaw. And he moved the same too, with the quiet confidence that came with more privilege than most people could ever dream about.

Jonah's mother carried the auburn hair gene. Hers was long and swept up in an elegant twist at the nape of her neck. She wore a long green dress that complimented her husband's eyes, and pearls collared her throat. "Jonah," she called. "There you are. You're late."

"I'm sorry." Jonah winced as he leaned forwards to greet his mother with a kiss to each cheek. "We had some lift trouble at the office."

"The office?" Jonah's mother cast a curious glance to Sacha, clearly absorbing the possessive hand on her son's back. "Is this...a friend from work?"

Tension rippled through Jonah. *He is not a good liar*, Sacha surmised. That pleased him too. And stirred him to take the heat for his cringing companion. He reached for Jonah's mother's hand and clasped it firmly, the way Russian women liked. "We met at work, yes. Our offices are in the same building. I am Sacha Ivanov. I am very pleased to meet you."

Jonah's mother glowed. "And I you. I'm Jonah's mother, Eleanor. This is my husband, Ralph."

Sacha shook Jonah's father's hand too, then stood back in the hope that he'd gifted Jonah enough time to gather himself.

"You didn't tell us you were bringing someone," Eleanor chastised Jonah, ruffling his already unruly hair. "In fact, you didn't even tell us you were dating anyone, though I can understand why you'd want to keep this one hidden away. How long have you been seeing each other?"

"A while," Jonah said. "I, uh, wasn't sure Sacha could make it, so I didn't want to get your hopes up."

"Is my fault," Sacha supplied. "I have been away on business a lot this month. It finished earlier than I thought."

"What do you do for business, Sacha? Do you work in advertising like Jonah?"

"No. Software development. Apps and social media."

"He works at Blutecc," Jonah said. "I can see him from my desk."

Sacha slid his arm around Jonah's waist, pulling him closer. "You never told me that."

"You never asked."

Eleanor Gray laughed and offered Sacha her gloved hand

again. "Well, isn't this nice? Did you know, Sacha, you're the first date my son has ever brought to this party? You must be very special to him."

"I hope to be," Sacha said.

"I'm sure you already are," Jonah's father chimed in. "Now, don't let us cramp your style. Go and mingle and drink. We'll catch up later."

Tension melted from Jonah's tall frame. He kissed his mother one more time, then grabbed Sacha's hand and tugged him into the glorious ballroom the Dorchester was famous for. It was decorated for the festive season, draped in gold and twinkly lights. A live jazz band played at the front where an area had been cleared for dancing. The rest of the room was filled with round tables and rich people. Wait staff floated around with trays of champagne, cognac, and orange juice.

Jonah grabbed two flutes from a tray and pressed one into Sacha's hand. "The first of many." He tipped his own glass to his lips. "You'll need to be drunk to get through this nonsense."

"Nonsense? You don't like this crowd?"

Jonah kept moving until they came to a vacant table. On the way, he waved to people who called his name, but didn't engage. "It's not that I don't like them. I don't know ninety percent of these people."

"But they know you."

"Of course they do. Famous, remember?"

"For what?"

"For being rich. It's not an accolade I'm proud of."

"Cursed by nepotism?"

"Not exactly, but my company is housed in a building my

family owns and I only started paying the full rent last year, so make of that what you will."

Sacha smiled and took a healthy sip of champagne. "You mistake me for someone who does not understand privilege."

"Are your parents billionaires, Sacha Ivanov?"

"Not quite. But I am from a wealthy Russian family. To be rich is to be born, yes? But you knew I would speak that language or you would not have asked me to accompany you tonight."

Jonah took a seat at the table and gestured for Sacha to do the same. Once they were both seated, he angled his chair, pointing his knees at Sacha's. "I was mostly joking. It didn't really cross my mind that it would happen."

"And yet here we are. That speaks to me of something unsaid."

"I like how you speak," Jonah said. "The way you phrase things is so different and yet the same."

"I will take that compliment. A man in a coffee shop called me something much worse yesterday."

"Why?"

Sacha shrugged. "I did not ask, but I was talking on my phone in Russian and I don't think he liked it."

Jonah snorted. "This is London. If he doesn't like mixing with a thousand other cultures on a daily basis he's in the wrong city."

Sacha said nothing. He didn't much care for the sensitivities of angry white men buying overpriced coffee. He did care about the sensation of Jonah's knees brushing his, though. It was nice. Pleasant. And any other bland descriptor he could think of to keep him from hooking Jonah's chair closer. *What is it about this man? He is hypnotising me.*

Or maybe it was the champagne. It was a drink Sacha

truly did enjoy, but lacking the time for socialising and hang-overs both, he didn't partake much. He'd had the same bottle of vodka in his freezer for over a year.

Still. He drained his glass and retrieved two more from a passing waiter. "You promised me canapés too."

"I did, didn't I?" Jonah eyed Sacha with the kind of smile that would look good wrapped around Sacha's cock. "Where can they be?"

He gazed beyond Sacha, scanning the room while Sacha fought the filthy images bombarding his brain. But it was a tough ask. Jonah was a beautiful man, tall, strong, and with those ridiculous eyes, and Sacha was but human. It would be a strange thing indeed if he didn't think about fucking Jonah, another pleasure he rarely had time for these days. He wondered if—

Something changed. Sacha blinked, mistrusting his assessment of a man he did not know, but the set of Jonah's jaw was unmistakable, and different to the tension he'd carried when he'd faced his parents in a lie. *He is unsettled.* But why? Was it Sacha? The stranger on Jonah's arm? The unfamiliar knee brushing against his?

No.

That wasn't it. The discomfort in Jonah's eyes was years old. Sacha knew like he knew the champagne they were drinking cost more per bottle than a regular person's monthly salary.

No one in this room was a regular person, least of all Jonah Gray, but whoever he was, he didn't deserve the anxiety that had suddenly seized him, stealing away his soft smile and kind eyes.

Sacha knew that too.

He followed Jonah's gaze, tracing it to the cluster of

people who had just entered the ballroom. Three pairs of heteronormative couples. The first two were old enough to be contemporaries of Jonah's parents, the last set were younger. Sacha eyed them, considering the man and the woman and pondering which had caught Jonah's attention. It was the man, it had to be. With his slick hair and sneering face, he had the air of someone Sacha knew he'd instantly hate if they were acquainted.

Sacha didn't want to look at him any longer, and he didn't want Jonah to either. "Hey."

Jonah jumped. "Sorry. What?"

"If something upsets you to see, don't look."

"I'm not upset."

Sacha stood, blocking Jonah's view of the man with preposterous hair. "Of course. Because you are not looking."

"That makes no sense."

"Does it need to?"

Jonah stared, his shoulders rising and falling too fast. He opened his mouth. Shut it again. And shook his head. "Maybe not."

"Come." Sacha held out his hand."

Jonah took it without seeming to think much about what he was doing. "Where?"

"That doesn't matter either."

"I thought you were hungry?"

"I am always hungry, Jonah Gray. You will learn this about me."

Jonah's tight features found the smile Sacha had somehow missed. "Is that right?"

"Yes. And do you know what else you will learn?"

"Um...no?"

Sacha made yet another impulsive decision and took

Jonah's hands in his. Considering they hadn't so much as shaken hands in greeting since they met a few hours ago, it was a bold move, but Sacha didn't care. Being bold had kept him alive. He eased Jonah close enough that anyone nearby would maybe think they were about to kiss. "No date of mine will ever have face like that."

"Like what?"

"Like this." Sacha put two fingers to Jonah's lips and pulled them down into a comical pout. "Or I will think you are maybe hungry too."

"I am hungry. If you stop yanking my face around we can do something about it."

"You don't like me touching your face?"

"I shouldn't. I don't know you."

"But?"

Jonah's smile returned full force. "How do you know there's a but?"

Sacha let his hand drop, disproportionately pleased he'd distracted Jonah from whatever had upset him. "I do not know you either and somehow I like touching your face. Perhaps you feel the same."

"I'm not confirming either way—shit, hang on."

They were interrupted by someone who seemed to know Jonah, and for the next hour or so, they just kept coming while Sacha drank more champagne and watched, occasionally rescuing Jonah from awkward questions about his existence.

It was late by the time Eleanor reappeared and towed Sacha away.

Jonah shot Sacha a panicked look.

Sacha smiled and hoped it translated to the three words Jonah so desperately needed to hear. *Ya poluchil eto.*

I got this.

"So..." Eleanor grasped Sacha's arm tightly, the way only mothers could. "I'm so sorry my son didn't see fit to tell us a thing about you before tonight. His father and I would've liked to spend more time with you before we leave the city for the festive season."

"Where are you going?"

"To our estate in the Cotswolds. We like a country Christmas. My husband misses the farm he grew up on."

"My father grew up on a farm too. It made him happier than his castles in the sky."

"Yes, it's the simple things, isn't it? Of all our children, Jonah perhaps knows this the most."

Sacha wanted to ask her how many children she had, but to do so would've given him away. Instead, he nodded and searched his brain for what little knowledge he'd gleaned about the advertising firm in the offices opposite his own. "He is very grounded. Works hard. You have to when you are the boss, no?"

"Indeed. Jonah doesn't enjoy life without a challenge."

This time, Sacha's nod was from the heart. "I do not understand a man that does."

"Or a woman, I hope. This world is for more than men."

Sacha chuckled. "I know. My mother was a strong woman."

"She's not with us anymore?"

"No." Sacha glanced away from Eleanor, searching for Jonah. He found him still surrounded, men and women both fawning for attention Jonah plainly didn't want to give, though his eyes remained kind.

Sacha did not possess such patience. He pondered what he might've done if this night had been something else. If

Jonah really was his date, his lover, his...person. And he didn't have to look far for the answer. Sacha would've rescued him in a heartbeat, hustled him back to their quiet corner so they could drink in peace, share morsels of tiny, pretentious food, and then bid the room goodbye so they could go home and—

"Oh dear." Eleanor's voice broke into Sacha's musings. "There goes William Ratner. He always seems to make a beeline for Jonah at these things, and Jonah doesn't care for him at all. You must rescue him."

Sacha didn't have to check to know the insistent man was the same as the one whose very presence had rattled Jonah so earlier in the evening. And he didn't need Eleanor to tell him to put himself between them.

He left her and strode across the ballroom, not giving a single fuck what anyone thought of him. *I don't know these people. They don't know me.* Neither did Jonah, but the relief on his face when he saw Sacha coming was all Sacha needed to see to know he'd made the right call.

Smiling, he stepped between Jonah and the man with the bad hair, cutting off any interaction before it could happen. He took Jonah's hands. "Come with me, *luchik*."

"Where?"

"Just come."

Without waiting for further response Sacha steered Jonah away. Jonah let him, and they eased through the crowds as though they'd danced this dance a hundred times or more. "You know," Sacha said. "Your English balls are very civilised. Even in Russian high society there would be some sort of fighting by now."

"I'm sure we could find you a pub brawl somewhere around here if you're feeling pugnacious."

"What does that word mean?"

"Combative. Quick to fight."

Sacha chuckled. "That isn't me. I don't waste my energy on people I don't care about, and I don't care about most people."

"No?"

"No. But you're not like that, I can see. Tell me, Jonah Gray, what did that man with the unspeakable hair do to you?"

"What man?" Jonah kept moving, but his bright gaze turned to glass.

Sacha accepted his answer, filed it away, and gestured around the ballroom. "My father had this money once. Now he has only enough to look down on others, but not to ever be satisfied. I don't know if there is a word for this in your language."

"I can't think of one."

"Then maybe there isn't."

"Are you close to your parents?"

"No."

Jonah turned his head, treating Sacha to a clear view of a face that seemed to grow more beautiful as the evening progressed. If their date had been real, Sacha would not have had much to complain about. "You said that with such finality, but you speak as if your father is still alive."

"He is."

"But you don't like him?"

"Not much. The feeling is mutual."

"Why?"

Sacha shrugged and looked beyond Jonah to the waiter bearing down on them. More champagne was tempting, as was the cognac now the hour was late enough to justify heavy liquor, but he resisted and forced himself to meet Jonah's gaze again. "Many reasons. None of interest to you."

"How do you know that?"

"Is first date, no? Complex conversations come later, or so I'm told."

"Second date?"

"I would not know. First date is usually the only date for me."

"Ah." Jonah nodded his understanding. "Busy man, I suppose. No time for romance?"

Sacha smirked. "What is this romance you speak of?"

"Beats me. I'm a busy man too." Jonah's lips turned up, his grin boyish.

And irresistible.

Sacha stopped walking, reclaimed his arm from around Jonah's waist, and dropped his hands onto shoulders that seemed to be made of steel.

Warm steel that soaked into Sacha's palms and nearly derailed his power of speech. "Was this date everything you dreamed it would be?"

"I didn't dream about it. I didn't know you existed until an hour before you got here."

"Yes, but you have dreamed of bringing a date here with you, haven't you? What was that like?"

The final strands of tension melted from Jonah, and his frown became one of amused speculation as he considered Sacha's question. "I don't date, so I never thought it would happen, but..."

"Yes?"

"But, when I did think of it, it wasn't as easy as tonight has been with you. This feels like..." Jonah rubbed the back of his neck. "I don't know. Like we've done this before. I barely know your name, but it doesn't seem to matter."

Sacha soaked in the words. They were sweet and made him feel good, and there weren't many people in the world who made Sacha feel that way. Actually, he couldn't think of anyone who made his stomach flutter quite the way Jonah did. *What a strange thing indeed.* "I am glad you have enjoyed your evening. And your mother too. That was your intention, yes? To make her happy?"

"I suppose." Jonah slid his hands to where Sacha's were still grasping his shoulders. He twined their fingers together and laughed. "I can't actually remember what I was thinking when I invited you here. It doesn't make much sense now."

"Or maybe it does and that is the confusion."

"Maybe. This isn't where I would bring a date, though, for the first time or otherwise."

"Where would you take them?"

"Anywhere but here. You?"

"Me?"

"Yes, Sacha Ivanov. Where do you take your first and only dates?"

"To the wine bar close to my home, and then..."

Jonah's auburn eyebrow ticked. He squeezed Sacha's hand and closed the minuscule distance between them. His whole body was as hard and warm as the handful of places Sacha had already touched him. "And then...? What do you do next?"

"I take them home and fuck them, Jonah Gray. Would you like me to do that to you?"

3

Jonah was high. There was no other explanation for the speed at which he'd yanked Sacha out of the Dorchester hotel and into the waiting limo. It would explain his stampeding heart too. And the sweat sticking his clasped hands together. *Calm down. It isn't like you've never had a one night stand before.*

It really wasn't, but this felt different. Perhaps it was the misplaced intimacy they'd already shared. The light touches and lingering stares. Sacha's gentle, guiding hands, and rapt attention to every word Jonah had spoken. He'd played his part to perfection, so much so that Jonah had almost forgotten it wasn't real. But...here they were, huddled on the backseat of the limo, gliding along the streets of London on their way to Jonah's penthouse apartment. *Maybe he didn't mean it. He'll come in for a drink. We'll laugh. Exchange numbers for no reason whatsoever, then see each other on Monday and pretend this never happened.*

It made more sense than the heat gathering pace in his veins.

"Jonah."

"Hmm?"

Sacha gave another of the deep chuckles Jonah had become addicted to as the evening had progressed. "We don't have to do anything. I can go home."

"I don't want you to go home."

"Then you should probably look at me."

Jonah turned in his seat. Sacha was spread out beside him, the picture of roguish relaxation. His grin was easy, and his obvious amusement was kind, not mocking. "Sorry," Jonah said. "It's just not how I expected this night to go when I woke up this morning."

"But the unexpected can be good, no?"

"Yes, I think so."

"Then let it happen. If you're worried you won't be safe with me, tell someone where we are going, and that you are with me."

"I'm not worried you're a serial killer. I've seen your company ID. Christ, we work in the same building."

Sacha's smile widened. "Yes, but you did not know that until today. Perhaps I faked it."

"Did you?"

"What do you think?"

"I think you don't expend energy on trivial things, so either you really are a serial killer, or I'm perfectly safe inviting you into my home."

"So..." Sacha sat up from his sprawl and leaned closer. He still smelled of clean cotton and, well, *man*, and to Jonah's champagne-hazed eyes, the scruff on his jaw seemed to have darkened as the evening had progressed, leaving him more alluring than ever.

Jonah wanted to touch it. To run his fingers through it, and rub it with his own face. He wanted to bury his nose in Sacha's elegant neck and breathe him in.

He settled for a snatched inhale. "So what?"

"So," Sacha repeated. "If I don't kill you, what would you like to do instead? We can do as we said before we got in this car, but it doesn't have to be so...literal."

"Literal?" Jonah flicked a glance to the privacy screen that separated them from the driver his parents used for all their events. "You mean you're not going to fuck me?"

"That's not what I said. But I like how you say it. Say it again."

"Which part?"

"The part about me fucking you."

Jonah's pulse kicked up a gear. They were nearly at the exclusive apartment building he called home and despite his nerves, he was glad of it. The anticipation was killing him. "To answer your first question," he said. "I'd like you to come in and make good on what we agreed when we left the ball. What you do with that is entirely up to *you*."

The car stopped as he finished speaking. Like magic, the doors opened, and Jonah got out before Sacha could respond.

He strode towards the entrance of his building. The concierge greeted him. Jonah barely heard himself respond, too keenly aware of Sacha a heartbeat behind him.

They found themselves in another lift. Sacha smirked again and this time, Jonah did too. "This is nicer than the one we spent twenty minutes in earlier."

"It is," Sacha agreed. "And let me guess, you live in the penthouse?"

"I do. It's not mine, though. It belongs to my family."

"But you live alone?"

"Isn't that what a serial killer would ask?"

"A serial killer would already know, I think."

"It should worry me that you know that."

"Maybe it should." Sacha reached around Jonah to press the button for the top floor. "But I think I'm not the first man you have brought home, so perhaps it doesn't."

It didn't worry Jonah in the slightest, but he was enjoying the game—Sacha's twinkling eyes, and teasing smile. It made the desire fast building in him easier to handle, though the lift ride to the top floor seemed to take as long as their disjointed one earlier that evening.

Eons had passed by the time the doors opened to the landing that housed only one door—the one to Jonah's apartment. They stepped out of the lift. Sacha drifted to the window and gazed down at the Christmas lights that had lit up the city since the middle of November. "It's nice from up here. I don't like it at ground level. It's too...crowded with the colours. I can't distinguish one from another. Up here it is just light, like the stars."

Jonah came up behind him, drawn to Sacha's back in ways he couldn't explain, but Sacha spun before he could touch him, leaving them face to face and inches apart. "I've never really thought about it," Jonah said. "Christmas is something that happens, like the weather. We have no say in the matter."

"You do not like it?"

"Oh no, I do. But I think I take it for granted."

Sacha nodded. Jonah couldn't tell if it was agreement or not, and he didn't much care. Now he had Sacha so close, his nerves were beginning to fade. He wanted him on the other side of that door, damn it.

As though he'd read Jonah's mind, Sacha grasped Jonah's lapels and backed him across the small landing and into the door. "Where's your key?"

"Coat pocket. The left."

Sacha reached down and retrieved the key. He pressed it into Jonah's hand. "Open up."

Jonah obeyed, spinning around and jamming the key into the lock of the heavy door. It swung open, revealing the entrance hall to his apartment in all its high-class glory, but Sacha didn't seem to notice the solid wood floors and priceless artwork on the walls. He pushed the door shut behind him and took his coat off, motioning for Jonah to do the same.

Both garments fell to the floor.

Jonah stepped out of his shoes and Sacha bent to untie his boots.

Impatient, Jonah stooped to help him. Sacha chuckled again and kicked the offending footwear aside. Then he straightened, bringing Jonah with him, and gripped his shirt.

He's going to kiss me.

But not on the lips. Sacha brought his mouth to Jonah's neck and gently sucked while he loosened Jonah's bow tie and collar. The sensation was light, but maddening, and Jonah's dick thickened, hardening sharp and fast, straining against his perfectly tailored trousers.

Sacha undid the bow tie entirely and let it drop. Then he unbuttoned Jonah's collar with deft fingers, working his way down his white shirt, revealing Jonah's torso.

He slid his hand inside the shirt, splaying his palm across Jonah's abdomen. "I knew this."

"Knew what?"

"That you had the body of a dream beneath this suit you do not like."

"How do you know I don't like this suit?"

"Because you do not care that I am about to leave it on the floor."

Jonah couldn't deny it. He pushed Sacha's suit jacket from his shoulders and to the floor too.

Sacha let it happen. Apparently he didn't care about his expensive clothes either. "Where is your bedroom?"

"Last door on the left."

"Show me?"

Jonah took his own jacket off and dumped it on top of Sacha's. Then he took Sacha's hand from inside his shirt and entangled their fingers again. He led Sacha further into his apartment and along the corridor that led to the bedrooms. His was the last door at the end. He kicked it open, leaving the main lights off, and flicked on the lamp at the side of his queen-sized bed. A warm glow illuminated the room. Jonah let go of Sacha's hand and spun to face him again.

Sacha eyed him and his gaze held a hint of a challenge.

Jonah wanted to jump him, to tumble him to the bed and kiss him until his lips were raw. But he didn't move. Couldn't, while Sacha's dark gaze pinned him in place.

"How do you feel," Sacha said slowly, "about taking orders?"

"During sex?"

"Yes." Sacha ran a fingertip along Jonah's jaw. "You seem like a man who would be good at it, and I find that...interesting."

Jonah shivered. Couldn't help it. "I've never thought about it, but I'm not into S&M, so don't get any ideas about that."

"I did not mention S&M, only the notion of you doing as I say. That is not pain, no? Only pleasure."

"I like pleasure."

"So do I, and I think I will like yours very much."

"My pleasure?"

"Yes." Sacha reached into Jonah's pocket and fished out his phone. "But I can still hear your heart racing. Do us both a favour and tell someone you are here with me. Perhaps then you will stop worrying."

"I'm not worried."

"Do it anyway. It is the safe thing to do."

"Does anyone know you're here? Maybe I'm the serial killer."

Sacha snorted. "Of course you are. Make the call."

Jonah rolled his eyes and tapped out a quick text to Lily.

Jonah: *Brought someone home with me tonight. If he kills me during sex his name is Sacha Ivanov. Tell my mother I loved her.*

He held it up to Sacha. A smirk was his only response. Jonah hit send, then sent another less sinister text to follow up.

Jonah: *I'm joking about the murdering part. He's a nice guy, just being safe. Missed you tonight. Call me when you fly in next week x*

He didn't show Sacha that message. He dropped the phone onto the bedside table and instantly forgot about it and everything else that wasn't the way Sacha was looking at him. A breath caught in Jonah's throat. His dick was still hard from Sacha's lips on his neck in the hallway, but it was a different throb now. Anticipation had morphed into something more imminent.

They were really doing this.

While Jonah had been tapping at his phone, Sacha had

unbuttoned his own shirt and removed his wristwatch. His chest was lean and strong, and dusted with dark hair. Jonah yearned to touch it, but Sacha moved first. He stripped Jonah of his shirt, then gently tugged him to the floor-to-ceiling windows at the foot of the bed. Again, the city sprawled out before them. It was a view Jonah largely ignored, perhaps spoilt by it. But with Sacha behind him, roaming his hands over Jonah's body, it seemed brand new, and he drank it in, until Sacha's touch ventured to his waistband.

"You know," Sacha said lowly, "I was not serious about ordering you around. But I am enjoying you like this, here, where the whole city could see you if they would look your way."

"They'd need X-ray vision," Jonah choked out. "We're on the thirty-fifth floor."

"But you still worry they can see you, no?"

"Define 'they'. And no, not really. This glass is tinted."

"I don't believe you."

Jonah closed his eyes, unwilling to admit that Sacha was right. No one could see them, not even the birds, but he felt eyes on him all the same, and he couldn't decide if he was mortified, or so turned on he could barely hold himself upright.

Perhaps both. And did it matter?

No. No it didn't. Nothing mattered while Sacha was touching him like this. Jonah forced his eyes open and found their combined reflection in the glass. Sacha was behind him, concealed by Jonah, but his gaze at Jonah's shoulder was hot and hungry, and Jonah shivered. "I don't care who sees us. Do you, Sacha Ivanov?"

"I do not think so. But I do care about how you feel, so if I do something you do not like, you must tell me to stop, yes?"

A near hysterical laugh built in Jonah's chest, and escaped in the form of a strangled grunt. Sacha had hardly touched him and he was already in danger of blowing his load in ten seconds flat. He couldn't imagine their encounter lasting long enough for Sacha to make him uncomfortable.

But as Sacha's deep gaze bored into him, his amusement faded. He sucked in a breath and nodded. "I will."

"That is good. You have obeyed your first order. Do you like it?"

"Yes. What's next?"

"Shh." Sacha tapped Jonah's lips. "Perhaps you will make no sound."

"That's speculation, not instruction."

"Quiet." Sacha spoke softly, but with an authority that sent new heat fizzing through Jonah's veins.

Jonah swallowed and dropped his head, revelling in the new sensation that was like nothing he'd ever felt before. His dick was a stone column, straining against his tuxedo trousers, and his nerves jangled, anticipation tingling across every millimetre of his heated skin. He didn't speak again.

Smirking, Sacha unbuttoned Jonah's trousers and slid his hand inside. His fingers brushed Jonah's cock, gently at first, then with enough purpose to roll Jonah's eyes, and force a groan from his gut that lodged in his throat.

Sacha's touch was maddening. Jonah clenched his fists against the window and pondered what on earth he'd signed up for. S&M was off the table, he'd made that clear, but this was torture of a new kind.

Seeking friction, he bucked into Sacha's hand.

Sacha chuckled. "Be still."

He removed his hand from Jonah's cock, and pushed Jonah's tuxedo trousers down his hips. They puddled at

Jonah's feet, fast joined by his underwear, leaving him naked while Sacha remained almost fully clothed.

It didn't seem fair, but at the same time, Jonah's senses were on overload. If Sacha's electric palms were anything to go by, he wasn't sure he could handle his skin against his anytime soon.

"Look at me," Sacha said. To punctuate the instruction, he placed two fingers beneath Jonah's chin and tipped his head upright. "That's good. You have an amazing body. You know this, yes?"

Unwilling to break the loaded silence, Jonah raised an eyebrow, lifting his shoulders in an understated shrug. He'd rowed at university, and used the gym in the basement of the building, but he didn't spend much time looking in the mirror.

Sacha growled as if he'd read Jonah's mind and he didn't like what he found. He pressed against Jonah harder from behind and brought his lips to Jonah's throat again, right below his ear. "I can tell you don't believe me, so I am going to show you. I am going to tease you until you can no longer be silent, and then I am going to fuck you until you scream my name. Is that okay with you, Jonah Gray?"

Jonah gazed straight ahead, transfixed by Sacha's reflection. Their eyes locked, and Jonah's heart struck up a faster tattoo, a heady thud that banged against his ribcage.

He nodded, and hoped Sacha heard the words he couldn't speak. *God, yes. Fuck me. Please.*

Sacha made good on his promise to tease Jonah beyond measure. He covered every inch of skin with his devilish hands, and kissed a sinful path up and down Jonah's spine.

He sucked his throat too, and pressed open-mouthed kisses to Jonah's jaw, his fingers tangling in Jonah's hair, his lips everywhere except where Jonah wanted them most—on his own. Jonah *ached* for his kiss, his lips tingled and his tongue darted restlessly over his gritted teeth as Sacha trailed his fingers over Jonah's dick, his balls, and dipped into his crease.

A layer of sweat built on Jonah's skin. He fought for breath, desire blooming in every dark corner of his body and mind. He'd never been so turned on. Never wanted someone with such crazed need. And all in the hushed quiet of his apartment while the city of London twinkled festively below them.

His hands were still in fists from Sacha's very first touch. Sacha reached over Jonah's shoulders and uncurled them, finger by finger. "You are tense," he whispered. "Would it help if I took my clothes off too?"

A strangled noise escaped Jonah. He couldn't help it. Then he panicked, the fear that Sacha would keep his clothes on after all leaving him dizzy.

Sacha's smirk morphed briefly to the kind of smile that had no place in an encounter so heady. He cupped the back of Jonah's neck and held his hand there, unmoving. Comforting, almost. Soothing. Jonah's pulse slowed, and breath moved freely in his lungs. Then wickedness returned to Sacha's deep gaze.

He stepped back from Jonah and retreated into the bedroom, logic drawing him to the bedside table where he found condoms and lubricant. He dropped them at the foot of the bed and unbuttoned the rest of his shirt. The expensive fabric fell away, revealing a strong torso that the hazed reflection did no justice.

Jonah clenched his fists again, desperate for more. *I need to see you.* It felt wrong to have a man inside him who remained such a mystery.

As if he'd heard the sudden doubt clouding Jonah's mind, Sacha moved into his eye line and slouched against the glass as he pushed his shirt over his shoulders. Up close, his body was even hotter. Long, lean, and hard. Jonah bit his lip. "More."

"You want to see everything?"

"Yes."

"As you wish."

Sacha's velvet voice wrapped around those three simple words like liquid sex. Jonah dug his teeth deeper into his lip, tasting the iron tang of blood. He'd already broken the silence, but he kept his groan in, letting it swell in his chest instead, suffocating him in the sweetest way as Sacha's hands moved to his belt buckle.

The leather slipped slowly through Sacha's belt loops, as if time had caught in Jonah's throat. He'd never been so eager to see a man's cock, to feel it pressed against him, and inside him. He wanted to taste it too, and grip it with his fingers, feel the weight of it. "Hurry *up*," he ground out.

"Why? Do you need to be somewhere else?"

Jonah made a low noise. Sacha paid him no heed and continued his unhurried dance with his belt. He let it fall to the floor and unbuttoned his fly, opening his trousers to reveal expensive underwear that did *nothing* to conceal the prominent bulge inside.

Jonah's mouth watered. Fresh sweat beaded his skin. "I want to see you."

"I know."

"So let me...please?"

Sacha's grin turned snake-like. He let his trousers fall and kicked them away, then he toyed with the waistband of his underwear. "Maybe I should keep them on."

"*Sacha.*"

"Or maybe not if you say my name like that. I like it. Say it again."

"Sacha."

"Again."

"*Sacha.*"

The underwear disappeared. Sacha's cock sprang free. Thick and long, it jutted out from Sacha's powerful hips, and Jonah yearned for it as much as he yearned for Sacha's kiss. Maybe more. A kiss was intimate, an act between lovers. This was sex. A casual hook-up that could just as easily have begun on an app. He had no right to demand affection from Sacha, but *god*, he wanted his cock.

Sacha licked his lips, appraising Jonah. His eyes were darker now, hooded with the desire that flowed between them. "I had grand plans to fuck you slowly, but I know now that you might test my control too much."

"Control?"

"*Self*-control," Sacha amended. "I have asked you to stay still and quiet. I will not force you."

Jonah knew that, and perhaps he had all along, but he kept his hands on the glass all the same. Moving felt like conceding, and he'd conceded enough tonight.

Perhaps.

Or maybe they'd barely got started. Either way... "You don't have to force me. I can take it."

"Take what?"

"You. I can take *you*."

Sacha hummed and pushed off the window. Upright, he seemed stronger than ever, but in reality, they were evenly matched pretty much everywhere. Sacha was an inch taller, Jonah a little broader.

"Turn around," Jonah blurted.

"Why?"

"I want to see your back."

Sacha gave him a long stare, then turned, showing Jonah the leanly muscled expanse of his back. His hair was neater than Jonah's and his elegant neck was exposed. A jagged scar stood out from his smooth skin. Jonah wanted to kiss it so badly his lips *burned*.

He settled for staring until Sacha faced him again.

"Did you see enough?"

Not even close. "Yes."

"Good. I am going to fuck you now. I will stop any time you wish. You say, yes? I will hear you."

"You've said that already."

"So? You think it can be said too much?"

Jonah didn't know what he thought. With Sacha's dick pointing at him it was hard to translate anything that flashed through his mind into something coherent. He shook his head, out of words to explain himself.

Sacha stepped closer and kissed Jonah's neck. "I will hear you."

Jonah nodded, but it was cut off by his low groan as Sacha's lips travelled south, along his collarbone, and down his chest. He hadn't been expecting so much attention, and was unprepared for the light pressure of Sacha's mouth on his nipple. The slow, pinching suck turned his brain to mush. His cock jumped, knocking Sacha's hip, and Sacha moved just enough so the impact switched to his solid length.

Wow. If Jonah hadn't been ready for Sacha's lips, there was no way he was equipped to deal with the sensation of his cock just about anywhere, let alone on his own dick. He pitched forwards, couldn't help it.

Sacha let him have his way, but briefly, and it was worse than if he hadn't let Jonah move at all. The friction was electric. Mind-bending. And then it was gone.

Sacha stepped back, taking his dick and his wicked lips with him, and Jonah was alone. At least, it felt that way without Sacha's touch, despite the reality that he hadn't gone far.

The tearing sound of a condom wrapper reached Jonah's ears, and the *click* of the lubricant bottle. He shivered, not because he was scared it would hurt, but because he knew how absolutely this man was about to take him apart.

He's going to dismantle me, and I'm going to love it.

How did he prepare for that?

Jonah had no idea. So he waited, head bowed, eyes closed, fists still pressed against the glass wall, and tried to make ready for a hurricane.

Sacha returned, pressing up behind him. His body heat warmed Jonah's skin, and he slid his palms up Jonah's back, all the way to his shoulders. "Okay?"

"Yes."

"How about if I do this?"

One hand left Jonah's back, and returned as slick fingers dipping into his crease, probing, searching. Sacha's touch was still devilishly light, but Jonah felt it *everywhere*. He groaned again, widening his stance with little conscious thought. "That's good. I like that."

"And this?" Sacha pressed a finger inside Jonah and found the sweet spot with laser precision.

At Jonah's nod, he added another finger and fucked Jonah with them, slow and sweet, massaging Jonah's prostate with every thrust, building a desperate pressure that unhinged Jonah's jaw.

Christ. It's just his fingers. How the hell am I going to handle his cock?

His subconscious had no answer, and for long minutes it didn't matter. Sacha worked him open with his fingers, then pulled back and rubbed his slicked, sheathed dick along Jonah's crease, brushing his hole, but not pushing inside. It was perfect torture, but Jonah needed it. Every nerve was screaming out for Sacha's cock inside him, but, *fuck,* his brain was lagging behind.

And Sacha seemed to know it, teasing Jonah for an endless stretch of time until Jonah was shaking with need, and unable to recall that he'd ever wanted to wait.

"Do it." He widened his legs again. "Please."

Sacha answered with his cock, dragging it along Jonah's crease one last time before pressing against his hole, sliding inside inch by slow inch, until he was *right there.*

The pressure was unbelievable. Sacha's dick was huge, and Jonah felt him in every facet of his body. It was dizzying and he staggered, lurching sideways.

Sacha caught him with a strong arm around his torso, steadying himself with a hand on the glass beside Jonah's. "Easy. I will fuck you lying down, but I do not want to fall to get there."

Jonah choked out a laugh. "Get a smaller cock then."

"There is nothing wrong with my cock. You can take it."

Jonah wasn't so sure. He was no stranger to bottoming, but Sacha was something else. More than size, Sacha was power. Strength. Poise. Everything Jonah had believed of himself until the Russian had stepped into the lift and turned his entire evening upside down.

In a good way, though. Without him you'd still be at the Dorchester pretending you wouldn't rather drown yourself than answer the same fucking questions over and over.

He didn't think about William Ratner. Hadn't since Sacha had blocked him out and given Jonah far better things to think about. Things like—"*Fuck.*"

Way ahead of him, Sacha began to move, eviscerating Jonah's brain power. He circled his hips, driving his cock in and out of Jonah at an infuriating pace. A leisurely pace, as if they had all night, though Jonah supposed they did if—

Sacha cut him off again, fine tuning the velocity of his slow thrusts until they were steady enough for the slap of flesh on flesh to drown out the thump of Jonah's racing heart. He fucked Jonah hard, holding him with one arm, and bracing himself on the window with the other. His breaths grew heavy, merging with Jonah's ragged moans. He pressed his forehead to Jonah's shoulder and tightened his arm around him. "Jonah Gray," he ground out. "You are something special, no?"

The power of speech had deserted Jonah the moment Sacha had put his hands on him. He had nothing. He pressed back against Sacha, taking him deeper, and his own cock ached to be touched, but stubbornness kept his hands on the glass even as Sacha fucked him harder.

More sounds fell from him that he didn't recognise as his own. His body became one with Sacha's cock driving inside him. Pleasure sluiced through his veins, melting every synapse in its path. His strangled gasps became drawn-out moans. "Oh god. I'm going to come."

"Do it." Sacha dug his fingers into Jonah's flank. "Come for me while I fill you up."

The dirty words shoved Jonah over the edge. His climax rushed him, eclipsing every sense. He yelled out a stream of curses, barely registering Sacha growling in Russian behind him, and his cock erupted, painting the window with wet heat.

"Fuckfuck*fuck*. Damn." Jonah wavered again.

And *again*, Sacha held him up, silent and strong, his only sound his laboured breaths.

Jonah was destroyed. His legs shook and his lungs burned, and beyond that, his brain was fried. He'd never come so hard in his life. What was this sorcery Sacha had brought to the table?

He didn't fuck you on the table. You didn't even make it to the bed.

The errant thought made him laugh.

Sacha chuckled too and slowly eased out of him. He disappeared, but was back before Jonah could blink.

He wrapped long fingers around Jonah's wrists and pried his hands from the glass wall. "You can let go now."

"I know."

"You seem like you maybe forgot."

Jonah hummed, enjoying the blood flow as it rushed back into his aching arms, and enjoying Sacha's soothing hands on him even more. "Well, it is hard to recall just about anything when you've just shot your brains out of your dick."

Sacha snorted. "Do you speak to your mother with that mouth?"

"All the time."

"Liar. You are a good son. She told me so."

"Oh yeah? What else did she tell you?"

"That is between us. Shall we use your shower?"

Jonah eyed the window and contemplated what *he* looked like after Sacha had fucked him so well. "Probably a good idea. Come on, I'll show you."

He took Sacha by the hand and led him to the ensuite wet room. The shower had four heads and room enough for two.

Jonah leaned against the tiles while the water heated, but the cool spray didn't seem to bother Sacha. He stood beneath it, eyes closed, and Jonah could hardly stand how glorious he was, naked, and still half hard. "Is it a Russian thing to take cold showers?"

"It is not cold."

Jonah begged to differ and remained where he was until steam began to rise around them and fill the room.

Sacha was already washing his hair with the citrus shampoo Jonah's housekeeper kept topped up. Jonah wanted to help him, but awkwardness threatened the easy energy that had carried them this far. What next? *Do I ask him to stay? Is it weird to spend the entire night with a stranger?*

No weirder than fucking against his bedroom window, but Jonah kept his thoughts to himself and took his turn with the shampoo. He washed his hair, turning his face to the hot spray as he rinsed.

He opened his eyes to find Sacha watching him, his golden gaze more speculative than Jonah was in the mood for. "What?"

"Nothing. Am just curious."

"About what?"

"About you. You have done this before? One-night stand?"

"Of course." Jonah shook his head, dispersing the water gathered on his face. "Not often, though. I don't have time for relationships."

"I was not talking about relationships. Why would you want one? You have Grindr, no?"

Jonah rolled his eyes. "I suppose, but I don't use hook-up apps much."

"Neither do I."

"No? Do you have a boyfriend?"

"No."

"Girlfriend?"

"Not for a long time now."

"You're bi?"

"Does that bother you? Some men do not like to be with another who fucks women too."

"It doesn't bother me," Jonah said. "I thought I was bi for a while."

"What changed your mind?"

"I like men too much to have room for anything else."

Sacha's slow smirk widened. "Is there such a thing as liking men too much in your country? You have so much freedom here."

"I've never thought about it," Jonah admitted. "I know it's different in Russia, though."

Sacha's shrug was inscrutable. "It is, but I do not live there, so I don't think about it much either."

"How long have you lived over here?"

"Eleven years."

Jonah wanted to ask how old that made Sacha. His strong jaw gave his face a maturity that didn't quite match his boyish features, but he had wise eyes too, the kind of eyes that would be the same until the end of time, giving idiots like Jonah no clue how long he'd been on the earth. "Do you have family over here?"

"Some. Not close, though. Cousins, and their children. I don't see them."

"Then why did you come here?"

"To study."

"Where?"

Sacha's lips rose a touch more. "That is many questions."

"Sorry."

"Is okay. I don't mind. I studied at Imperial College, then I like the city, so I stay and find work."

"In app development?"

"Not at first, but it is what happened."

Something was lost in the phrasing. Jonah tried to puzzle it out, but it was hard to make his brain work while Sacha was still so close and so very naked. He gave up and braved a step sideways, hoping Sacha would take the bait.

He didn't. He turned the water off and reached for a towel. "I should leave."

Still breathless from their first fuck, Jonah hadn't anticipated a second round, but the prospect of Sacha's departure disappointed him than he could explain. He followed Sacha out of the shower and snagged another towel from the shelf. He wanted to ask him to stay, but how? What was he supposed to say? *A sleepover would be weird, but please don't leave without fucking me again?*

No. Definitely not. Some things were better left unsaid. Right?

Reason warred with a stomach-clenching reluctance to let Sacha go. Jonah was a confident man—born to such privilege, how could he have been anything else? But the G&G

Christmas ball always left him unsettled, had done for years, ever since—

Stop. That's what you're thinking about right now?

Not literally. But it was impossible to deny that the disquiet his yearly encounter with William Ratner left in the pit of his stomach was largely absent. Jonah was flying, in a muted sort of way, and he didn't want to come down. Not yet.

He certainly didn't want to watch Sacha put his clothes *on*. It felt like sacrilege. "You don't have to go," he blurted. "I mean, unless you have somewhere else to be. I have food, um, and you said you're always hungry, so..."

Smooth, Gray. This is why you don't date, because you can't have a conversation with a beautiful man without making a fool of yourself.

There were other reasons, including the ones they'd already discussed, and he'd never found himself in conversation with *anyone* as devastatingly attractive as Sacha Ivanov, but tripping over his words was an old flaw.

An amusing flaw, if Sacha's dancing gaze was anything to go by. "I did say that, didn't I?"

Jonah nodded, not trusting himself with more words. He bent to retrieve his shirt from the floor, his underwear too, but strong hands gripped him before he could reach for his discarded clothes, and brought him upright again.

Sacha was right in front of him. Somehow, he'd crossed the room with no sound. "What food do you have?"

The question didn't match the intensity blazing in his liquid gold eyes.

Jonah swallowed. "Charcuterie, cheese, wine. Some smoked salmon, maybe. No caviar, though, I'm afraid."

"I do not like caviar. It's a cliché and it's disgusting."

"Agreed. What about the rest of it, though? Can I entice you to stay?"

For a long moment, Sacha said nothing, and Jonah feared he would leave after all. Then his fierce grip on Jonah's biceps slackened. "I will stay and eat," he said. "And after…"

"Yes?"

Sacha shrugged. "Eat well, Jonah Gray. I am not finished with you."

4

Incompetence irritated Sacha more than the stupidest person ever could. Stupid people were stupid, they couldn't help that. But the spectacle of a perfectly intelligent individual being monumentally moronic incensed him beyond belief.

He cast a baleful glare around the meeting room. "It is not a hard concept to grasp. If this app fails again, we will miss the soft launch date and cost this company a significant amount of money. Meaning operating capacity is reduced. Employment is reduced. *Your* employment. If you do not believe in the app itself, this is your motivation to be better. If it isn't, you should work somewhere else."

Silence met his statement, and the faces around him were a futile mix of slow comprehension, and the bored complacency that had brought them to this mess in the first place. They'd started with a simple brief: to build a fitness app that appealed to, and empowered, ordinary women. A recycled mission statement, bought for peanuts from a failed start-up. They hadn't even had to come up with the concept themselves. But somewhere along the line of bad decisions, laziness, and plain inanity, the message had been lost. The app didn't even work, let alone appeal to female consumers who, frankly, deserved better.

Sacha shook his head. "You're all idiots."

"What Mr. Ivanov means," Sacha's boss—the main investor of the failing app, and the man who'd hired Sacha to save it—broke in, "is that we have a lot of hard work ahead of us—"

"No," Sacha refuted. "I mean they are idiots."

More silence, but it wasn't uncomfortable for Sacha. He didn't care about massaging the egos of people who'd made such fundamental mistakes. Even the basic data aggregation was flawed. At this rate and with these clowns for company, Sacha was going to have to reengineer the whole thing himself.

The meeting dragged on. Sacha was blunt, and his boss wasted ten minutes after each eventuality, smoothing hurt feelings and explaining Sacha's intentions.

Stupid man. But the break in conversation that required actual brain power gave Sacha's mind the opportunity to drift to his current favourite topic: Jonah *Maximillian* Gray. That's right, Sacha had looked him up the moment he'd got home in the early hours of Saturday morning. Who needed sleep? Not Sacha. *Liar*. But after an evening spent in the company of the most charming man Sacha had ever met, it had been low down on his list of priorities.

Company? Is that what you're calling it? You fucked him on every surface of his penthouse apartment.

It was true. The only place he hadn't screwed Jonah was his actual bed, but that suited Sacha. After a long day topped off with too much champagne and several mind-blowing orgasms, Jonah's pristine white bed would've been a dangerous place to be. Sacha didn't do sleepovers.

Anymore. It had been a hell of a long time since he'd last broken that rule, and he didn't intend on doing it any time soon. Or ever. Sharing a bed for anything other than sex brought a shift in dynamics, a closeness that he didn't have the time or inclination to enjoy. No. He stuck to fucking. Drinks beforehand at a push. Nothing more.

Yeah? So how does a cosy picnic in Jonah Gray's kitchen fit into that?

Sacha hadn't decided. The only takeaway he had from that night was that there was zero chance of him not spending every precious free second daydreaming of fucking Jonah again. *And*, that despite two days of furtive glances across the foyer that divided their office space, he'd yet to catch so much as a glimpse of the auburn hair his hands had found such a welcome home in. If Sacha closed his eyes, he could still feel the silky locks tangled around his fingers as he'd fucked Jonah from behind, at the window, over the kitchen counter, against the front door.

"Sacha?"

"Yes?" Sacha turned without blinking to the woman who'd said his name, one of few employees in the room he'd deduced worth a second conversation. Her name was Helga, and she was beautiful. If not for the weight of the corporate world hanging over them, Sacha might've paid her more attention, but he didn't have time for distractions right now. Only for yet another quick glance to the glass partition between Flash Gray Media and Blutecc Ltd.

A pointless glance as there was still no sign of the auburn hair of his dreams.

Helga said something else. Sacha missed every word, but

was fairly confident that he could answer her question regardless. "We will have to find the time," he said. "If we do not make the soft launch before Christmas, this app will be dead in the water. The investment will be lost, and this company will be marked as one that does not deliver."

Another voice spoke. "What does that mean for working hours until then? Most of us are contracted for thirty-eight hours. You can't make us work overtime without fair compensation."

Sacha turned his gaze on the man not much younger than him, with wax in his thin moustache and terrible hand tattoos. "If that is your attitude this company will not survive long enough to pay you anything at all, fair or not. Perhaps it would be better if you worked somewhere else."

"You can't sack me."

"I haven't tried." Sacha smiled. "But thank you for bringing yourself to my attention. I look forward to analysing your performance in the weeks to come."

Moustache man spoke again, but Sacha was bored with him, and tuned him out, his attention, naturally, drifting back to the glass wall. This time, he was rewarded with a flash of copper, but it was gone before it became tangible enough for Sacha to say it was Jonah. It could've been anyone.

At least, that's what his brain said. The warmth in his chest said something else.

"I cannot *believe* you took a complete stranger to your parents' ball and got away with it, *and* managed to have incredible sex after it. Why do these things never happen to me? You didn't even want a date, did you?"

Jonah snorted into his drink and set it down, wiping his mouth before he answered Lily's admittedly fair question. "I didn't think I wanted one until I had one. I can't explain the rest of it. It just happened."

"It's never happened to me."

"Yes, well. He's bi, if it's any consolation. Maybe you can take him out too."

"And then have him ravish me? Don't joke about such things, boo. I'd totally do it."

Jonah knew she would. Lily Dawson had been his best friend since they were both in nappies and he was well aware of her insatiable appetite for amazing sex. Until Sacha, Jonah had believed he'd known the kind of sex she was talking about. Post-Sacha, he was fairly sure he'd been doing it wrong his entire life until the night of the winter ball. "Whatever. You're not fucking Sacha. I need to keep my memories pure."

"That good?"

Jonah drank more beer and shook his head. "It wasn't good. It was...wow, I don't have an adjective. It was like dream sex, you know? The kind that wakes you up in the middle of the night and you have to come to terms with it not being real."

"Oh yeah. Dream sex is the best. There aren't many men out there who can match up to your subconscious imagination."

"He did. I swear..." Jonah glanced around and lowered his voice. "I've never come so hard in my life, awake or otherwise. I was literally seeing stars."

"That's cute. What does he look like?"

"Moody," Jonah said. "But only if you don't catch him

right. He seemed quite sweet some of the time, it was fucking confusing."

"It must've been if you're swearing about it. Are you going to see him again?"

"Literally? I suppose so, we work in the same building. I don't know about, uh, socially, though. He didn't leave his number when he left."

"Have you looked him up?"

"Where?"

"On social media. Give me your phone. I'll do it." Lily swiped Jonah's phone before he could protest and opened his twitter account. "What was his name again?"

"Sacha Ivanov. I bet he's not there, though. He didn't seem the type."

"He must be the type if he works for Blutecc. Social media and apps are what they do."

"That's work, not personal. Reading his business account wouldn't tell me anything about him."

Lily rolled her eyes and tapped at Jonah's phone. Despite absolute certainty that he was right, Jonah leaned forwards and peered at the screen, watching Lily type Sacha's name and scroll through the search results.

His heart skipped when her eyes lit up.

She held up the phone. "Is this him?"

Jonah squinted at the screen. The profile avatar was small, but there was no mistaking the chiselled features of the stranger who'd fucked him against his bedroom window. Dressed in a shirt unbuttoned to his chest, Sacha had perfected the look of a man who'd woke up as ridiculously attractive as he'd gone to sleep. And he was smiling in the photograph. Laughing, maybe. *Damn, he's gorgeous.*

Lily smirked. "I'll take that as a yes. I can't stalk his tweets, though. They're all in Russian."

"That's his first language."

"Ooooh, does he have an accent?"

"Yeah. It's sexy as hell, especially when, well. You know."

"Dirty talk?"

"I think so. It was the right time to be saying something filthy."

"While you were fucking him?"

"Other way round."

"Really?" Lily lowered the phone and reached for her glass of Chablis. "You don't do that very often."

"How do you know?"

"Because you tell me every sordid detail I ask for."

"You don't always ask me that."

"I don't need to. Based on past evidence I'm usually confident making an assumption."

Jonah laughed. "Well, you know what they say about assumptions."

"I do. And I also know what you say about getting fucked. What was different about this bloke?"

"I don't know. I didn't really think about it. It just happened."

"Is it going to happen again?"

"You asked that already and I still don't know the answer."

"The Russian Twitter account didn't help?"

"Shockingly no." Jonah reclaimed his phone and shut down the app, resisting the urge to scroll through any pictures Sacha had posted. His likes and retweets. Any clue to who he actually was. It felt wrong without Sacha's sardonic smirk for company. Besides, without the context of actual words, what was the point? "I very much doubt it, though. He was pretty clear about second dates."

"As in?"

"They don't happen. He's a one-night kind of guy."

"But it wasn't a real date, not officially, at least. Surely he can spare you another one?"

"That's what you think I should go with when we finally cross paths again?"

Lily sipped her wine. "Sure. Why not? What's the worst that can happen?"

"He could say no, and then a perfectly good one-night stand would be tainted by rejection."

"Counter proposal: he might say yes and then a one-night stand turns into an extended run of amazeballs sex. If you don't think it's worth the risk then he wasn't nearly as good in the sack as you're claiming."

Jonah laughed—couldn't help it—and leaned forwards again. "He wasn't good in the sack, Lily, he was off the stratosphere."

"Then find him and ask him to fuck you again. Seriously. That kind of sex doesn't come to call that often. Don't let it go without a fight."

"I don't need to fight for him. We're not star-crossed lovers."

"Not yet. But mark my words, sunshine. Office romances get super complicated super-fast—"

"It's not a romance. Christ, it was a one-night stand."

"Yeah. Okay." Lily gave Jonah the look she'd been giving him since they were twelve and she'd decided he needed to kiss the son of her live-in housekeeper, just to make sure he really wanted to kiss boys. The look that let him know he was an idiot.

But she wasn't always right, and this time, she was wrong. His night with Sacha had been a once in a lifetime experience. A magical, never repeated experience that Jonah wouldn't ever forget.

Right?

The conversation moved on. Just. Lily pulled it back to Sacha a few times, but Jonah had nothing left to share. Eventually, she let it go.

It was still early when Jonah put her into a cab. He had every intention of going home, but a quick pat of his pockets revealed he'd left his keys in his desk. *Damnit.* Jonah had never been good at "popping in" to the office. Even a five-minute dash to retrieve his keys from the drawer would result in him somehow finding more work to do, and he wasn't in the mood. It had been a long week, and it was only Thursday. But unless he wanted to chase Lily down for her spare key, he had little choice but to go back for his own.

Sighing, he made the short walk from the bar to the office. Though the hour wasn't that late, it was late enough that the Flash Gray side would be deserted. Jonah tried to remember if they'd left anything in the break room Curtis could take home for his kids, but the day had been a blur of meetings and storyboards, and after two hours of beer and sex talk, he was fried.

He waited for the lift in a daze, trying not to think about the last time he'd ridden it after office hours. That heady night with Sacha had been less than a week ago, but it felt like a lifetime, not helped by the fact that Sacha seemed to be a ghost. His picture was up on the Blutecc wall of fame, but Jonah had yet to catch a glimpse of the man himself. If not for his scowling mugshot, he'd have wondered if the entire evening had been a dream. Christ, he'd even woken the next morning to find the window wiped clean of any evidence and every scrap of detritus around his apartment picked up and cleared away. *What if it did happen in my head? What if the story I just told Lily is nothing but wishful thinking?*

The lift arrived. Jonah glanced up, half a mind still questioning his sanity as the doors opened.

In the same moment, Sacha Ivanov raised his gaze, and somehow everything fell into place, as far as his actual existence, at least. But still, Jonah stared. In person, Sacha was even more attractive than he remembered and he found himself rooted in place, caught in the vortex of his killer gaze.

Sacha didn't move either. He stared too, until his lips rose in the smirk Jonah recalled from the sweaty dreams he'd had every night since their fake date. "Jonah Gray, we meet again."

5

Jonah unglued his tongue from the roof of his mouth. "You sound surprised, as if it wasn't inevitable given that we work on the same floor."

"If it was inevitable it would've happened by now," Sacha retorted. "You are the invisible man."

"That implies you've been looking for me, and also that you haven't looked that hard as my office is twenty metres from yours."

Sacha's smirk deepened. "I don't have an office."

"Semantics."

"Facts. I have spent all week in a goldfish bowl and have seen no sign of you. It made me think that perhaps *you* were the one with the fake security badge."

"Seriously?"

"No. You were right the first time. I did not look for you that hard."

Jonah didn't know whether to be amused or offended, and the lift doors started to close before he could decide.

He shot out a hand to stop them and stepped into the lift,

pressing the button for the thirteenth floor before it occurred to him that Sacha hadn't moved.

The doors closed and the lift began to rise through the building. "Sorry," Jonah said. "Want me to let you out at the next floor?"

Sacha shrugged. "I don't mind. I have fond memories of this lift with you."

Jonah's belly warmed and he didn't care for it. Irritation threatened the thrill of finally being alone with Sacha again. Why did he have to say things like that at the same time as making it obvious he didn't give a shit? Talk about mixed signals. Or no signals, actually, as there was every chance Sacha was merely making conversation now Jonah had taken him hostage in the lift, and that was as irritating as his first conclusion.

Stop drawing conclusions then. Act like a normal person.

Jonah sighed and shook his head.

Sacha's keen stare pierced holes in him. "Something wrong?"

"Hmm? What? Oh. No. Just a long day. I thought it was over, but I forgot my keys."

"I didn't see you leave."

"Hardly surprising when you said you didn't look that hard."

"Maybe I was lying."

Jonah forced himself to face Sacha's smirk, the one that was equal parts intense and amused. "Do you do that a lot?"

"Lie?" Sacha pushed off the lift wall he was slouching against. "No, not really. I am lazy and the truth is easier."

"So which is it? Did you look for me or not?"

"Does the truth matter to you?"

"Maybe. I'm not sure it should, though."

Sacha was suddenly close enough that Jonah could smell him, and his clean, masculine scent took him right back to the moment he'd realised Sacha was serious about coming home with him. Like then, Jonah's heart jumped, and more frustration built in his gut. Sacha was toying with him, but why? He said himself the truth was easier, so why the hell was he still in the lift?

As the thought completed, the lift stopped. Jonah turned away from Sacha, waiting for the doors to open. They duly did and Jonah stepped out, lifting his hand in a cursory wave. "See you then. Thanks for the chat."

He walked away without looking back. The lift doors closed. Jonah made his way to his office. It had glass walls, like most of the floor, but he'd shut the blinds before he'd left for a lunchtime meeting, and he took sanctuary in the darkened space, despite the fact that Sacha was already gone and unable to see him regardless.

Shaking his head, he let out a long, slow breath and rubbed his chest, coming to terms with the full body trip he apparently endured every time he was in the Russian's company. It was... something else. Perhaps it was just as well they seemed destined to avoid each other during office hours. Jonah had too much on his plate to make time for daily meltdowns.

"So this is where you work."

Jonah startled, and his slowing pulse picked up pace again. "You followed me," he said brilliantly.

Sacha chuckled. "I did. I don't know why, though. Maybe I left something here too."

"What?"

"I don't know. I haven't thought of it yet."

"That makes no sense."

"Precisely."

"What is?"

Sacha stared at Jonah like he was the world's stupidest mutant.

Jonah fought the urge to squirm and rounded his desk, flicking on his computer for something to do before he remembered he'd come for his keys.

He fished them out of the drawer as his iMac flashed to life. The screen filled with the storyboards he'd spent all afternoon pitching to his most high profile client, and more vexation roiled in his gut. The concept Flash Gray had created was cutting edge and crisp—Jonah had lost enough sleep making sure of it—but the client had barely glanced at the images Jonah had brought to the table, instead making it clear that he'd signed with FG because of Jonah's last name. After months of hard work, it had been a kick in the dick he hadn't prepared for.

"Death by nepotism?"

He shook his head. *Damn you, Sacha Ivanov.*

"What is this?"

Jonah blinked. Sacha was beside him, peering at the computer screen. "Storyboards for the next La Glo launch."

"The perfume?"

"Yes. Their summer scent."

Sacha squinted closer at the screen. "Did you design this?"

"Not entirely. I have a creative team in place these days. But…"

"You have trouble delegating?"

"How can you tell?"

"Because this is the beating heart of what you do here,

no? You didn't found this company to sit in an office and watch the dollars roll in. You could've done that anywhere."

"It's pounds, but yes, I get what you're saying." Jonah turned his back to the screen and leaned against his desk. "I like the artistic side. I was good at it and I'd probably have preferred to work for someone else and do it full time."

"So why didn't you?"

"It's not how we do things."

"Who?"

"My family. We don't work for other people."

Sacha rolled his eyes. "But you're a slave to expectation. How is that any different?"

"It's not, but at least I can pick my own hours."

"I heard a rumour that you are always the last to leave, and yet you were not today."

"Lunch meeting. And not to be pedantic, but I'm still here."

"*We're* still here."

Jonah laughed. "And I'm the pedant? Did you figure out what you left here yet?"

Sacha finally tore his gaze from Jonah's computer. The warm light coming from the La Glo boards made his eyes gleam, like a wolf by firelight. "Not yet. I'm thinking maybe it was something I neglected to do."

"You don't strike me as a forgetful person."

"No? How do I strike you?"

Hot. Sharp. Deadly. Kind. Jonah couldn't decide until he settled on a new word: *Conflicted.*

He licked his lips, more aware of Sacha's closeness than ever. "You strike me as efficient. If you didn't do something before you left, it was deliberate."

"Deliberate." Sacha repeated the word slowly, as if

turning it over in his mind to see if it fit. His expression was unreadable, but Jonah was growing used to that, though it made him ache to realise he hadn't seen Sacha's face when they were fucking. *I wish I'd seen him come.*

"Are you all right?" Sacha waved a hand in front of Jonah's face. "You are flushed."

"It's warm in here."

"It is not. The heating shuts off at six o'clock."

"How do you know that?"

"Because there is an idiot in my office who tells me it means it is time to go home."

"And does he? Go home, I mean."

"Of course. There is an idiot-shaped hole in the door at six o'clock sharp."

Real irritation darkened Sacha's features. It was dangerous, and sexy as hell. Jonah's fingers itched to trace the frown lines on Sacha's handsome face. To maybe smooth them away with his lips, then slide along his jaw, and to his mouth. They hadn't kissed when they'd fucked. There'd been a few moments when Jonah had thought they might, but each time Sacha had pulled back and pressed his lips somewhere else, leaving Jonah waiting and wanting.

That hadn't changed.

Stop. If he wanted to kiss you he'd have done it already. Put your keys in your pocket and go home.

Jonah didn't move.

Sacha straightened, but didn't step away either. He sank backwards into Jonah's desk chair and fiddled with it until it was adjusted to his liking, his eyes dancing with challenge, as if daring Jonah to stop him.

Jonah didn't. It was just a chair. Who cared if Sacha had moved every component beyond recognition? While Sacha was this close to him, not Jonah. It was hard to care about anything that wasn't his heated gaze and addictive scent. "Do you want to go for a drink?"

The words were out before he could catch them. *Damn it.* But he couldn't bring himself to regret them. Their second ever encounter had proved stilted and strange, but he didn't want it to end. He wanted to spend the rest of the evening in Sacha's unique company, so much so that he laughed as Sacha began to shake his head. "Come on, Ivanov. It's one drink. I'm not asking you to marry me. Or does one night of sex mean we can't be friends?"

"You want to be my friend, Jonah Gray?"

"Maybe. Unless you don't want to be mine."

A beat of silence stretched between them. Jonah waited for Sacha to pull back and shake his head. To get up and walk away to wherever he'd been headed when the lift doors had opened downstairs, but Sacha didn't shake his head. He didn't say no.

He reached forward, gripped Jonah's desk, and rolled forwards on Jonah's chair until he was neatly inserted between Jonah's legs. "I do not have many friends," he said slowly. "I don't need or want them. But...you and I, with benefits, no? I do not think I could spend time with you without fucking you again."

Jonah's eyebrows shot up. He felt them disappear into his hairline as he digested Sacha's words.

His pulse banged against his eardrums, brain reeling from the abrupt shift in subject matter, despite the fact that he'd been thinking of Sacha fucking him non-stop since it had happened the first time. "You want to fuck me again? Thought you didn't do second dates?"

"I don't really do dates at all. But we would not call it that if you were my friend. We would just be hanging...out? Is that the phrase?"

"It's *a* phrase," Jonah countered.

"A bad one?"

"No. Not at all. It's unexpected, that's all."

Sacha nodded. "For me too. I never say this to anyone else."

"What's different about me?"

"We are from the same life. And you said yourself you don't want to marry me, so I don't have to worry about you misreading my intentions. You would know what we are... acquaintances who have sex, yes?"

"I didn't say—" Jonah pursed his lips and took a deep breath. "Acquaintances. Right. Are you saying that we share an apathy for relationships? And that I'm rich enough in my own right that you don't have to worry about me being after you for your money and status?"

Sacha laughed and it changed his face entirely. His features softened and his eyes shone. "I have no status in your world, but yes, I suppose that is what I'm saying. I feel safe with you, Jonah. We speak the same language."

"About sex?"

"About many things. I do not have to explain myself to you. We can hang out and have sex. I would like that, and I think you would too."

He wasn't wrong. Jonah could think of nothing he'd rather do than spend his scant free time in Sacha's company, especially if it revolved around them fucking again. But disquiet bloomed in his gut, a prickling sensation he'd never felt before, and it confused the hell out of him. He had no doubts about having sex with Sacha again—*lord* no—but the idea of a friendship that didn't go anywhere or mean anything set his teeth on edge. "We don't have to hang out," he said. "We could just fuck and call it what it is. Don't pander to my sensibilities."

"'Sensibilities'?"

"The terminology isn't important. And I didn't ask you for a drink because I wanted to fuck again."

Sacha's brow flickered with brief confusion before he schooled his features, but Jonah sensed the cogs turning in his brain all the same. "I do not understand."

"Why not?" Jonah said. "It's fairly simple. I enjoyed your company the other night and ninety percent of it wasn't fucking. Why wouldn't I want to do that again?"

"I have answers to that question, but I am stuck on your division of our time together. We were at your parents' ball for four and a half hours. I left your apartment at five o'clock the next morning. Explain to me how the time we spent there equates to a figure of ten percent."

It was a demand, not a question. Jonah almost laughed, but Sacha's expression stopped him, and he rolled his eyes instead. "I was making a point, not doing specific mathematics."

"Be specific. Don't make statements that are not true."

"Okay. *Specifically*, I want to have a drink with you. And I want to have sex with you again. I don't care what particular combination that comes in and I don't care what you call it. Oh, and I like that you feel safe with me. You should. I'd never do anything to hurt you."

"I am not worried about you hurting me."

"Then what *specifically* do you feel safe from when you're with me?"

Sacha grinned a little. "Nothing...*specific*. It was a feeling and I voiced it. It doesn't have to be tangible."

"It does if we're fucking. Where's the fun if you don't feel it?"

"You'll feel it."

"What about you?"

Sacha rolled Jonah's desk chair again, bringing himself closer. For a moment, he looked as though he might stretch up and kiss Jonah. Then he reached for Jonah's belt buckle and began to undo it. "I feel plenty or I would not want to do this again."

A flashback to last Friday bulldozed into Jonah's brain. Sacha's hands on his cock, and then his mouth as he'd held Jonah against the kitchen counter, the contents of Jonah's fridge spread out around them. He'd sucked Jonah until he was hard again, then spun him around and fucked him a second time, fast and sharp, jackhammering into Jonah until he'd shouted his release loud enough for the neighbouring apartment block to hear him. He shivered, and it took every ounce of willpower to still Sacha's hands. "Stop. We can't do this here."

"Why not?"

"Because we're in my office."

"So? The blinds are closed. No one is here."

"Curtis is. So is Samson downstairs."

"The security guard is asleep. He does not wake up for his walk-around for another hour."

"How do you know that?"

"I have worked late this week. He is the creature of habit you said he was when we met."

"And Curtis?"

Sacha shrugged. "He is less predictable. I can shut the door if you wish."

Jonah couldn't think of a single thing he wished for

beyond Sacha's hands on him again. The prospect of Curtis or Samson catching him with pants down seemed a distant concern, and he *knew* his office wasn't covered by CCTV. Only the landing and the elevators were. If no one came, no one would see. Besides, the smugness in Sacha's gaze was obscene. Jonah wasn't going to give him the satisfaction of demanding he shut the door. "Leave it."

"Are you sure?"

"I'm sure."

Sacha's amusement dialled down, replaced by a clear intent that sent more hot shivers down Jonah's spine. He tugged on Jonah's belt again. It came loose from the buckle, inch by inch, and Sacha didn't seem to be in a hurry.

He undid the belt and moved onto the buttons of Jonah's trousers with *criminal* slowness. He had deft, elegant fingers, but he seemed to make them clumsy on purpose.

Jonah sucked in a shaky breath. Perhaps Sacha was giving him time to think. Time to back out, despite being the one to goad him into this in the first place. And what was *this*? Were they going to fuck right here in his office? Was Sacha going to bend him over the desk? It wasn't as if he hadn't shown his fondness for that position when he'd fucked Jonah all over his apartment.

"Shh," Sacha said.

Jonah glanced down at him. "I didn't say anything."

"You don't have to when your jaw tics like that."

Jonah made an effort to relax his face. "Perhaps I'm excited," he hedged. "It's not every day someone blows me in my office."

"No? Shame."

"Is it?"

"Yes. Everyone should get blown in their office. It makes coming to work worthwhile."

"You don't like your job?"

"I love it. But perhaps I would love it more if I could keep you under my desk."

"Charming."

Sacha's lips turned up. "I try."

"Try harder."

"At what? I never said I was going to blow you."

"But you are."

Jonah grinned. Sacha smirked back, dark and deadly. He leaned forwards and unzipped Jonah's trousers, pushing them open, revealing the black underwear Jonah had dressed in that morning. They were plain and expensive, but apparently no barrier for what Sacha wanted. He slid them down, and Jonah's dick sprang free, already half hard.

And wanting. Sacha's mere gaze was enough for him to harden fully, his balls drawing up, anticipation leaving him dizzy. Jonah could hardly stand it, but he forced himself to keep silent and still. Sacha was a predator, and Jonah the prey, but it made no sense to make a meal of himself so fast. There was a difference between playing dead and lying down to die.

Why are you thinking like he's a lion stalking you? You want this. You basically asked for it.

All true. Jonah had no answers for the devil on his shoulder. Just a building heat thrumming in his veins, and lips that ached to be kissed—another errant thought he'd have to ignore if he wanted to enjoy this.

"*Focus,*" Sacha said softly. "On me and what I'm going to do to you. Don't think about anything else, just what's real."

"You don't know what I'm thinking."

"I don't need to." Sacha closed the conversation with his mouth on Jonah's cock, and coherent thought abandoned Jonah as if he'd never had it.

Ever.

As if he'd lacked the skill since the day he was born, and his brain was a void. A black space filled only by the dismantling sensation of Sacha going to town on his dick.

Wet.

Hot.

Hard.

Then he switched it up and sucked slowly up and down Jonah's shaft, his gold-flecked gaze as teasing as his tongue.

Jonah groaned, and his hands flew to Sacha's head, fingers tangling in his perfectly dishevelled hair. It was as silky as he'd imagined it, no product weighing it down. It would be so easy to bury his fingers in it, and cant his hips, fucking Sacha's mouth. But he didn't. He kept his hands loose and his hips still, ceding control to the man bent double between his legs.

He didn't stop to think about why. Just closed his eyes and *felt* and tried not to consider the possibility that Curtis or Samson, or any other employee who'd forgotten something, could walk in on them at any moment.

As the pressure in his gut built, not thinking became easier. Pleasure unfurled, beat by beat, curling his toes and stealing his breath. Harsh pants escaped his lungs, and spasms rocked every muscle as he fought to keep still.

Sacha slid his free hand up Jonah's leg, gripping his thigh. Jonah let one of his drift from Sacha's head before he caught himself and put it back. *Don't try and hold his hand. He's blowing you in the office, not declaring undying love.*

The reality of the situation almost made Jonah laugh, but

there was nothing funny about what Sacha was doing to him. He'd never felt anything like it. Shivers became full body shudders. Gasps became groans. Jonah tipped his head back and screwed his eyes shut, no longer caring if the building staff heard him shout. "Fuck. I'm going to come. Pull off if you don't want it down your throat."

Sacha hummed and stayed where he was.

Jonah tried to warn him again but his roaring climax choked him, barrelling through every part of him with a strangled shout. He emptied into Sacha's hot mouth, still warring with the urge to buck his hips and ram his cock down Sacha's throat, and winning the battle was exquisite. His climax stretched out, held by the ropes of his tight muscles, and he was seeing stars when it finally faded.

Sacha pulled back, his self-satisfied smirk returning full force.

Mourning the loss of his soft hair, Jonah rolled his heavy eyes. "Don't be smug. It doesn't become you."

"Yes, it does."

"Okay, maybe it does, but I don't like it."

"So?"

"So..." Jonah glanced around for something to throw, but settled for fixing his clothes back in place, standing to buckle his belt with shaky hands.

Sacha helped.

"Thanks." Jonah gazed down at him, heart still racing, thumping the tattoo that seemed to be his constant companion when they were together.

Sacha blazed back, his lips reddened and wet. The urge to lean down and kiss him sent new dizziness through Jonah. He rocked on his heels. Sacha caught him, standing to bring them eye level again. "If nepotism does not kill you, maybe blow jobs will."

"Very funny."

"Am I?"

"No. But you're hard. Can I return the favour?"

Sacha stared at him for a long moment, then shook his head. "Not tonight. It's late, we should both go home."

His length pressing against Jonah's thigh told another story. Jonah opened his mouth to protest, but Sacha silenced him with a single finger to Jonah's wanting lips. He tucked a damp lock of Jonah's hair behind his ear. "Next time, Jonah Gray."

Next time. "How long are you going to whole-name me for?"

"Until it bores me."

Jonah nodded and absorbed the words unsaid: that it wasn't just Jonah's name on borrowed time, it was Jonah himself too. But still.

Next time.

6

Sacha was a listener. Sometimes he talked, but most days he preferred to scowl at people until they left him alone forever. Monday morning had started as one of those days, but as it passed in a haze of emergency coding and fraught meetings, he found himself longing for the kind of conversation he'd only had in recent memory with one person. The kind that was teasing and intense, shadows and light.

The kind that he didn't have a single minute to spare for right now.

It was annoyingly ironic that since his last true encounter with Jonah at Jonah's desk, he now saw him every damn time he looked up. Which was often as the company Sacha was keeping in his own office space was irritating enough that he needed a distraction.

"Are you even listening?" Helga asked. "*You're* the one that said this was important."

Sacha tore his gaze from the glint of copper hair he could just about glimpse in the neighbouring offices. "It is important. The app cannot launch if the website isn't strong enough to support it."

"So we need to hire a team to recode it?"

"No." Sacha shook his head. "There is no time for that. We will have to take it apart ourselves and shore it up. It can be rebuilt properly after the soft launch in a few weeks."

"Okay, but *who's* going to do that extra work? We don't have enough capacity in our web development team."

"I'll do it," Sacha said absently, his brain still fixated on Jonah. He'd seen him about twelve times today, the man never seemed to stay in one place for long. He was constantly on the move, checking in with his staff, brewing coffee for anyone and everyone. At one point, he'd gone out and returned with enough doughnuts for the entire floor, the Blutecc teams included.

Sacha had ignored the doughnuts out of a principle that hadn't solidified yet, but it hadn't surprised him to learn that Jonah's generosity was a weekly occurrence. He had kind eyes that didn't belong in the cut-throat world of corporate advertising.

Does he, though? Or is this the version of him you've created in your own head? You hardly know this man.

But Sacha wanted to. Which made the odd pact they'd come to last week all the more complex to swallow. Sacha rarely met anyone he wanted to talk to as much as he wanted to fuck them. And it was even rarer that he wanted to fuck someone more than once. He possessed a scant attention span when it came to peopling because people were boring. Vacuous. Dull. It irritated him that Jonah Gray was anything but.

I don't have time for this. Especially not if he was committing to the extra work of recoding the weakest parts of the website supporting the cursed fitness app, but regardless of Sacha's feelings on personal relationships, he liked a challenge. No. *Loved* a challenge, and this was one he couldn't resist.

The day dragged on. Sacha's offer to recode the website was approved at a tense management meeting, but even if he worked day and night, there was still no guarantee the website would hold. And Sacha had no intention of working day and night. He had an auburn-haired friend with benefits he wanted to reconnect with before he began to wonder if their encounter last week had been an empty promise.

They hadn't spoken since. It wasn't deliberate, but they'd stumbled out of the building that night too dazed to exchange numbers, and they hadn't crossed paths in person. *So? Go into his office and shut the fucking door. Or ask him what he's doing tonight.*

But Sacha did neither. He stayed where he was, huddled in the corner of Blutecc's office space with the few employees he could tolerate without throwing things, and worked like a dog until even Helga deserted him.

"Go home," she said. "It's only Monday."

"What does that matter?"

"You have the whole week ahead of you. There's no point exhausting yourself now."

Sacha rolled his eyes. "I am not exhausted. But you go. I will see you tomorrow."

"Are you sure? I can stay if you—"

"Go," Sacha insisted. "I cannot talk when I'm coding anyway so it would be boring for you to stay."

Helga fetched him more coffee then left. Sacha inhaled the strong black brew, and got up to pour himself some more. It was his sixth cup of the day, something he'd pay for if he wasn't careful, but he needed the stimulation to keep his heavy eyes sharp. Despite everything he'd told Helga, he was aware of his lack of superpowers.

It was late by the time a warning flicker passed through his vision. A flash of pain that would need a bulldozer to stop it if Sacha didn't catch it in time.

He opened the desk drawer he'd claimed as his own and found the pill bottle stashed at the back. It was nearly empty. He popped two and made a mental note to refill his prescription, then dropped the bottle back into the drawer.

The temptation to keep working was strong, but Sacha knew himself well enough to know he at least needed the break of his journey home. He shut his laptop down and packed it into his bag. His coat was on the other side of the office for reasons he couldn't quite remember.

He retrieved it. Jonah's box of doughnuts was by the water cooler. Sacha strode past with every intention of heading straight for the lifts, but, of course, as it had done all day long, a mere glimpse of Jonah's hair threw his entire brain off course.

Sacha was at Jonah's office door before he could stop to make sense of what he was doing. "Midnight oil, yes? That's how you say it?"

Jonah glanced up from his computer. His hair was a riot and he looked as tired as Sacha felt. "Something like that. Why are you still here?"

"Why are you?"

"My team wrote a terrible pitch for an important summit tomorrow. I have to redo it or we're going to crash and burn."

Sacha nodded. It was a scenario he knew well, though the context was different to his own work. "How far have you got?"

"About halfway. It's going to take me all night, but I need to take it home so I can eat and shower."

"So take it home."

"I'm going to. I'm waiting for it to transfer to the cloud so I can access it remotely."

"What are you going to eat?"

The first flickers of Jonah's smile warmed his lovely face. "I don't know. Whatever's at the top of my delivery account, I suppose. I don't have time for anything else. What about you? Why are you still here? Or did you tell me already and I'm too scatty right now to remember?"

"I did not tell you, but it is the same. I must do something no one else can do in a short space of time."

"How long?"

"How long what?"

"How long do you have?"

"A few weeks. We soft launch the app just before Christmas and the website isn't strong enough to support the influx of traffic. I have to fix it."

Jonah frowned. "I don't know what your actual job is, but isn't web design a little below your pay grade?"

"It's not design, it's functionality. The website is not attractive at this stage, but it does not need to be—it just needs to work. That is my job, to make things work."

"Fair enough. It makes more sense when you put it like that. I don't know much about websites beyond the pretty bits."

Sacha chuckled. "That is charming, Jonah Gray."

"Why, thank you. Are you heading out?"

"Yes."

"To go home and keep working?"

"Yes."

Jonah tapped a few keys on his computer, then shut it down with the mouse. A pause stretched out between them. Sacha wondered if he should leave, then Jonah appeared in front of him, his previously tired eyes wide and expectant. "Come on then," he said. "Let's go."

Sacha blinked. "Go where?"

"Home. *My* home, I mean."

"For what?"

"For work. Dinner. Companionship." Jonah's smile was boyish and sweet. "It's what friends do, Ivanov, unless you have a pressing desire to be alone."

"I don't."

"Then let's *go*."

They took a cab to Jonah's building, then rode the elevator to his penthouse apartment. At the top, Sacha found himself drawn to the window again, transfixed by the Christmas lights that had multiplied since his last visit. "Do you have a fir tree in your apartment?"

"I do, actually," Jonah said. "I wasn't going to bother, but Lily made me get a massive one."

"Lily?"

"My friend. She thinks my apartment is too much of a bachelor pad."

"What is wrong with that if you *are* a bachelor?"

"You'd have to ask her. Are you coming in?"

Jonah unlocked his front door and waited. Sacha backed up and preceded him inside, and as promised, a huge decorated tree took up most of the hallway. It was colour-coordinated and smelled of the forest. Sacha stepped closer and examined a bauble that had the face of a baby imprinted on it. "Is this supposed to be Jesus or you?"

"I dread to think," Jonah said. "Lily got it from my mother, so it could be either."

"And what is that?" Sacha pointed to the top of the tree. "An angel?"

"Yes. You don't have those in Russia?"

"Angels? Yes, but my family did not have Christmas trees. We are...secular, yes? Not religious."

"Oh. So you don't celebrate Christmas?"

"We do, but not with religious symbols. Our tree is a *yolka*. It celebrates the New Year and we don't put it up until after your holiday has passed."

Jonah shed his coat and gestured for Sacha to do the same. He took them both and hung them by the door, then he took Sacha's laptop bag from him and tucked it under his arm. "Come on. Let's have a drink and order some food before we start work."

He disappeared into the open living space Sacha only remembered as the cool marble and smooth walls he'd braced his hands against when he'd fucked Jonah over and over until he'd been at the point of collapse. A booze-hazed memory of toppling Jonah onto his bed pushed into Sacha's mind. He remembered the feel of Jonah's clean sheets in his hands as he'd wrapped them around Jonah and then crept away, haunted by the temptation to climb in beside him and go to sleep.

Fool.

Sacha forced his legs into motion and followed Jonah to the sitting room where Jonah laid Sacha's laptop bag on the antique coffee table. "Why is your tree not in here where you can see it?"

Jonah glanced up. "Because I don't spend much time here. I can see it better from my bedroom if it's in the hallway."

"You spend a lot of time in your bedroom?"

"Not especially. It's just the place I frequent most when I'm home."

"And you like your tree? Even though you didn't want it?"

Jonah smiled enough to warm Sacha's blood. "I do like it, actually. My family isn't particularly religious either, but it's more about being together than anything else, and having the tree reminds me that I don't have much longer to wait for that."

"That's what it was supposed to mean in my family too... the together part. For those who still follow the Soviet holiday, they are a symbol of happiness and prosperity."

Jonah shrugged out of his suit jacket. He draped it over the back of the couch and gestured for Sacha to sit. Sacha ignored him and wandered to yet another floor-to-ceiling window. The devil in him pondered if he could make Jonah come against this one too, but his mind was fighting the heaviness the medicine he'd taken at the office often left him with. It was hard to keep track of one thought as it flowed into the next. He wanted to feel Jonah's skin slide against his as much as he wanted to fuck him again.

"Sacha?"

"Hmm?"

Jonah appeared beside him and waved in front of his face. "I've got wine, but I'm thinking we might need coffee if we're going to last all night."

It took a moment for Sacha to remember he was talking about work. He fought the dirty images pooling in his imagination and nodded. "Yes. Coffee. Would be nice."

"I'll get it. Have a look at this and see what you want."

Jonah pressed an iPad into Sacha's hands. It was open on a food delivery app Sacha had helped launch a few years ago. The interface had changed, but Sacha still knew it like the back of his hand. "You should not use this. The security is weak."

"How do you know that?"

"I tell them when they built it. They do not care. Use this one instead." He swiped into the app store and pointed at another logo he knew intimately.

Jonah raised a brow, half amused, half perplexed, but downloaded the app anyway and handed it back to Sacha. "Same request. See what you want."

He vanished again.

Sacha took the iPad to the oversized couch and sat down. The cushions nearly swallowed him whole. They were too comfortable even for fucking.

Stop thinking about fucking.

Sacha snorted softly. It was a big ask even without Jonah's entrancing presence. Sacha liked sex. A lot. And sex with Jonah? Yes. Indeed. It was like nothing he remembered for a very long time.

I want to fuck him again. Hardly a new conclusion, but it was solid enough that Sacha pushed it aside and focused on the iPad screen. His left eye still flickered, as if he had static in his retina. He rubbed at it, knowing it would pass but still dreading what would happen if it didn't. *Put the screen down.*

Sacha poked hurriedly at the first option that seemed vaguely appetising, then loaded his credit card details into the payment screen as Jonah came back in the room.

"Coffee is brewing. What did you get?"

"Noodles. Chicken and rice. I got a lot, but I left it open in case you wanted something else."

"No. That sounds good. Pass it here, I'll send it."

Sacha nudged the iPad to Jonah. "Don't pay. I already did."

"Why?"

"Why not?"

"I'll get the next one."

"If you say so, Jonah Gray."

"I do." Jonah tapped the iPad a few times then set it down next to a laptop Sacha hadn't noticed. It was a MacBook wrapped up in a Deadpool case. He grinned when he saw Sacha's brows rise. "I have a thousand nieces and nephews. They gave me this for my birthday and said they'd cry if I didn't use it."

"You take that into meetings?"

"Of course. I have no interest in being bland. It's not a good look for my company."

"You couldn't look bland if you tried."

"That's sweet," Jonah said. "Is it wrong that I think the same of you right now when you're clearly unfed and in need of a nap?"

"I do not need a nap. I need coffee and to see you naked again."

"Before or after work?"

"I want to say before, but I think when you are naked again I will forget I have work at all."

Jonah shook his head. "All this talk of me being naked. Are you fully clothed in this scenario?"

"Maybe," Sacha hedged, ignoring the desire to feel Jonah's skin against his for the split second he could bear to. "Perhaps I cannot wait long enough to strip."

Jonah snorted. "As if. It was me who couldn't wait last time. You drove me wild."

"Good. I like wild Englishmen."

"Hmm." Jonah got up and abruptly left the room.

He returned with two mugs of strong coffee and passed one to Sacha. He set the other by his Deadpool laptop and Sacha took it to mean the fucking talk had passed.

Sacha reached for his own computer and opened it. The mess of code he'd abandoned filled the screen and he waited a moment to see if his eyes would hold up. They did, and it wasn't long before he was immersed in his work again.

The buzz of Jonah's intercom startled him sometime later.

"It's the food." Jonah got up. "I'll get it."

The evening seemed to be punctuated by Jonah leaving the room, Sacha missing him, then him returning with something else to make Sacha's life brighter. This time it wasn't just his lovely self, it was cardboard containers of Cantonese food.

Sacha took the chopsticks Jonah brandished and dug into a box of salty chicken noodles, laced with chilli, soy sauce, and ginger. Across from him, Jonah claimed a plastic fork and made short work of the fried rice.

Sacha couldn't look away. "You're sexy when you eat."

"Says you using chopsticks like a pro."

"It's not hard."

"I'm sure it's not, but I don't fancy throwing rice all over my laptop while I figure it out."

"I can teach you."

"I'd rather you ate your dinner and did your work so you can fuck me later."

Jonah had a soft, low voice. It was deep, and masculine, but he spoke so smoothly every word wrapped around Sacha like silk. He swallowed the food in his mouth, taking a moment to gather himself. It wasn't often he found himself floored like he was with Jonah, and he wondered if Jonah knew the effect he was having on him.

He doubted it. Jonah was charismatic and warm, but unassuming when it came to how he saw himself.

Sacha wanted to change that. He wanted Jonah to know how beautiful he was.

It was a shame he had at least another hour of work to do before he could show him.

They polished off the food and got back to it. Jonah finished first and left Sacha to clear away the rubbish from dinner, and take a shower.

When he came back, Sacha was still working, but he'd moved from the couch to the floor.

Jonah dropped down beside him. "How much more do you have to do?"

Sacha shrugged. "I must do as much as I can as long as I am not too tired to carry on tomorrow."

"How much is that?"

"I do not know. I am not good at judging that."

"Do you need an intervention?"

"How so?"

Jonah took Sacha's hand and eased it away from the laptop. When Sacha didn't protest, he did the same with the other. "I mean, do you need someone to tell you stop?"

"Always."

"I mean work, Ivanov."

"I know, Jonah Gray."

"Why are you smirking then?"

"Because I like it when you are assertive. It's cute."

"Cute?"

"Yes. And optimistic."

"That sounds...interesting."

Sacha laughed and felt the shackles of his work loosen a touch, perhaps proving Jonah's theory, not that he was going to admit it. He wrenched one hand free and shut his laptop. Then he gave Jonah his full attention. "I am interesting. And interes*ted*."

"In what?"

"In you."

"What do you want to know? Ask me anything, I'll tell you."

Sacha believed him. Trouble was, he couldn't think of what question he wanted to ask first. If it was verbal, or something he wanted to ask of Jonah's strong supple body.

They were still holding hands. It blew Sacha's mind a little, tender intimacy wasn't his style. Not even close. But every moment with Jonah, naked or otherwise, seemed loaded with the unexpected. It was a game of chicken with Sacha's impersonal bad habits.

He squeezed Jonah's fingers, testing the theory. The lone wolf in him wanted to rip his hand free, throw Jonah down, and do what he'd come here for. But the man still holding Jonah's hand argued that his motives had been unspecific. Jonah wanted sex, but he'd mentioned companionship too. Could Sacha do that? Did he even know how?

Jonah reclaimed Sacha's other hand and stood, bringing Sacha with him. He walked them to his bedroom, where they'd fucked the first time. It had barely been two weeks, but somehow it seemed an age had passed since that night. And the grand winter ball? Sacha could hardly recall it, his memories overwhelmed by what had happened after in this very room.

Desire rippled through Sacha. He tugged Jonah to a stop and flattened himself against Jonah's back, moulding their bodies together. Jonah's alabaster neck was a temptation he couldn't ignore. He pressed his lips to pale skin that smelled of nothing but Jonah, and left a trail of open-mouthed kisses until he came to the hollow behind his ear. Then he stopped and took another breath. "You do not wear cologne."

"No."

"Neither do I."

"I know. I like that."

"Why?"

Jonah shrugged. "I like how you smell without it."

"And how is that?"

"Like a man."

Sacha felt himself smile, though Jonah couldn't see him. "It is like you are in my head. That is what I would've said if you had asked me."

"Is it?"

"Yes. I like how you smell too."

Jonah leaned back, arching his neck to give Sacha more skin to explore. "What else do you like?"

"About you?"

"Maybe. Or in general. I don't mind. Just tell me something."

Sacha lost himself to Jonah's jaw for a moment, considering his answer. "I like watching us fuck in the reflection of your obnoxious windows."

Jonah sucked in a shaky breath. "My windows aren't obnoxious. How can glass offend you so much?"

"I am not offended."

"You called them obnoxious."

"They are."

"Are they? Or do you mean something else?"

"I know what I mean."

"I don't doubt that, Ivanov."

"So why do you question me?"

Jonah let out a laugh that Sacha gladly cut off by sinking his teeth into Jonah's tender flesh. He sucked—not hard enough to leave a mark, but with enough force to make Jonah groan.

The heady sound lit Sacha on fire. He no longer cared about conversation and he pressed a hand over Jonah's mouth to tell him so.

Jonah spun in his arms, fighting him. He was as tall as Sacha, and just as strong. Whoever won would be the man who wanted it most.

And that man was Sacha. He held firm, keeping his hand where it was until he was sure Jonah would not speak. Then he travelled lower, unbuttoning Jonah's shirt as he went, revelling in the fact that they were safe in Jonah's apartment, not holed up in his office, restricted by the threat of the elderly security guard snoozing downstairs.

He rid Jonah of the shirt that fit him so perfectly. Jonah's chest was as pale as the rest of him. Sacha slid a hand across it and down, traversing to his defined abdomen.

Jonah shivered.

Sacha smirked. "You like that?"

"I like you touching me."

"Why?"

"It makes me want you."

"You did not want me before?"

Another shudder passed through Jonah. "Stop talking in circles. You know you make my dick hard."

"I know nothing."

"Liar. You've had my cock in your mouth."

Jonah had a way of speaking filth that made Sacha's head

spin, ridding him of the migraine he'd been fighting all evening. It was magic, or it would've been if Sacha had believed in such things. But he didn't. He believed in science, and the biological reaction his body had to Jonah. In the pulsing heat sluicing through his blood, and the slight shake of his hands as he turned Jonah again and pressed his lips to the nape of his neck.

It wasn't magic, it was inevitable.

Sacha trailed his lips down Jonah's spine, gripping Jonah's hip, pinning him in place as long as Jonah wanted him to. And then it occurred to him that his conclusion on their earlier struggle had been wrong. Or at least, biased. Sacha hadn't won just because he wanted to, *Jonah* had wanted it too. He'd wanted Sacha, with his bruising grip and biting kiss. His rough touch. His teeth.

His cock.

More heat flooded Sacha. He undid Jonah's suit trousers and shoved them down his hips, taking Jonah's underwear along for the ride.

Jonah was hard, his dick jutting out, straight and long. Sacha wanted him in his mouth again, but more than that, he ached to be inside him, and his characteristic patience deserted him. He'd tease Jonah later. Perhaps. Maybe. If they did this again. But if they were only doing it once, Sacha couldn't wait. He wanted him now.

He pushed Jonah onto the bed and unbuttoned his own trousers while Jonah stretched across the bed to the bedside table. Lube and condoms appeared within Sacha's reach. His pulse kicked up a gear. He freed his dick and laid a hand on Jonah's back, drawing him closer.

"Wait," Jonah said.

Sacha stilled. "What is it? You want to stop?"

"No. I want to feel you."

"What do you mean?"

"Your clothes, Ivanov. Take them off."

A slow smile curled Sacha's lips. "You want me naked?"

"Of course I do. I can't remember everything from last time we did this, but I remember how you felt, and I want that again."

It was probably the sweetest thing anyone—man or woman—had ever said to Sacha. And he recalled Jonah's earnest desire to see him that night too, and the fleeting fear in his gaze when Sacha had kept him waiting. For whatever reason, Sacha fucking him with most of his clothes still on dampened his smile, and Sacha wasn't here for that.

Give him what he wants. If only everything in life was so easy.

Sacha shed his clothes, taking care to toss his shirt where Jonah could see it. Then he crawled onto the bed behind him and melded their bodies together again, his cock finding home in Jonah's crease as if they'd been born to fit together this way. "Better?"

Jonah let out a low hum and dropped his head. "Much. Sorry, I—"

"Shh. You can have what you want. Always. I am just bossy."

"I like that."

"I know. Is why I do it. Not to keep you quiet."

"You told me to be quiet last time."

"Yes, and you asked me to take my clothes off, so we both get what we want, no?"

"I'm not being quiet now."

Sacha rolled his eyes, feeling Jonah everywhere from his toes to his fingertips. "I did not ask you to be."

It was an exchange that could've lasted forever, and if not for the burning arousal making his eyes mist, Sacha might've let it. But his desire for Jonah won out. He pulled back and rubbed his hands over Jonah's pale skin, leaving marks that built a possessive growl in his chest. The lube was close, but he found himself ignoring it and dropping to his knees behind Jonah, pressing his face to his hole.

His mouth made contact and Jonah jumped, perhaps expecting something else. Something harder and thicker than the feather-light touch of Sacha's lips and tongue. "*Fuck.*"

Sacha smiled and slipped his tongue further inside Jonah, probing, circling, searching for the cadence that made Jonah's strong thighs shake, and Sacha's own cock pulse with need.

The sounds Jonah made were everything. Sacha had long been addicted to mapping the pleasure points of the souls he shared a bed with, but Jonah was a whole new thrill. Sacha had never wanted someone so much. Had never trembled with want like he was right now.

His own moans escaped him. Shocked him. *We're not even fucking yet.* And they wouldn't ever get to that if Sacha couldn't tear himself away from taking Jonah like this. He wondered if Jonah could come this way, with just Sacha's tongue inside him. Then he flipped the consideration to himself and pondered the ridiculous level his arousal had already reached. If Sacha didn't fight it, it wouldn't have taken much to push him over the edge.

Unbidden, Sacha's hand drifted from Jonah's hip and to his own dick. He took himself in hand and squeezed, but the rush of pleasure was too much. If he wanted to fuck Jonah, he had to stop. Like, *right now*, and it was another new sensation Sacha didn't quite understand. He'd always prided himself on restraint. He could fuck all night if he wanted to, not coming until the final throes of an encounter. His self-control was absolute, his edging game flawless. But...this was Jonah Gray. Apparently, his bewitching powers extended beyond the fact that he'd coaxed Sacha into a third encounter.

Far beyond.

Sacha drew back, leaving wet kisses in his wake, and up the wicked path of Jonah's spine again.

Jonah shook beneath him, a layer of sweat dampening his skin.

Sacha's dick *ached*. He grabbed for the condoms with clumsy hands. He ripped one from the strip and tore it open with his teeth. "I'm going to fuck you now. Is that okay?"

"I'd murder you if you didn't."

Sacha laughed, deep from his belly, in a way he hadn't for a very long time.

Jonah raised his head and turned his gaze over his shoulder, snaring Sacha in a trap of forest green and surprise. "Deadly rage amuses you?"

"*You* amuse me, *luchik*."

"Yeah? What else?"

"What else do you do to me?"

"Yes. Tell me."

Sacha didn't usually talk so much when he was fucking someone, but giving Jonah what he wanted had become so important that words spilled out with little thought. Raw. Unfiltered. "You make me think less and think more at the same time. It is very strange."

"Strange how?"

Sacha rolled the condom onto his dick and finally reached for the lube. "It is strange because I have never felt such things until I met you," he said, but in Russian, so Jonah could not understand him.

"That's not fair."

"I know, but I don't always know how to say things in your language."

"So you cheat."

"No, I say them anyway. It is not my fault you don't speak Russian."

Jonah laughed, as deep and free as Sacha had done. His eyes blazed at Sacha a moment longer before he dropped his head.

Sacha missed the connection, but the feeling was brief as heat rose between them again. Jonah called to him like a siren. He gripped his cock and guided it to Jonah, easing inside with a slow slide, closing his eyes as Jonah's tight warmth enveloped him.

It was as consuming as he remembered, traversing every muscle and nerve, wiping all thoughts from Sacha's brain except the overwhelming need to move. To drive in and out of Jonah with a rhythm that made Jonah groan and arch his back.

Sacha fucked him with steady thrusts, intensity building with every snap of his hips. He'd had wild plans to draw it out and fuck Jonah for hours and hours, until the sun rose and it was time to go to work, but Jonah's spell on Sacha was complete.

Perhaps he did believe in magic after all.

No. It is science. It is my body responding to his. We are just more compatible than any that has come before.

Yes. Compatibility. That was it. Sacha pushed Jonah down so his chest hit the bed, and nudged his legs wider. The change in angle took Sacha deeper. Jonah *moaned*, and it stirred the inferno in Sacha's blood. He fucked Jonah harder, chasing Jonah's climax so he could do battle with his own, but he was still unprepared for the sensation of Jonah clenching tighter around him, or the shudder of hot flesh beneath his hands, or Jonah's gasped curse.

Sacha was closer to the edge than he'd ever imagined. He fell, growling in Russian, the words tearing from his throat, and he came hard, flinching from the impact.

For a long moment, he couldn't move. He remained hunched over Jonah, panting, as he watched their reflection in the window. Jonah's face was buried in his arms. Sacha wished it wasn't. He wished he'd rolled Jonah over before he'd pushed inside him so they'd fucked face-to-face.

Next time.

The thought made Sacha's heart flutter. It had been a strange two weeks since he'd turned his life upside down to take the job at Blutecc. The last-minute decision had led him to this, thinking about a *fourth* date with a man he was now calling his friend. A man who'd enchanted him so entirely in that fucking lift that Sacha hadn't been able to let him go since.

Two weeks. You are...preposterous. It was one of Sacha's favourite English words. But still. Two weeks. How could so much have shifted in Sacha's brain since then? He didn't go on multiple dates. He didn't have many friends. And he certainly didn't cuddle after sex like he was doing right now.

He shifted, releasing his death grip around Jonah's waist, and sat back, heart thundering. Disposing of the condom gave him something to do. He got up, threw it away, and washed his hands in Jonah's bathroom.

Go home.

Pick your clothes up off the floor and go the hell home.

He found a clean wash cloth on the shelf and dampened it with warm water.

Go home.

He took it back to the bedroom. Jonah had rolled onto his back. His skin was flushed and shiny. Sacha gazed a moment, spellbound, then handed him the cloth.

"Thanks." Jonah cleaned himself up, then shifted up the bed to drop his head on the pillows. The bedsheets were a mess. Sacha retrieved them and dragged them to cover Jonah's legs.

Jonah grinned. "Tucking us in?"

"Tucking *you* in."

"You're leaving?"

"Yes."

But Sacha didn't move. He stood stock still while Jonah ran his sweet gaze over him, unabashed by his nakedness. This, he could do all night long. And Jonah seemed to know it. He rolled his eyes and patted the mattress beside him. "Don't go just yet. Lie down a while. I promise I won't jump you again."

"You think I would mind?"

"I don't know what you mind, Ivanov. You don't say much that makes sense."

"That is not true."

"Then come here."

Go home. Sacha lay down on the bed, sliding his legs beneath the rumpled sheets. He stretched out on his back, and gestured for Jonah to come closer. "This is what you want, no? To lie together?"

"What do *you* want, Sacha?"

To sleep for twelve hours then wake up and fuck you all over again. "I want my friend to be happy."

"That's sweet."

"I am precious. Come here."

Jonah smirked and followed Sacha's direction until they were entwined, Jonah beneath Sacha's arm with his head on Sacha's chest. He danced his fingers on Sacha's abdomen. It was a nice distraction from the faint headache blooming at Sacha's temple. He closed his eyes, letting himself drift. *Just for a moment. Then I will leave.*

7

———

Jonah woke with a jump. Déjà vu hit him hard and he knew before his eyes fully opened that he was alone. Again. It was the second occasion Sacha had left him in bed before dawn broke, and the second Jonah couldn't clearly recall it happening. But this time there had been no alcohol involved. Jonah had woken with a clear head, and he was a light sleeper, dammit. Was Sacha moving around his apartment like an assassin?

It was the only plausible explanation as to how he'd yet again managed to put Jonah's apartment back together without being heard. He'd even washed and put away the coffee cups, and loaded the machine ready for the morning. *He's a ghost.* If not for the tell-tale soreness of a wild night in, Jonah might just have believed it.

Dazed, he shuffled around, getting ready for the day, and bypassing the coffee machine with a daft sentiment that he didn't want to disturb where Sacha had been too much. He dressed in a dark suit and a white shirt, and fastened Disney cufflinks—another present from his niece and nephews—at his wrists.

His hair was a lost cause. Even the shower couldn't save it from looking as if he'd just tumbled from his bed. *I should cut it.* But he lacked the time and the inclination, so he let it be, and left the apartment, trying not to fixate on Sacha as he glanced from the window on the landing. He had back-to-back meetings ahead of him, on top of his usual workload. It was going to be a *long* day.

Jonah was habitually the first to arrive at the office, both at FG and Blutecc. He walked his routine on autopilot, flicking lights and computers on. Starting the coffee machine in the lounge area both companies shared. But this morning, someone had beaten him to it. The jug was full, and beside it were two boxes of festive pastries, one for each company.

Curious, Jonah filled a mug with java that had been brewed like rocket fuel and tasted like Christmas, and took it on a tour around the office, searching for whoever had been so thoughtful, but he found the FG side of the floor still empty. The only signs of life were coming from the Blutecc side, and Jonah rarely ventured over there unless there was a problem with the building.

Still clutching his cinnamon-scented coffee, he slid the dividing door open and stepped into Blutecc territory. It was quiet and dark, no lights had been switched on, but the glow of a computer lit up the back corner, and the *tap tap* of a keyboard guided Jonah in. He rounded the wall of the small alcove. Sacha was there, dressed in a fresh suit, his hair as disrupted as Jonah's.

Jonah blinked. "It's you."

Brilliant, Gray. Just brilliant.

Sacha eyed him, his handsome face giving nothing away. "It is true, I am me. Good morning."

"Um. Morning. You don't usually get here this early."

"How do you know?"

"Because I do, and for the two weeks you've worked here I haven't seen you."

"Maybe you have not looked."

"I've looked."

"Why?"

"Because—no. Fuck off. Stop talking in circles."

Sacha grinned a little. "I have not really heard you curse outside of your bedroom."

"Not true." Jonah glanced over his shoulder, checking they were still truly alone. "I said fuck a lot when you blew me at my desk."

Sacha's hazel eyes glittered. "Okay. Perhaps I mean outside of that kind of conversation."

Jonah didn't much care what Sacha had actually meant. He wasn't caffeinated enough yet for convoluted banter. "*Any*way. I came to say thank you for the coffee and the pastries. I assume it was you?"

"It was."

Jonah nodded. It was on the tip of his tongue to ask why, but he didn't. The words stuck in his throat, as though Sacha was a stranger, not the man who'd fucked his brains out last night.

For something to do, he swiped Sacha's empty mug and returned to the break room. He filled the mug with coffee and took it back to Sacha with one of the pastries from the Blutecc box.

Sacha was no longer alone. A striking platinum-haired woman Jonah had seen around was now beside him, leaning over his shoulder, peering at the laptop screen. She glanced up as Jonah paused in the doorway. Sacha didn't. His frown was deep. Whatever was on the screen was irritating him.

Jonah forced himself to continue his path to the desk. He set his wares in front of Sacha and smiled at the woman. "There's coffee, and Sacha brought pastries. Can I get you anything?"

A bemused flicker passed over the woman's striking features. She shook her head. "No, thank you, Mr. Gray. I'm fine."

"Okay then. Well, have a good day." Jonah backed up and left the alcove without waiting for a response, if there had even been one. He strode through the Blutecc space, not releasing a breath until he was safely back on FG turf. Carl, the director of his creative team, waited for him with more bemusement.

"What were you doing on the dark side?"

"Delivering the coffee they made us this morning," Jonah said dryly. "And stop calling it the dark side. I've told you about that before."

Carl snorted softly. "Yeah, and I told you they shun daylight and eat bats for breakfast. You said the moniker was fair game after that."

"Was I drunk?"

"A little. It was at the management Christmas party last year."

"Christ. You're holding me to something I said a year ago at that horrible club you dragged me to?"

"Only because it's true. They're all weirdos over there. Even the new guy."

"What new guy?"

"The one with the cheekbones and the resting bitch face. Apparently he's a—"

"All right, all right." If Jonah wasn't caffeinated enough to deal with actual conversations with Sacha, he certainly wasn't ready to deal with second-hand gossip from the break room. It was a place Jonah usually avoided, given that he expected half the bitching to be about him. "We have the Fairside meeting at ten. I've finished the pitch. Are you ready to present it?"

"You're not doing it?"

Jonah shook his head. As tempting as it was to spearhead every pitch himself, especially the big ones, he'd learned long ago that micromanaging his company didn't work, for him, his staff, or the firm's bottom line. He'd nurtured his teams to be competent—more than that, the best in their field. He paid them well, and as such had to trust them to do their jobs.

Besides, Jonah didn't have time to attend the Fairside meeting. He had a far more boring engagement to endure with his financial operations manager. *Kill me now.* Jonah hadn't been joking when he'd told Sacha he preferred the artistic aspects of his job to the point where he'd rather work for someone else, and it was never more apparent to him when he had to spend time in the clutches of the money men. Was there anything more dull?

Jonah couldn't think of much.

With Carl in tow, he decamped to his office and opened up the pitch he'd vomited out last night with half a mind on the enigmatic Russian on the opposite couch. A lifetime seemed to have passed since Jonah had last looked at it. He barely remembered pulling it together, and the words on the screen seemed to belong to someone else.

"Wow. This is good," Carl said.

"Is it? I was a little distracted when I put it together. I wasn't expecting to have to write it myself."

"Yeah. I'm sorry about that. I honestly thought the guys could handle it. They did so well with the Nestlé pitch."

"Don't apologise. It's important that you can come to me if something isn't working so we can fix it. Much better than showing up to the meeting with the nonsense we had on the table yesterday." Jonah spoke absently, reading through the powerful presentation he'd neglected to proofread last night. Or had it been the early hours of the morning? Christ, he couldn't remember. Sacha Ivanov was amazing in bed, but he was playing havoc with Jonah's cognitive function.

Luckily, Jonah was a clean writer. His words made sense, even if he didn't much remember typing them. If Carl was on form, the pitch was in the bag.

They went through it together, sipping on the spiced coffee Sacha had made, and eating the festive pastries. They were loaded with dried fruit and apple and unlike anything Jonah had ever eaten before. He ate two and licked icing sugar from his fingers while Carl added notes to the presentation. By nine-thirty, they were ready. Jonah transferred the pitch to the company cloud and left the office for the financial meeting elsewhere.

It was a nice day—cold, but bright. He forewent his usual black cab ride and walked across Waterloo Bridge. The fresh air cleared his mind of the haze his late night with Sacha had left him with. He was still in no mood for number-crunching, but all the sunshine in the world wouldn't change that.

Enjoying the sharp breeze in his face, he let his mind drift back to Sacha and the quiet few hours they'd spent working side by side before Jonah had all but dragged Sacha away from his laptop. Sacha's work was a mystery to him, but it had been clear to see he was as committed to his job as Jonah. Perhaps more. Outside of looming pitches, Jonah rarely had a problem switching off at night, a state of mind that after many *many* mistakes, he'd battled hard to win. Sacha Ivanov had the air of a man without that luxury, and Jonah wondered why. Was Blutecc that important to him? Or was he awash with the bad habits Jonah had fought hard to quit?

Either way—

Jonah's phone rang. He fumbled in his coat pocket and fished it out in time to miss the call from Carl's extension at the office. "Dammit."

He called straight back, but no one answered, and reception didn't pick up either. After a few tries, the calls stopped connecting. Jonah called Carl's personal phone. Automated voicemail kicked in.

Puzzled, Jonah resumed his walk across the bridge and checked his messages. There were three from Carl, all sent in the twenty minutes Jonah had been gone from the office, and escalating in panic with each one.

Carl: *where did you save the pitch and the notes? I can't find them in the usual folder.*

Carl: *Seriously. Where are they? The Fairside team just arrived and I need to go in. Did you save it on your laptop instead of the cloud? Is there another copy on your desktop?*

Carl: *JONAH. Call me as soon as you're out of that blackspot by the bridge. I need the pitch and my notes or we're going to crash and burn.*

Alarmed, Jonah checked his call records. There were none in the last half hour, save the unanswered calls he'd placed of his own. But the walk across the bridge had taken him through an area well known for having no data coverage or call signal, and by the time he'd stepped out of it, the office lines had stopped connecting too. *What a shit show.*

Jonah turned on his heel and headed back in the opposite direction, dashing through the blackspot until the office was in sight again. He hurried into the building and stepped into the lift, cursing as it stopped on every floor until it came to the FG/Blutecc landing.

His laptop was in the bag he carried over his shoulder. He retrieved it as the lift shuddered to a stop, tapping on the cloud, but he couldn't get in. The WiFi connection was down. *"Shit,"* he exclaimed, glad the lift was empty. Sacha had been right to note that Jonah rarely swore in general conversation —only during sex, and situations of high stress, which this was fast turning out to be.

The lift doors took an age to open. They clunked halfway there. Jonah wrenched them the rest of the way and stumbled onto the landing. The reception desk for FG was empty. At the Blutecc desk, they cast brief stares in Jonah's direction before they respectfully returned to their work.

Jonah rounded the FG desk and pushed into the office. At first, nothing struck him as out of the ordinary, then he saw the smartphones balanced on every desk, and the tense frowns of every face in sight. "Where's Carl?" he asked the room. "And what the hell is going on?"

"WiFi's down," someone called. "And the cloud crashed too. We thought it was wiped, but the new guy next door restored it in time for Carl to get the Fairside pitch. He's still working on the rest."

The influx of information made Jonah's head spin. He soaked it in, piece by piece, battling to prioritise. He needed to know what they'd lost, both in time, content, and personal data, and figure out a recovery plan, but as he opened his mouth, the least important question bubbled up his throat. "What new guy?"

"The Russian one with the eyes."

"The eyes?"

"Apparently so." The voice from across the room materialised as Nico, Jonah's IT specialist. The stress in his face mirrored Jonah's, but there was humour too. His eyes had the twinkle of someone who'd survived a crisis. "I haven't seen them myself. I was too busy shitting a brick when we couldn't access the cloud."

"But you've accessed it now?"

"Yeah. He hacked into my portal and accessed everything remotely using Blutecc's network. Some stuff is still missing, but he said he'd come back later if we don't get back online before then and see what he could do."

"Wow." Jonah blew out a long breath. "Sounds like we owe him a drink."

Nico nodded. "And then some. Carl pretty much had a heart attack when the Fairside people turned up. We all did. I don't know how they didn't notice."

"Doesn't matter if they did. What matters is what happens in that room." Jonah pointed at the conference room, the windows obscured by the same blinds Jonah had in his office.

"Nothing would've happened without the written pitch," Nico said. "Carl's a visual presenter. He'd have died on his arse if he'd had to wing it."

Jonah was inclined to agree, but he said nothing and retreated to his office to take a deep breath and eat another of the pastries Sacha had gifted that morning. It went down in three bites, leaving Jonah to lick his fingers—again—and spend the rest of the day mediating between Nico and the IT providers who seemed to want to set each other on fire.

It was late when he finally came up for air. He'd missed every meeting he'd had scheduled and added a million things to his list of things to do, and worse than that, the only glimpse he'd caught of Sacha had been as Sacha had left the building at lunchtime.

He hadn't come back—Jonah knew it because he'd glanced up every ten seconds to check, giving himself neck ache—and when he came in the next morning, there was still no sign of him, even in the hidden alcove where Sacha, according to office legend, spent most of his time.

It was lunchtime on Friday when Jonah finally sensed his presence. The Blutecc team were gathered in their main space, shoulders hunched and tense as Sacha addressed them.

His shoulders were tense too, but his back was turned to the FG windows, leaving Jonah unable to see his face, a state of affairs that frustrated him enough to pour hot coffee on his hand.

"Bollocks." He slung the empty jug back under the machine and moved to the sink to rinse his hands.

Carl shot him a curious glance. "Everything okay?"

"Why are you asking me that?"

"Because you've been glaring at everyone and everything all day and that's totally not your style. If it was, I'd work for Saatchi & Saatchi and make the big bucks."

"I pay you big bucks."

"Yeah, but I could get more there if I wanted to wake up every morning and stick my head up my arse."

"Charming."

"I try." Carl grinned, then his features fell serious again, and expectant.

Jonah shook his head. "I'm fine. It's just been a long week.

I'm sorry if I've been difficult. Let everyone know I'll buy them a drink across the road after work, all right?"

"That wasn't what I was getting at, but okay. I'll let the hordes know it's a free bar."

"One drink." Jonah searched for a stern expression and plastered it on his face. "You're not dragging me to that gin pub again. I don't have time for that kind of hangover."

"But it's Christmas, boss."

"*One* drink."

Carl snorted and wheeled away to give the team the good news.

Jonah watched him go, torn between amusement and irritation that he still couldn't see Sacha's face. He fiddled with the coffee machine some more, changing the filter, and setting it up for whoever came to it next with the Christmas coffee Sacha had supplied that morning. It was from a specialist shop in Chelsea, close to Jonah's flat. He wondered if Sacha lived there too—he'd never said, and Jonah hadn't got round to asking. In fact, he didn't know much about Sacha at all, save that he called a Christmas tree a *yolka*.

The Blutecc meeting broke up. People drifted back to their desks. Sacha migrated to the back and Jonah finally caught a glimpse of his face, his features cut into severe lines. He opened a drawer and reached for something. His frown deepened, and he shut the drawer again with more force than seemed necessary and disappeared into the nearby alcove, leaving Jonah with the distinct impression that he could do with a drink.

I can fix that.

Jonah returned to his office and shut down for the day. He packed his laptop into his bag, slung his coat over his arm, and made for the exit, slowing only when he reached the sliding door to the Blutecc side of the office. He reached for the handle, but Carl reappeared before he got there, and clapped him on the shoulder. "Ready?"

"Think so. Go ahead without me, though. I just need to check I switched the coffee machine off."

Carl stared like Jonah had grown antenna on his head. "Since when do you do that?"

"Since now. *Go.*"

Jonah gave Carl a gentle shove. He was close enough to him, and perhaps Nico, that he considered them friends, but until they left the office, he was their boss, and Carl knew it.

He left. Jonah considered the Blutecc door, and then the team members still hunched over their desks, clearly dealing with a crisis. What was he about to do? March through them and ask their boss out for a drink?

Leave it. He'll find you if he wants to.

But would he? Jonah tried to picture Sacha showing up at his apartment unannounced with a pizza and a bottle of wine, and just couldn't do it. The simplest solution was to lift Sacha's contact details from the Blutecc wall of fame, but that felt wrong too. If Sacha had wanted Jonah to have that information he'd have handed it over by now...right?

Jonah had no idea. Sacha was no ordinary man, and if Jonah didn't want Carl to come back for him, he was running out of time to fret over it.

Mind made up—kind of—he backtracked to the coffee machine and propped his business card against it, close to the mugs, hoping Curtis wouldn't find it first and throw it away. Then he left, forcing himself to keep his gaze to himself and not sweep it around the Blutecc office one last time. There were only two ways this could go: Sacha would call, or he wouldn't, and Jonah resigned himself to spending the rest of night pondering which way it would go.

He was twenty feet from the office when his phone buzzed.

Unknown number: *later, Jonah Gray.*

8

"Are you sure you don't want to come with us?" Helga asked Sacha again. "This place has the best vodka in the city, at least that I can afford, and you've been saying you need one all day."

Sacha shook his head, only half listening as he poked at his phone on the descent to the ground floor. "I have vodka at home. I don't need to waste my money on someone else's opinion of what is good."

"So come and be social then. It might make your grim reaper impersonation at staff meetings less traumatic."

Sacha sighed and pocketed his phone, still waiting on Jonah to send his current location. "Traumatic for who? I am not traumatised."

"I meant the rest of us. You've got everyone running scared that they'll be made redundant before Christmas."

"They will be if we do not make our deadline. And they should be scared. If they are not, they should work some-where else." Sacha was bored of saying it. In fact, today, he was bored with his own voice entirely, especially as no one seemed to be listening. *Why would I want to spend more time with these people?* Helga aside, he stood by his initial assessment of them. *They're all idiots.* "I cannot come with you," he stated. "Even if I wanted to, I have other plans."

"With who?"

"Why do you care, Helga?"

"I don't." Helga's gaze flickered as close to humour as her stern, beautiful features ever got. "I'm just curious about whoever has you itching to get your phone out again. I've never seen you text and smile at the same time."

"You've known me a matter of weeks. You have never seen me do many things."

"*Sacha.*"

"Helga. What do you want from me?"

"I want to get drunk with you."

"Why?"

"Because..." Helga slid a sly look to Sacha's pocket. "I want to see how long you can hold out before you run out on us for whoever is blowing up your phone."

"This long." The lift doors opened. Sacha stepped out and strode to the revolving doors that would take him outside.

Helga followed and chivalry made him wait and walk her across the street to the pub where the Blutecc team had decamped after the day from hell.

"Just one drink," she said.

Sacha shook his head. "No. Thank you. You have my credit card, yes? Use it to pay for the drinks and I will see you on Monday."

"But—"

"Goodnight."

Sacha pushed her into the pub, pulled the door shut behind

her, and walked away. Helga had proved an unflinching ally in recent days, and he was glad to know her, but he had zero interest in confirming her suspicions about his phone were correct.

He walked to the tube station before he let himself look.

JG: *Come to Farringdon. Castle Inn, by the sandwich shop.*

Sacha navigated the busy underground station to the correct line and caught the next train. It was jam-packed, and he squeezed himself into a gap at the end of the carriage. Bodies pressed against him, elbows and knees digging in. Scowling, Sacha squared his shoulders, claiming the space around him, and scanned the message thread between him and Jonah again. Despite all he'd said to Helga, he couldn't help questioning his sanity at ditching his own team's Friday night drinks to join whatever fuckery the Flash Gray staff called fun. It said a lot about Jonah's bewitching powers that Sacha was even considering it, let alone that he was halfway to Farringdon already.

Sacha: *later, Jonah Gray.*

JG: *Given that you're using my whole name, can I assume it's you, Ivanov?*

Sacha: *you can assume whatever you like.*

JG: *Can I buy you a drink too?*

Sacha: *maybe. I thought you were out with your team*

JG: *I am...for now. And I think they want to buy you a drink too, especially Carl and Nico.*

Sacha: *I do not know these people.*

JG: *And yet you saved the day for them this morning. Let them spend money on you.*

Sacha: *and then what?*

JG: *Then I believe your...friend owes you dinner.*

Sacha: *I believe he does.*

JG: *Come to Farringdon. Castle Inn, next to the sandwich shop.*

Sacha hadn't replied to confirm he was on his way. His fingers hovered over the buttons, but hesitation stilled them. Disquiet. Doubt. Dashing across the city for an unspecific rendezvous was as ludicrous as it had been to go home with Jonah the night before, and this time, they'd have an audience, a prospect that made Sacha's skin crawl. *Go home then. No one's making you go.* But Sacha stayed on the train. Got off at Farringdon and emerged above ground with laser focus on the pub across the street.

Maybe it is you who is the idiot.

Sacha had no answer to that. He crossed the road and entered the pub, absorbing the wall of noise from the lively weekend crowd, and familiar enough with the FG team to believe he would spot them easily enough, but as he scanned the faces around him, bracing himself against the overloud Christmas music, he found none that he recognised, not even Jonah's.

The bar called his name. He ordered the vodka he'd been craving all day, with ice, and pulled out his wallet to pay for it.

"No, you don't."

Warmth settled in Sacha's bones before he'd even turned his head. A solid body pressed up beside him and pushed the hand clutching his wallet aside.

"I'm getting this," Jonah said. "Don't fight me."

"Or what?"

"You'll lose."

Sacha let the transaction happen. Jonah ordered a rum on the rocks for himself and paid for both drinks with the swipe of a black card. Then he turned with the grin Sacha dreamed of when his mind wasn't full of website code, bandwidth disasters, and clunky interfaces that had failed from the start.

"I wasn't sure you'd show," Jonah said.

Sacha shrugged and reached for his drink. "You left your card where I would see it for a reason, no? Maybe I want to know that reason."

"You know the reason."

"Say it."

Jonah glanced around, then leaned closer. "We're friends. That's reason enough. And, I wanted to thank you for helping my team today. It's crazy what can happen when you leave the office for an hour."

"It would not have mattered if you were there. The problem would have been the same."

Sacha didn't add that he'd probably have left his post and gone to Jonah's aid a lot quicker than the ten minutes it had taken him to decide to intervene that morning. Or that he'd only done that because Helga had told him FG were about to flunk the pitch Jonah had spent all night writing. He didn't add anything at all. Just tracked Jonah's mouth as he sipped his drink. Followed his tongue as it darted out to lick his pillowy lips.

"Anyway," Jonah said. "Thank you. That pitch was important to me—to us."

"I know. I watched you sweat over it all night."

"I did not sweat."

"Yes, you did."

"That had nothing to do with the pitch."

"I know that too, Jonah Gray. You are so easy to rile."

"Am I?" Jonah stepped closer, invading Sacha's personal space.

Sacha took a slow sip of his ice-cold vodka and stole a

glance beyond Jonah to the rest of the pub. He still saw no one he recognised. "Yes. You are. But never mind that. Where are your team? I heard they want to buy me vodka too."

Jonah smouldered for another few seconds, then stood down, retreating to his own bubble. "They're next door in the student place."

"Why aren't you?"

"Christmas karaoke and technicolour shots aren't my style. I only came to buy them a few drinks for their hard work today. I was happy to see them go."

It pleased Sacha more than he was ready for to learn that he had Jonah all to himself, that they were alone, even in the crowded bar. He tipped his vodka down his throat and ordered another, along with a rum for Jonah. "Let's sit. It has been a long day."

Sacha took Jonah's arm and steered him through the bar. It reminded him of the ball and the night they'd met, but this was Farringdon, not Mayfair, and an altogether different crowd. The pub was dark and sticky, decked out in tacky plastic for the festive season, not the regal gold of the Dorchester, and Sacha liked it just as much. Only the growl of his belly made him long for something else.

They found a couch in a quiet-ish corner and huddled together out of a necessity that Sacha enjoyed. Jonah's leg pressed against his and they were close enough that an inch more would mean a kiss.

Sacha's lips tingled. He blamed the vodka, drank more, and asked Jonah banal questions about his work that neither of them cared about.

For a while, Jonah appeared to humour him, but his roaming fingertips said something else as they danced on Sacha's thigh, leaving fire in their wake.

Sacha fought the burn, and zeroed in on Jonah's anecdote about the reality star FG had used in the campaign they'd created for a rainbow condom company. "It was crude, really," Jonah said. "But if you understood that, you weren't the target audience."

"You were targeting stupid people?"

"No, more those easily influenced by shiny images on social media."

"And where did your "celebrity" fall on such things?"

Jonah laughed, soft and low. "I'm not altogether sure. He was too busy chatting up Nico."

"Nico? The computer man with the tattoos on his neck?"

"That's him. I think he would be a better model than anyone we've ever hired, but he's too shy about stuff like that. He'd literally rather die."

"I thought he was straight," Sacha said absently, not bothering to deny that he'd noticed how attractive the tall computer geek was when he'd found himself hunched over his laptop that morning, hacking into FG's secure portal.

Jonah snorted. "Yes, well. We know how that goes, don't we? Is anyone ever anything until they meet their person?"

"You think there is a person out there for everyone?"

"Maybe. Ask me another day. All I know for certain right now is that you, today, were some kind of angel for me."

"An angel?"

"Yes. I need to repay you. What do you want, Ivanov? What can I do for you?"

Sacha glanced at the long, elegant fingers still tracing patterns on his leg. *You are already doing it, luchik.* "I am hungry," he said. "I had four slices of *krendel* this morning, but it is not enough for what I have in mind for you later."

Jonah smirked. "Okay, let's unpack that. What's *krendel*? Am I saying it right?"

"No. Not even close, but to answer your question, it is the fruit bread I saw you eating this morning. Is Russian Christmas food."

"It's divine."

"I know. It is the only thing my mother ever cooked."

"She's a bad cook? I can relate to that."

Sacha shook his head. "She was not bad, but my father's mother was better, so she never got the chance."

"You're speaking in past tense. She's dead?"

"Yes. Long time now."

"I'm sorry. Without the rum, I might've phrased that better."

"What would be the point of that?" Sacha drained his glass and set it on a nearby table. "She would still be dead."

Jonah flinched. "Yes, but perhaps I could've asked more gently."

"My point stands."

"Only if you want it to."

"What does that mean?"

"Whatever you want." Jonah finished his drink too. He leaned in, but stopped a hairsbreadth away from kissing Sacha, uncertainty flickering in his warm gaze.

He wants to kiss me.

I want to kiss him.

Sacha had feelings on public displays of affection, but with Jonah so close he forgot every sensibility that had ever crossed his mind. He forgot about everything except how it might feel to cup Jonah's neck and press their lips together.

After all, he'd kissed Jonah everywhere else.

Sacha's eyes grew heavy, as if a smog of desire had settled over him. He took a breath, leaned in, and—

"Jonah!"

Sacha jumped back, startling Jonah as much as the shriek of his name had. He gripped Jonah's shoulder, holding him in place, searching for the source. For a moment, there was nothing and he feared they'd imagined it. That their combined subconscious had objected to what Sacha already knew was going to be the best kiss of his life.

Then his gaze fell on a wild-eyed FG staff member who'd become Helga's best source of gossip. Her name was Winona? Maybe? He couldn't quite remember.

"Jonah!" she called again.

Jonah rose from his seat, already reaching for his coat. "What is it?"

"It's Carl," she said. "He got punched."

9

Jonah pushed through the crowds milling between the mellow pub and the rowdy bar next door. In the chaos, he lost sight of Winona and her raven hair, and panic clawed at his chest. He was younger than some of his staff—a lot of them, actually—but still felt a responsibility for them that made his stomach clench.

And Carl was among the few Jonah counted as friends. The thought of him being hurt made Jonah want to vomit.

Disoriented, he rose on his toes, fighting to see over the throng, but it was no good. He couldn't see a thing, the Friday night bustle was too thick and he rocked back with a stagger.

Strong hands caught him. Steadying him. Sacha gripped Jonah's shoulders and used him as leverage to conduct his own sweep of their surroundings. "Over there," he said. "Come on."

He towed Jonah on without waiting for an answer, elbowing a path through the masses until they came to a small clearing where they found Carl propped against a lamp post, blood dripping from a nasty gash in his scalp.

Jonah dropped to a crouch beside him. "What the hell happened?"

"Some arsehole put his hand down Winona's pants. I pushed him away so he slammed a bottle into my head."

"A bottle? Jesus." Jonah put gentle hands on Carl's face, tilting his head to inspect the messy wound. "Who did it? Where are they?"

Carl pointed beyond Jonah to another body he hadn't noticed in a heap on the pavement. Nico stood nearby, arms folded, scowling as security staff tried to back him against a wall.

Jonah knew him well enough to join the dots. "Wow. Maybe you should've let Nico handle it from the start."

Carl offered him a weak grin. "Maybe, but he wasn't around, and the dude was already assaulting Winona, so I didn't think."

Jonah shivered, disturbed by both the blood oozing out of Carl's head, and the visual of what had brought them to this moment. He searched for Winona and found her crying into Sacha's chest. Around her shoulders was Sacha's expensive coat, while Sacha spoke too quietly to her for Jonah to hear what he was saying.

He couldn't see Sacha's face either, and it was as frustrating now as it had been at the office. Or maybe it was something else. Jonah forced himself to focus on Winona, on her tear-streaked face and trembling shoulders. He felt sick, but he didn't have time to choke on it. Carl was still bleeding and there was no sign of the paramedics a passer-by had called.

Jonah shed his coat and his suit jacket, and unbuttoned his shirt to reveal the fitted T-shirt he wore beneath. He yanked it over his head, leaving him briefly bare and exposed to the chilly night air. Loud whistles reached him, but he ignored them, zeroed in on Carl, and folded the T-shirt to press to the wound on his head.

Carl flinched, but grasped the makeshift dressing while Jonah put his clothes back on.

When Jonah looked at him again, his pained gaze was still amused. "What?"

Carl cocked a bloodied eyebrow. "Nothing. Just absorbing the fact that the Russian computer nerd was looking at you like he wants to eat you."

Jonah forced himself to keep still and not spin around to check out whatever Sacha was doing to make Carl's face light up. "I don't know any computer nerds, so whatever you thought you saw is probably the result of concussion."

"Oh yeah, so why is he even here? I don't see any other Blutecc weirdos floating around."

"Don't call them weirdos. Sacha saved your skin this morning. Without his intervention, you'd have gone into that meeting blind."

"Sacha now, is it?"

"Stop." Jonah replaced Carl's hand on his balled up T-shirt with his own. "Unless you're mouthing off to distract yourself from the pain, in which case carry on, but at least change the subject."

"Okay, Lord Reasonable. Still think he was checking you out, though."

Blue lights interrupted them before Jonah could verbalise a response. Police and paramedics arrived on scene, quickly separating them. Jonah found himself corralled by a burly police officer, but had little to add to the discussion. "I didn't see anything. I came out of the pub next door when Winona came to find me."

"What's your relationship to these people?" The officer gestured to Carl, Nico, and Winona whose face was still streaked with tears.

"I'm their employer." Jonah dug ID from his wallet and handed it over. "We came out for a drink after a successful day at the office."

"That went well," the officer deadpanned. "What about him?"

Jonah followed the policeman's jerked head to Sacha as Sacha happened to glance in his direction. Their eyes locked. The melee faded, and for a split, heart-pumping second, it was just them. Jonah smiled a little. "He's my friend."

Sacha smiled too.

It took an age to unpick the carnage of a quiet after-work drink. The assailant Nico had put down wasn't seriously hurt. He was arrested and taken away, as was Carl in the back of an ambulance with another FG staff member for company.

Jonah stayed behind to negotiate on Nico's behalf while Sacha remained with Winona as she gave her account to the police.

An hour had passed by the time Nico was free to leave the scene, the police believing Jonah's assurances that they could find them all, Nico included, at FG if they needed further information.

"Thanks, boss," Nico said. "I thought they were going to arrest me."

"They probably would have if the door staff hadn't backed you up. They didn't take a blind bit of notice of me."

Nico shook his head and rolled his gaze to the heavens. "You really have no idea, do you?"

"About what?"

"Never mind. I'm tired. I'm gonna go home. Will you make sure Winona's okay?"

"Of course. Do you have cab fare?"

"Yes, Jonah. I'm not twelve." Nico stomped away, leaving Jonah to find Sacha and Winona who'd decamped to a bench on the other side of the street.

Sacha regarded Jonah, his golden eyes narrowed with something Jonah was too tired to decipher. "I called a car for Winona," Sacha said. "We go with her, yes? Take her home?"

"Of course." Jonah dropped onto the bench and wrapped a platonic arm around Winona. "I'm sorry this happened to you. And that Carl and Nico got caught up trying to help. I should've been there."

Winona snorted. "Why? We're not your children. Stuff like this happens all the time."

"Well, it shouldn't. It's not okay for random drunks to put their hands on you."

"I know that, but you being there wouldn't have stopped it happening, and it might've been you who took a bottle to the head instead of Carl."

Sacha made a low noise and stood, drifting away from them and across the road to buy pizza from the cart by the pub.

Winona watched him go. "He's nicer than I thought he'd be."

"Why would you think he wouldn't be nice?"

"Dunno. He seems kind of moody when I see him at the office, and I've never seen him smile."

"He smiles plenty."

Carl would've asked Jonah how he knew, and seen straight through whatever bullshit answer Jonah's tired but wired brain spat out. But Winona didn't ask. She put her head on Jonah's shoulder and stared into space until Sacha returned with pizza slices and cans of lemonade.

The carbs and sugar sobered Jonah to the point he could hardly recall the four drinks he'd sunk before Sacha had joined him. The jolt in his belly when Sacha had walked into the pub felt like it had happened to someone else.

Winona stopped shaking too. She came back to herself and walked to the car that rolled up sometime later with steady legs.

They took her home.

Jonah escorted her into her building while Sacha waited in the car. Winona lived with her brother. Jonah explained the turn the evening had taken, then escaped the fraternal rage-storm brewing and jogged down the stairs. At the bottom, his hand shook on the door handle. He took a breath and retracted it, shoving it into his pocket as he backed up to the bottom step.

He sank down. Nausea bloomed in the pit of his stomach, and darkness threatened his vision. He leaned forwards, hunching over his knees, only half aware of the door opening and light from the street brightening the dim hallway.

"Jonah." Sacha dropped down beside him and pressed a warm hand between Jonah's shoulder blades. He didn't say anything else, just rubbed soothing circles into Jonah's back as they sat in the unfamiliar hallway, cloaked in a silence Jonah hadn't known he needed until it was there.

"I'm sorry," he said after a while. "Clearly I can't handle my booze."

Sacha snorted softly. "I have seen you drink more and be

fine. Perhaps it is seeing your friends attacked that has rattled you."

"I'm not rattled."

"Then you are a liar."

Sacha spoke without malice, but his hand on Jonah's back stilled, as if the tiny fib had offended him too much to keep moving.

Jonah missed his warm touch and sighed. "Yeah. Okay. I'm rattled. Not about the boys, Carl and Nico can handle themselves. It's what happened to Winona that bothers me. Why do people think it's okay to violate women like that?"

"I cannot explain why the world works the way it does," Sacha said. "It is not okay, though. It will never be okay."

"Thank you for being nice to her."

"It was not hard. She is nice girl."

"I know, I just—"

"What?"

Jonah wished there was a wall behind him he could bang his head against. "I couldn't look at her."

"I know."

"You do?"

"Yes, Jonah. I do."

How could he? He'd asked Jonah about the "man with the unspeakable hair", but Jonah had never answered him. How was it possible that Sacha had watched events unfold tonight and seen them mirrored in an insignificant, years' old incident Jonah had spent most of his adult life trying to forget?

It *wasn't* possible. And to think anything else was ridiculous. *Jonah* was ridiculous, shivering against a man he barely—

"*Jonah.*"

"What?"

Sacha grasped Jonah's chin with insistent fingers, forcing Jonah to look at him with the lightest touch. His gaze seem to have darkened as they'd huddled on the stairs, and the gold in his eyes shimmered with the gaudy Christmas lights someone had wrapped around the worst Christmas tree in the world. Warmth and conflict battled for dominance, and it was an even fight. No winners. No losers. Just Sacha leaning ever closer as Jonah's pulse hammered his eardrums.

He's going to kiss me.

Sacha's lips on his surprised him all the same. A staggering shock that lit a new fire in the inferno of desire Jonah already carried for this man. Sacha's lips were soft and smooth, contrasting with the scruff on his unshaven jaw, and his kiss was dizzying. Even sitting down, Jonah swayed with the gentle impact, blood rushing, veins hot with pleasure. Behind the scenes, his brain still ran a thousand miles an hour, but the noise was quieted, snuffed out by Sacha's lips.

Jonah reeled, snatching a breath. Then his faculties returned to him and he kissed Sacha back, shifting on the cold stone until they were facing each other.

His hand found its way to the nape of Sacha's neck. The change in angle deepened the kiss. Jonah opened his mouth, Sacha's tongue slipped between his lips, and his giddiness reached new heights.

A soft moan pierced the quiet air. Him or Sacha? Christ, he had no idea. All he knew was the longer they kissed on the stairs of a building where neither of them lived, the further they were from a place where kisses could become something else.

Something magical.

He pulled back. Sacha stared, unblinking, as if frozen in time.

Jonah kissed him again, soft and sweet. "It's cold," he whispered. "Will you come home with me?"

"Why?"

"You know why."

"Be specific. I like it."

"Okay then. Because you've been an angel tonight and I don't want to let you go."

"I am not an angel, Jonah Gray."

Jonah kissed Sacha's lips again, and then his jaw, and his cheek. Sacha smiled a little and it was the kind of smile that changed his whole face. It softened his masculine features and hard jaw, and it was all Jonah could do not to kiss him again.

They scrambled to their feet—at least, Jonah did. Sacha moved with grace and poise Jonah had never had—and ducked out and into the waiting car. It took them to Jonah's penthouse apartment, then slipped back into the city traffic as unobtrusively as it had arrived.

The lift ride was quiet. On the landing, Sacha was, as ever, transfixed by the view. Jonah didn't like to disturb him, not even for another kiss. He opened his door and waited. Eventually Sacha came. "I like it up here," he said.

"I know."

"Do you?"

"Yes. I see the lights in your eyes every time you look down on them. The view...it pleases you."

"You please me too. Do you think I could use your shower before I show you how? It has been a long day."

Jonah swallowed thickly and pushed his door further open. "Of course."

Sacha preceded him inside. Jonah followed, heart beating

a slow tattoo as they took their coats and shoes off, then moved through the apartment to his bedroom.

After a brief moment where he appeared enchanted by Jonah's Christmas tree, Sacha disappeared into the bathroom. Jonah sat on the edge of the bed and stripped to his under-wear, glad he hadn't reclaimed the bloody T-shirt he'd pressed to Carl's head. Another shiver passed through him, but not from cold, and only the sound of the shower turning on kept him present.

Idiot. It's been years, and he's not even here. Sacha is. Focus on him.

Jonah shifted and lay down on the bed, gaze fixed on the ceiling as he listened to Sacha move around the bathroom. It was as familiar as it was brand new. Comforting, almost.

Closing his eyes, Jonah chased every sound, from the groan of pipes, to Sacha's low humming. His body buzzed with anticipation, craving the wildness Sacha brought out in them both whenever he made good on his filthy promises.

It was a nice place to be, and Jonah fought to stay there.

"I'm not an angel, Jonah Gray," Sacha had said.

You are tonight.

10

It was an accident to wake up in Jonah's bed, one that had started when Sacha had fallen asleep. He hadn't meant to. In fact, he hadn't meant to wind up in Jonah's bed at all, at least not to sleep. But then he'd come back from the bathroom to find Jonah already passed out, and slipping under the covers beside him had happened before Sacha comprehended what he was doing.

Now it was morning—early, just before dawn. Jonah was still asleep, and Sacha was still in his bed. And they weren't even naked. *How is this my life today?*

Sacha knew how. Because he'd been so perturbed by the disquiet in Jonah's usually sunny gaze he hadn't been able to leave him. Still couldn't, despite the fact that he'd had no trouble leaving him in bed before. And wasn't that an odd case of affairs?

About as odd as spending most of his day placating agitated FG employees he neither knew nor cared about because he couldn't bear the stress lines—both imagined and real—on Jonah's lovely face.

You are overtired. It makes you emotional.

Sacha couldn't argue with that, but with no way of lightening his workload in sight, the butterflies in his chest any time Jonah was near weren't going anywhere.

And neither, apparently, was Sacha.

He settled back in Jonah's comfortable bed. There was plenty of space for both of them, but somehow they'd wound up sleeping with a Bible's width between them, less in some places, like their feet that were pressed together.

The contact made Sacha warm inside. Before Jonah, he'd had frequent sexual partners, but never sleepovers. It had been *years*, and he couldn't clearly recall a time when he'd simply slept with a man. Shared his bed and body heat. Counted his breaths and watched him dream.

In fact, he'd never done that with *anyone*.

You are overtired. It makes you emotional.

Sacha closed his eyes and went back to sleep.

Not much time had passed when he woke again, but it was light. The sun had broken through the winter clouds and streamed through the gap in the curtains. Jonah had rolled onto his side. His back was to Sacha, exposing the wide expanse of creamy skin.

It was irresistible. Too exquisite to ignore.

Sacha placed his palm between Jonah's shoulder blades and slid it down, ghosting over Jonah's flank to the waistband of his underwear. His fingers curved around Jonah's hip, glancing over his abdomen, and Sacha's body came to life...if it had ever truly simmered down from the night before.

Jonah's hair was unruly enough to cover his neck. Sacha

brushed it aside and pressed a tentative kiss to the tender point left behind.

A quiet hum was his reward. Then a deep chuckle as Jonah shifted beneath his touch. "Am I awake right now, or am I dreaming a world where you didn't run out on me in the middle of the night?"

"I have never run anywhere in the middle of the night. I walk, in an orderly fashion, while you sleep like a baby."

Jonah laughed again. "But not last night. You're still here."

"I am," Sacha said as much to himself as to Jonah. "Your bed is nice. I like it."

"What else do you like?"

"This." Sacha grasped Jonah's shoulders and rolled him over, straddling Jonah's waist before either of them could blink.

Jonah's morning wood was beneath him. Sacha revelled in the sensation a moment before shifting away and leaning forwards to capture Jonah's nipple in his mouth.

"*Fuck.*" Jonah groaned, his body arching from the bed. "Okay. Now I'm awake."

Sacha released him. "You were already awake. You were talking to me."

"I thought I was dreaming, remember?"

"And now?"

"Now I know I am."

Smirking, Sacha traversed down Jonah's body, enjoying the daylight opportunity to explore. Jonah was glorious in any light, but like this, with his hair tousled and his eyes heavy, he was more beautiful than ever. His cock was hard and waiting for Sacha's mouth, but first, his chest, abs, and fine hip bones demanded attention Sacha could not help but give.

Beneath him, Jonah gasped, and his flesh jumped. "You're wicked."

Sacha's grin widened. "I know."

"I thought you were an angel last night. I've changed my —*fuck!*"

His second curse was punctuated by Sacha swallowing him whole. He did not often crave to have a man's cock crammed in his throat, but since the first time with Jonah it was something he thought about even when they were not together. The sounds Jonah made were addictive, and Sacha drew his climax out, edging Jonah as much as he could bear, just to hear more of his snatched moans and deep sighs.

"You're killing me," Jonah ground out.

Sacha wondered if Jonah knew it was killing him too.

He held Jonah's trembling thighs and worked him harder, teasing his cock with his tongue.

Jonah tensed, and choked out a warning, then he came hard, jerking in Sacha's grip, and his shout of pure pleasure went straight to Sacha's dick.

He swallowed all Jonah had to give, then rose and straddled him again, taking himself in hand.

Jonah panted, eyes wet from his climax. "I want to watch you."

"Watch me what?"

"Come. I want to watch you come."

"I can help you with that." Sacha jacked himself with every intention of going slow, but taking Jonah apart had left him on edge. He was so hard it hurt and only the pressure of his tight fist gave him any relief

His breath quickened, and his pulse thumped in his ears. Sweat coated his skin and he couldn't help the quiet groan that escaped him.

Surging, he fell forwards, bracing himself on one hand while the other flew up and down his cock. He locked eyes with Jonah and another jolt of heat rattled through him. "Where do you want me to come? In your mouth? On your chest?"

Jonah licked his lips, desire burning in his gaze. "Stay where you are. I want to see you."

"As you wish." Sacha's muscles began to seize, fibre by fibre. He pumped his cock, pleasure ripping through him hard and fast. The notion of spilling on Jonah's chest was one he hadn't considered before this moment, but now it was all he could think of, the sole reason he was awake and alive in Jonah's bed.

His vision darkened and his free hand curled into a fist. Orgasm battered his senses, from his toes to the top of his head, and with a final deep, gravel-laced groan, he came.

Release spurted over Jonah's lily-white skin, his shoulders, his chest, his throat. It was everywhere, as if they were two teenagers caught up in the very first moment. Breathing hard, Sacha fell slack. Jonah wrapped his arms around him, tight and consuming, and for long seconds his embrace was everything.

But the sticky mess between them couldn't be ignored for long. With heavy reluctance, Sacha pulled back, detangling from Jonah's hold. "May I use your shower again?"

"Of course. I'll come with you."

It was a fair compromise. Sacha climbed off Jonah and slid off the bed. He headed straight for the bathroom, stopping only to flick the lights on Jonah's Christmas tree, his spine tingling at the sensation of Jonah right behind him, in spite of the fact that showering together for only the second time since they'd met felt remarkably normal. If a man could call being naked with Jonah Gray anything close to normal.

He turned the shower on, embracing the cold as Jonah hung back with his toothbrush in his mouth, waiting for the water to heat before he joined Sacha under the spray.

"How do you do that and not shrivel up and die?"

Sacha rolled his neck and shoulders, letting the frigid water travel down his spine. "Habit. Conditioning. I come from rich family, but I went to a school that believed in punishment as personal development. No hot water for boys, even in winter."

"That's barbaric."

"It is different. And I am okay. I like the cold, it reminds me to live."

"Do you forget?"

"Forget what?"

"To live?"

"No. Is figure of speech."

Jonah stepped under the warming spray, his presence alone enough to raise the temperature of Sacha's blood. He looked as though he had more to say, but he reached for the shampoo instead and washed his hair.

Sacha eyed the suds running down his fit body. If they were true long-term lovers, it would've been so easy to grab the oil from the shelf over the sink, lube himself, and push Jonah against the tiled wall, but even thinking about it felt too intimate.

Too intimate for what? You already kissed him and slept in his bed—

Sacha drowned his clamouring subconscious by turning his face into the hot spray. Jonah's shower was powerful and it pummelled his senses with heat and noise. He could almost pretend he was alone, then soft fingertips brushed his neck and his scalp, and the scent of Jonah's shampoo returned.

He's washing my hair.

Sacha swayed on his feet.

Chuckling, Jonah steadied him. "Easy now. I've got you."

They were simple words. Sacha liked them. His body strained to lean back against Jonah, to absorb his sturdy warmth, but his brain said no, as if the sensation of Jonah's fingers carding through his hair was already too much.

Too much for what?

Sacha had forgotten the answer.

Jonah rinsed Sacha's hair, then rubbed body wash with the same scent over his skin. His cock was half hard and pressed against Sacha's thigh, but Sacha didn't react. Couldn't, or they'd be in the shower all day.

So what? You have nowhere to be.

That wasn't entirely true. He'd left his laptop at the office, and he had a full day of coding to fit in before Monday morning rolled around—coding he'd planned to be halfway through already. He had no time to bang Jonah in the shower. He had no time to spin and drop to his knees. He had no time to kiss Jonah again, but *god,* he wanted to.

He wanted it more than anything.

Jonah shut the shower off. He slid his hands over Sacha's hips and turned him around. His lips were pink and full, and he bit down on the bottom one, mauling it with his straight white teeth.

Sacha fixated on it, leaning in, then the obnoxious blast of a phone ringing made Jonah jump a mile, and the moment was gone.

"That's my mother. Damn it. Hang on."

He stepped out of the shower and dashed, naked, from

the bathroom. Shaking his head to clear it, Sacha stepped out too, and opened the vanity, searching for a spare toothbrush—Jonah seemed like a man who'd have one or twenty.

Or three, as it turned out.

Sacha claimed one and unwrapped it, tucking the box in the bin under the sink. He dried his hair while he brushed his teeth, and tried not to eavesdrop on the conversation filtering out of the bedroom.

It went well until he heard his own name, then curiosity got the better of him.

Leave it. You have no reason to barge in there and invade his life.

But Sacha had never listened to anyone, least of all himself.

He finished up at the sink, wrapped a towel around his waist, and padded silently to the bedroom.

Jonah was on the bed, dressed in charcoal drawstring pyjama bottoms that made his hair gleam. He was holding his phone up and gesticulating to whoever he was speaking too—his mother, presumably, a video call.

Sacha glanced around for his clothes, but he'd left them in the bathroom the night before.

Jonah got up and opened a drawer. Inside were more pyjama bottoms. He pulled out a black pair and passed them to Sacha with a wink.

"Who are you winking at?" Eleanor's voice came immediately. "Is it Sacha?"

Jonah's cheeks flushed. "Ma, stop it. You don't get to interrogate everyone who's ever in my home."

"I don't want to interrogate him. I want to see him. You've barely mentioned him since the ball. It's as though he doesn't exist, and it's rude, Jonah. We liked Sacha a lot when we met him. Why would you keep him from us?"

Jonah rolled his eyes and moved back to the bed, giving Sacha space to drop his towel and pull the pyjama bottoms up his legs. They fit perfectly and the symmetry with the loop Sacha's brain was on left him reeling.

Eleanor was talking again.

Jonah looked as though he wanted the bed to swallow him up.

Sacha pointed at the phone. "You would like me to speak?"

Jonah angled the phone away from his face and muted it. "You don't have to do that. She's always like this."

"Because she worries you're lonely."

"I'm not lonely."

"I know. Because I am here, no?" Sacha climbed onto the bed and claimed the space beside Jonah. He pried the phone from his hand and unmuted his mother, before turning the camera on himself. "Hello, Eleanor. I am sorry to keep you waiting. I was in the shower."

Surprise widened Eleanor's eyes. "It really is you. I was beginning to think my son had made you up."

"How could that be when you have met me yourself?"

"It was quite a night after all that champagne, dear, and you were such a beautiful man on my son's arm, I was convinced I'd dreamt you."

Sacha smiled. In her own way, Eleanor was as adorable as her strapping son. "What can I do to convince you I am real?"

"You should come home with Jonah for Christmas. He's never brought anyone and it's high time that changed."

"Is that right?"

"Yes," Eleanor asserted. "He's a man now, not a teenager."

"Oh my god." Jonah rolled off the bed and left the room.

Sacha laughed. "I think you embarrass him."

"My son is ridiculous," Eleanor retorted. "It's not an unreasonable question of the only man he's ever introduced us to."

"Maybe he is not ready to be that serious about me."

"I very much doubt that. He blushes every time I mention you."

Sacha felt heat creep into his own cheeks, but a different kind. Jonah was a good man, mortified at being caught in a lie, and this conversation was only prolonging it, but Sacha liked Eleanor. Her nosiness reminded him of his own *mama*, and he couldn't seem to let her go.

So he didn't. He let Eleanor grill him and gave her answers based on truth. They were both working hard, and taking care of each other when they could. Yes, Jonah was getting enough sleep and remembering to eat during the day. And no, he wasn't working all weekend.

Jonah came back into the room as Sacha made that promise. He waved a mug of coffee under Sacha's nose and dipped back into shot. "Ma, I'm stealing him back. I'll talk to you later."

Eleanor feigned theatrical disappointment, but said her goodbyes all the same. "Let me know about Christmas, Sacha. We'd love to have you."

"I will," he promised. And then she was gone, leaving Jonah to toss his phone on the bed with a groan.

"I'm so sorry. She's obsessed with you. But in her defence, you are wonderfully charming."

"Is that so?"

"Yes. Don't pretend you don't know it."

Sacha snorted and sipped his coffee. Silence threatened, but his stomach growled, puncturing the quiet.

Jonah laughed. "I have the answer to that."

"You have food?"

"Of course. Do you think I don't know you by now?"

The question was rhetorical, and Jonah was up and out of the room before Sacha could respond, but it stuck in his mind all the same. *Do you think I don't know you by now?*

It was a stupid question. Jonah didn't know Sacha any better than Sacha knew him. A few weeks of casual sex, brief workplace encounters, and twelve text messages didn't tell you who a man was and what had made him that way. It was superficial. Meaningless.

Easy to walk away from.

Sacha sat up to track down his actual clothes. His feet hit the floor, but he didn't go anywhere. A conflict he didn't understand raged beneath his skin. The instincts that kept him happily lonely were loud and strong, and telling him to get dressed, go home, and get back to work, but as much as he heard them, he couldn't make himself move.

Jonah was upset last night. Stay a while longer. Make sure he's okay.

"Are you okay?"

The echo in Sacha's head made him jump. He swung his gaze up from the floor to find Jonah in front of him, clutching a paper bag from Sacha's favourite Russian-owned bakery. The scent of *kolbasa* reached him. "You bought a Russian breakfast?"

Jonah smiled, though concern still coloured his bright gaze. "For you. I didn't know what any of it was, so I got eggs and bacon on mine."

"Show me."

"Move over then, unless you're going somewhere?"

"I am not."

A pause stretched out while Jonah waited. Sacha blinked and collected himself, and somehow sliding back into Jonah's bed was easier than it had been in his head.

Jonah emptied the bag. He'd ordered open sandwiches with sliced egg and *kolbasa* sausage for Sacha, and eggs and bacon for himself, topped with tomato and dill. Bastardised for Englishmen, it wasn't an exact translation of the simple *zavtrak* he'd once eaten back home, but it was close enough that his heart suffered another gentle contraction. "What made you choose Karaway for your breakfast, Jonah Gray?"

"Is that what it's called?" Jonah claimed his sandwich and set it on his lap. "I just googled Russian breakfast places that delivered. I don't even know where it came from, though it didn't take long, so it can't be far."

"It is ten minutes from here," Sacha said. "Walk south and turn right."

Jonah side-eyed him. "Do you live nearby?"

"To what? You, or the bakery?"

"Both."

"Yes, that is my answer."

"You don't want me to know where you live?"

"That is not what I said. I gave you the answer to your question."

"I know. But it sounds like you're being mysterious on purpose."

Sacha unwrapped his sandwich, biting his lip to contain his grin. Jonah likely didn't know it, but he was just like his mother. A people person. "I am not being mysterious. It is very clear. Walk south from here and turn right, and you will find my home."

"Do you live alone?"

"Of course. Do I strike you as someone who would share his space?"

Jonah didn't answer for a moment. He bit into his breakfast and chewed thoughtfully. "Honestly? When I see you scowling around the office, *no*, I can't imagine you living with anyone. But you're not always like that. You seem happy enough when you're here."

"That is with *you*," Sacha retorted without thought. "I do not spend this time with anyone else."

"Why me?"

Sacha shrugged, reaching for a nonchalance that didn't exist. "Why not?"

"See? Mysterious." Jonah let it go and polished off his breakfast. Then he left Sacha alone while he made more coffee.

Go. Leave. You've stayed long enough.

But Sacha didn't leave. He drank more coffee and sank further in Jonah's bed with him. They watched bad films on the TV in Jonah's bedroom and took their clothes off. Sacha fucked Jonah in his bed, rolling him onto his belly and taking him hard and rough, the way they both liked. Jonah ordered more food. They slept and showered, then slept again.

It was Sunday evening before Sacha went home.

11

Monday morning marked a return to snatched glimpses of Sacha through glass walls, while Jonah battled the workload closing in on him before the Christmas break. Good news came in the form of a contract for the La Glo project. Bad news came from Carl who'd be off work for a week, and Nico, who was currently crawling under Jonah's desk, trying to fix the shaky Internet connection.

"I don't know what's wrong with it," he said from somewhere near Jonah's feet. "That Russian guy said it's the VPN, but I've checked all that. It doesn't make any sense."

"That Russian guy has a name," Jonah said absently, immersed in the legal documentation from the La Glo project. "And why do you need him to tell you what's wrong anyway? *You're* the IT person around here."

"Not by choice. I'm the digital content director. I do this stuff as a favour, remember? Because we ran out of budget for someone who actually knows what they're talking about."

Damn. Nico was right, but his information was two years out of date. FG could well afford to fill the role Nico was floundering in, Jonah had simply forgotten to do anything about it. "Okay, scratch everything I just said. You're doing amazing work considering it's not your job. I'll send a hire request to Rochelle this afternoon. I'm sorry, Nico."

Nico grunted. "What's with you and the Russian dude anyway?"

"Sacha."

"What?"

"Sacha. That's his name."

"Okay. *Sacha* then. I heard he was a moody fuck, but he seemed pretty chill when he was with you."

"Did he?"

"Yeah. I mean, he still glares like a serial killer, but I didn't get vibes that he wanted to, like, actually murder anyone."

Contracts forgotten, Jonah pushed his chair back and stooped to glower at Nico's bent knees. "He doesn't glare."

Nico snorted. "If you say so, boss. I won't ask how you know."

"Don't." Jonah didn't much care if Nico had put two and two together and come up with the right number. There were any number of FG staff who might've seen him with Sacha when they'd come to Carl's aid. But he could only speak for himself, and he had no clue where Sacha stood on the matter.

Jonah didn't know much about him at all.

That's not true. You know he drinks black coffee and likes cold showers. That he picks olives off his pizza and drinks vodka with ice. And there were other things too—that he liked sucking Jonah's cock, and fucking him from behind. That he groaned deeply and shuddered when he came.

Nothing important, though, save the fact his mother was dead and he didn't like most people.

Jonah straightened up and fished his phone from his pocket. It had been fourteen hours since Sacha had left his apartment, and he'd resisted reaching out, taking Sacha at his word that he sometimes preferred his own company, but the silence gnawed at him.

Jonah: *it was real, you know...the invite to my parents' place for Christmas*

It wasn't what he'd meant to type, but he sent it anyway, firing it off into the ether before he could take it back.

Maybe Sacha wouldn't answer, especially if he was as busy as the rest of the Blutecc team seemed to be. For all FG liked to rib them, no one could fault their work ethic.

Jonah's phone buzzed, startling him back to the present.

Ivanov: *I know it was real. Your mother said so.*

Jonah: *I didn't mean her.*

Ivanov: *What did you mean?*

Now there was a question. How had they gone from a bizarre lift encounter to a fake relationship Jonah was now imagining could be real?

It's not real. And he doesn't want it to be. It's just sex.

Amazing sex. Mind-blowing sex. The kind that stayed with Jonah long after it was over.

He let his thumbs fly free over his phone screen again.

Jonah: *She thinks you're my boyfriend*

Ivanov: *I know this. We told her so together.*

Jonah: *So...*

Ivanov: *So what? Do you want me to come, Jonah Gray?*

Jonah: *I want to know what you'll be doing if you don't.*

Ivanov: *Why?*

Jonah: *I don't know.*

Sacha didn't reply straight away. Head spinning, Jonah

dropped his phone into a drawer and ducked out of his office, gaze roaming as always, searching for Sacha.

And as almost always, he was nowhere in sight. But he was definitely close. Jonah could feel it.

Fool. You can feel no such thing.

Jonah filled his coffee mug and helped himself to a Christmas-spiced flapjack from the box that had appeared that morning—an actual, tangible clue that Sacha was in the building.

He took it back to his office and opened the drawer he'd dumped his phone in. A message lit up the screen, too long for the preview to make sense.

Jonah swiped it open.

Ivanov: *If I am not with you I will be where I always am, at home.*

Jonah: *Alone?*

Ivanov: *Yes.*

Jonah: *Why?*

Ivanov: *Because that is how I live.*

Jonah: *But it's Christmas*

Ivanov: *I am aware. It is the same day every year, no?*

Jonah: *You shouldn't be alone.*

Ivanov: *It does not mean to me what it does to you.*

Jonah: *I don't believe you. You like my tree. You stare at it all the time. I saw you.*

Ivanov: *Yes, it was your Christmas tree I was staring at all weekend.*

Jonah: *Are you being sarcastic?*

Ivanov: *Maybe.*

Jonah couldn't think of a reply that didn't involve pushing Sacha to do something he clearly didn't want to do, but he wasn't buying his insistence that Sacha didn't care. He was too entranced by the sparkly view from Jonah's building for it to mean nothing.

Right?

In truth, Jonah had no idea, and he was no closer to figuring it out by the time the end of a very long day came around.

He was the last FG employee to leave. Blutecc were still working and didn't look to be going anywhere anytime soon. Out of habit, Jonah searched the sea of hunched shoulders and frowns for Sacha, and for once his gaze landed on the face he so wanted to see.

Sacha was bent over a desk, frowning deeply, tapping on a keyboard while he spoke on the phone. He had a pencil behind his ear and a collection of empty mugs around him.

Coffee mugs.

Doubling back, Jonah returned to the break room and cleared away the detritus of the day. He washed mugs in the sink and stacked them ready for their next outing, and loaded the coffee machine to its full capacity.

He set it to brew, then perched on the arm of a couch and pulled up his trusty food delivery app on his phone. FG had an account at the nearest wood-fired pizza place. He ordered a ridiculous amount to cover the Blutecc staff still working, and added a couple more for Samson and Curtis.

It was a small gesture, but as the man going home with the luxury of not checking his emails until the following morning, it was least he could do.

With a final glance at Sacha, he left, letting Samson know on his way out to expect a van load of pizzas.

The night was damp and cold. He took a cab home and hurried inside when he reached his building, stopping only to gaze out of the landing window that had held little appeal until he'd met Sacha.

Concealed by mist, the lights were harder to see tonight. Jonah strained his eyes and imagined he could see the building where Sacha was, picturing the frown he'd still sported when Jonah had left. They'd shared the same work space for barely a month, but somehow leaving him there felt all wrong. As if Jonah's soft heart believed he'd have been any use to Sacha if he'd stayed.

Idiot. You forgot to replace your IT manager. What use would you be to a development team?

None, obviously. It was a stupid thought that made no sense. Jonah knew it like he knew it was *cold* in his fancy apartment without Sacha to keep him company. That despite living happily alone for *years*, somehow he was lonely.

Call Lily.

He didn't. He took a shower and made a sandwich for dinner, eating it on the couch in front of a Netflix original about lawyers and murder trials. Eleanor sent her daily message, asking—*again*—about Sacha and Christmas. Jonah let out a strangled laugh and flopped back on the couch, a weight settling over his chest. *Lesson learnt. Don't tell lies.* Sacha seemed to find the whole thing amusing, but for Jonah, any humour in the situation had long ago faded, leaving behind a stark dose of reality—he had an accidental fake boyfriend he needed to set free.

But the trouble was, he didn't want to set Sacha free. He wanted to keep him, for Christmas, and beyond.

Oops.

The realisation, though not entirely new, sank Jonah deeper into the couch. It was all very well deciding he wanted to have Sacha for himself, but what about *Sacha*? What did *he* want?

Aside from mind-blowing sex, Jonah had no clue.

So ask him.

But he didn't do that either. He drowsed on the couch until his phone buzzed a little while later.

Ivanov: *perhaps you are the angel, Jonah Gray.*

In the darkness, Jonah smiled. The weight lifted a little, and he went to bed, leaving his reply unsent.

Only for you, Sacha. Only for you.

Sacha sat on his bathroom floor, coding with one hand and rubbing his temple with the other, willing the migraine-induced nausea he'd staggered home with to fade. It was the third day in a row he'd forgotten to bring his refilled prescription to the office to tuck in a drawer, and the third day he'd paid the ultimate price.

Don't puke. You know how this works. Keep the pills down.

Easier said than done, though he'd managed it the last two days, perhaps helped by the fact he hadn't had time to eat much since Jonah had ordered a lifetime supply of pizza to be delivered to the office. Good pizza, with no olives.

How did he know?

Sacha knew the answer to that. Jonah Gray was observant. Empathetic. Kind. And he didn't discriminate either, not like Sacha who picked and chose who to share his finite affection with.

Sacha stared at the stack of pizza boxes on the table. There were too many to count. "Take some for yourselves," he told Samson and the janitor who'd staggered into the office with them.

"No need," Samson replied cheerfully. *"Mr. Gray always takes care of us."*

Always. Of course he did. Even the two nights they'd slept side by side, Jonah had regularly flailed a hand out in his sleep, resting it on Sacha's chest a moment, as if checking his cynical heart was still beating.

Sacha smiled at the memory, the pills in his belly finally softening the sharp pain in his temple. He hadn't noticed Jonah leaving the office the night of the pizza delivery, and the disappointment at knowing he'd missed him had been... disarming until Samson had arrived laden with boxes. A silly thing, really. A simple goodbye would've been more tangible, even snatched and stilted in front of an audience.

Nothing about how Jonah made Sacha feel was simple.

I like him.

But then, who didn't? Sacha didn't partake in office gossip, but he listened, and he'd heard enough to discern that Jonah's FG employees adored him. That he was the sweetest, kindest boss he could be while running a fledgling advertising agency.

Sacha? He could clear a room with his glare and he liked it that way, but he couldn't deny the spell Jonah had put on him too. Or how long the last three days had been without him, which made no sense at all considering he'd spent an entire lifetime without Jonah's company, and only a handful of occasions with it.

You're overtired. It makes you emotional.

God, Sacha was bored with that mantra, despite the fact that it was truer today than it had been since he'd stepped into the same broken lift as Jonah Gray.

Eventually, the storm in Sacha's brain passed, muted enough by medication for him to ignore it and get on with his work. Another late night loomed ahead of him. After four hours of straight coding and all the bullshit snags that came with it, he finally opened his emails. Most were pertinent to the current project that was teetering on the edge of disaster. One was from his cousin letting him know Sacha's father was unlikely to be alive by the end of the year.

Sacha deleted the email without reply, numbness creeping into the irritation he carried with him ninety percent of the time, unless he was with Jonah. Nausea returned. He pushed it down. Sacha reached for his phone and opened the message thread he had with Jonah. They hadn't spoken since the exchange about Christmas, a conversation that Sacha had seemed to observe from afar, watching his fingers tap out messages he didn't recognise as coming from his own brain.

The notion of accompanying Jonah to his family home for Christmas was preposterous, and yet...Sacha would go if Jonah wanted him to.

I wish he was here now.

The errant through caught Sacha off guard. He'd grown used to the yearning in his belly that deepened after every sexual encounter they shared, but the ache in his chest was new.

I don't just want to fuck him. I want to—

Sacha's phone buzzed.

JG: *Are you awake?*

Sacha typed an answer without thinking.

Sacha: *Yes. Are you?*

JG: *It would be hard to send you this message if I wasn't.*

He had a point, but Sacha's brain wasn't working as well as it usually did. Fatigue and drug fog had seen to that.

Sacha: *Okay. I will ask why you are awake instead. It is late.*

JC: *It's early, actually. I just got up.*

Sacha blinked and checked the time. Sure enough, it was four-thirty in the morning—an hour before he usually rose on a regular work day—and he'd missed his window to go to bed.

Sacha: *Maybe it is late for me.*

JC: *You say strange things.*

Sacha: *I am okay with that.*

JC: *I thought you might be. Do you want to get breakfast?*

Sacha: *With you?*

JC: *No. In general.*

Sacha: *I think perhaps you are being sarcastic now.*

JC: *Maybe. Regardless, I'll be at Rosa's in half an hour if you change your mind.*

Sacha: *I never made up my mind.*

Jonah fell silent. Sacha thought about leaving it alone and crashing for the few hours he could spare before he was due at the office, but his scratchy eyes were nothing on the churn in his gut at the thought of missing out on alone time with Jonah.

You won't be alone. It's a café on a busy street, even at this hour.

Sacha took a shower and got dressed all the same, and he was out of the door with ten minutes to spare.

The breakfast café was a five-minute walk from the loft apartment he called home. Sacha expected to arrive first, but Jonah was already there, seated in a window booth with two coffees in front of him.

"You are presumptuous, Jonah Gray," Sacha grumbled by way of greeting, and slid into the seat opposite.

Jonah glanced up from his phone. A half smile warming

his lovely face. "You like coffee, food, and me, perhaps in that order. Why wouldn't you come?"

"The order of my preference should concern you. I could take my coffee and leave."

"You're forgetting the food. At least wait until it gets here."

"Why?"

"Because you're hungry."

"How do you know?"

"I listen, Ivanov."

Sacha settled into his seat and claimed his coffee. "I should not like it when you call me by my father's name."

"No? Why's that? I can stop if it truly offends you."

"It does not. That is my point."

"Okay..." Jonah sipped his coffee, eying Sacha over his cup. "Where does the possibility that it might come from? You don't like your dad?"

"I don't care enough about my father to dislike him."

"Why not?"

"He is a bitter old drunk."

"I'm sorry."

"Why? It is not you."

"I meant I'm sorry your relationship with your father is like that. I don't speak to my dad much, but I love him. I respect him. And I'm confident the feeling is mutual. I can't imagine not having that in my life."

"Well, I have never had it, so your experience seems bizarre to me."

"That's sad."

"It is true. There is no need to be sentimental about it."

"Here we go." Jonah rolled his eyes. "Do you repeat that narrative about everything?"

"What narrative?"

"That you don't care."

"I do not care about my father. You are pushing your own emotions onto me."

Jonah snorted. "If only. But I didn't just mean your dad. I meant everything. Why do you pretend you're this unfeeling, emotionless android? I know you're not."

"How do you know that?"

"A mixture of instinct and evidence."

Sacha shook his head slightly, as much to clear it as in disagreement. He had not prepared for such a convoluted conversation. "Your instincts are misguided, and your evidence is based on what? The short time you've known me compared to the lifetime I've known myself?"

"You help people," Jonah countered. "I've seen you."

"Perhaps for my own gain. Nothing is ever truly altruistic, no?"

A server came to the table with plates of poached eggs, crisp bacon, tomatoes, and fresh avocado. On the side was rye bread almost dark enough to be Russian. Sacha smiled and lost control of his leg as it hooked Jonah's under the table, entwining their ankles. "It is like you know what I need before I do," he said softly.

Jonah slid cutlery across the table. "Or maybe I'm greedy enough to eat yours if you don't want it."

"Greedy? You? No." Sacha closed his fingers around his knife and fork, using the cool metal to ground himself, to tie him down to the world when the simple contact of Jonah's leg against his was enough to send him spinning out of orbit. "You listen, Jonah Gray, even when others do not speak."

Jonah let it go. They ate in the companionable silence Sacha enjoyed so much when he wasn't in the mood to talk. The food was good, just the right balance of naughty and nourishing. *It is a parallel. Of your friendship with him. You want to fuck him, but you want this too—to eat with him while he stares at you and tries to figure you out.*

Sacha swallowed the last bite of his breakfast and pursed his lips. The idea of Jonah ever figuring him out was laughable. Sacha had a one-forty IQ and twenty-eight years of trying, and he was still no closer to understanding the contradictory nature of his brain.

"You are a cold man," a girlfriend had once told him. *"You take intimacy to make yourself feel good, but give me nothing in return."*

Sacha had given up on relationships after that, and had never regretted it. Walking away from affection was easy. At least, it had been until now.

In his head, he reclaimed his leg and pulled it back under the table. Pushed his plate away and leaned back. Thanked Jonah for breakfast and left with a resolve not to waste time waiting on flashes of auburn across the office to make his day more bearable. In reality, he pushed his plate aside and leaned forwards, grinning as Jonah met him in the middle. "Thank you," he said. "In case I was not clear."

Jonah smiled too, softer than Sacha's sharp edges as he moved his own plate aside. "You were clear. I hear what you don't say, remember?"

"I remember."

More silence stretched out between them, loaded this time, hot and heavy. Jonah's lips called to Sacha, soft and pink. He wanted to bite them, and feel them on every part of his body. He was more tired than he'd been for a long time, but with Jonah so close, the binds of fatigue loosened. New energy surged in his veins. Addictive energy. Was this how friends with benefits worked? Or was their friendship clouded by the fact they'd started out pretending to be something more?

Figuring it out was more complicated than Sacha had time for, but the sense that he was in too deep was a cold, creeping wave that felt all wrong against the heat simmering where his leg touched Jonah's.

You're overtired. It makes you emotional.

Sacha groaned and sagged back in his seat.

Jonah's fair eyebrow ticked. "Are you okay?"

"Yes. Why do you ask this?"

"Because you look tired and I'm your friend."

"You are not my friend. We sleep together. That is all."

"Okaaaay." Jonah leaned back too, widening the much-needed distance between them. "If that's how you feel, I should probably get to work, but—"

"But what?" Sacha snapped, already hating himself. "Go to work, Jonah."

Jonah stared, both brows rising in tandem, hurt colouring the uncharacteristic irritation in his emerald gaze. Surprise, too. Sacha's harsh words had shocked him as much as they had Sacha. "Are you—?"

Sacha glared.

Jonah shook his head. "Forget it. I get the message. Have a good day, Ivanov."

He left, ending their encounter so abruptly it took Sacha a moment to remember it was all his fault. That the frigid gust of wind that blew through the café door in Jonah's wake wasn't an accident. *He'd* engineered it. Forced it. And now he was alone again and everything was supposed to be easier.

It wasn't. And he was having a hard time recalling how and why and when he'd come to the conclusion that it would be. His brain felt glitched. As if it had short-circuited and blasted Jonah with the consequences too fast for Sacha's heart to catch up. Or he'd dreamt the whole thing and he was about to wake up on his couch with his laptop keyboard imprinted on his cheek.

He dreamt about Jonah a lot.

12

———

"Pick up, pick up, pick up." Jonah paced his office, phone pressed to his ear, willing Lily to just answer her phone already. He'd called her three times and her voicemail, however cute, was starting to irritate him beyond belief.

"Hey there, stranger."

"Finally," he ground out. "Where've you been all morning?"

"Um, I don't know. Asleep? It's still the middle of the night in California."

"Balls. I'm sorry. I forgot you flew out yesterday. I thought it was tomorrow."

"That's okay. My schedule changes so often *I* can barely remember it. What's up, boo? You sound stressed."

"I'm not stressed."

"You're blowing up my phone on a weekday for a chat? What happened? Is there a Tube strike or something?"

"I don't use the Tube."

"Well, you should. That way you'd get to see all your hard work out in the wild. I saw your Superdry billboards in every station from Kensington to Hampstead while I was home."

"I don't need to ride the Tube to see my billboards. I walk places too."

"No, you don't. You use the gym in your building and take cabs everywhere. Don't lie to me, Jonah. I know you too well."

Jonah wasn't in the mood to point out that Lily was rarely home enough these days to know what his actual habits were. He'd called to sound off about Sacha, not bicker about his non-existent pedometer. "When are you coming back?"

"Christmas Eve. Why? Do you miss me?"

"You know I do."

"Then you should answer your Skype calls. I've buzzed you twice this week."

"I'm sorry. It's been crazy at work."

"And?"

"And what?"

"*Jonah*," Lily drawled. "It's arse o'clock in the morning over here. Please don't tell me you really have called just to talk about the weather. What's the matter?"

"Nothing's the matter."

"Liar."

Jonah sighed and ran a hand over his unruly hair. It needed cutting, but he lacked the enthusiasm for a trip to the barber. "You were right about office romances."

"Ah ha! I knew it. So it wasn't a one-night stand?"

"More like a three-night stand, or four...I can't remember."

"Are you in love with him?"

"What? No. Of course not. I just..."

What? How are you going to explain this?

Jonah had no idea, so he went back from the start and

vomited out every encounter he'd shared with Sacha until he came to the part where he'd stormed out of the breakfast café.

Lily whistled. "Wow. That sounds dramatic."

"It really wasn't. I left for work, he followed half an hour later."

"How do you know that?"

"What? That he followed me? It stands to reason as we work in the same building."

"I meant the fact that you know exactly how long it took him. Are you spying on him at the office? Because I have to say, even if things were going well, that's creepy. Let the man live."

"I'm not spying on him. I just happened to be near the door when he walked through it."

"I'm not convinced."

"I don't care."

"No? So answer me again. Why are you blowing up my phone in the middle of the night?"

"I told you why."

"You told me what happened. Not why it's upset you so much."

I'm not upset. But Jonah's heart wouldn't speak the words, because they weren't true. "I'm just...confused, I suppose. We were supposed to be friends with benefits, but the friendship part seems to freak him out."

"Which part? Specifically?"

"I don't know. I didn't realise it was making him uncomfortable until this morning."

"When you asked him if he was okay?"

"Yeah, I mean, I wasn't trying to dissect him or anything." Jonah drifted to the window and gazed out over the city, noticing the Christmas lights more than he ever had before he'd met Sacha. "He just looked like he hadn't slept all week, so I asked him if he was okay."

Lily sighed. "You're too sweet, boo. It always gets you in trouble."

"It does not. We've never had this conversation before."

"Not exactly, but you are never going to be in a room with someone you care about and not let them know. True story. So if Sacha doesn't like that kind of attention, you're always going to clash."

"So what do I do? Ignore the fact that he looks like shit?"

"Yes, if you want to respect his boundaries and carry on with whatever you're doing with him. And double yes if he wants to forget the friendship part and go back to being a casual hook-up."

"He was never a casual hook-up. He was my fake boyfriend for my parents' winter ball." *Dear god, don't say that out loud again. Like, ever.* It was Jonah's turn to sigh. "I get what you're saying," he said. "I'm just messed up by the whole thing. I never meant to make him uncomfortable, but I didn't say anything to him that I wouldn't have said to a friend I wasn't fucking. Sacha—"

"Mr. Gray?"

Jonah spun around. A Blutecc executive he vaguely recognised was hovering in the doorway. *Christ.* "I have to go," he said into the phone and hung up.

His phone buzzed immediately with an angry text from Lily.

Lily: *don't you dare hang up on me!!!*

Too late. But Jonah could handle her outrage. He just had to hope the Blutecc suit had rocked up to his office with his mind elsewhere, or he'd be in Sacha's bad books more than ever.

"You're joking, right?" Jonah flipped his gaze between his office window, and the Blutecc executive currently taking up space in his office. It wasn't Sacha, but somehow the mild-mannered man was proving to be every bit as frustrating as the rest of his morning had been. "You're asking me to find room on our books to conceive a campaign for your product within the next *three months*. Are you out of your mind?"

"Probably," the executive said. "But in all honesty, we were expecting the development to bomb, or at least be so delayed we wouldn't have a launch in place before next autumn. Our team have caught us off guard with their progress."

"Your team? Or the person you hired to save this project?"

Person? That's what you're calling him? Lord. It had been three hours since Jonah had left Sacha in the café and he was still no closer to understanding what had happened to derail their breakfast so entirely. And now he had Blutecc's director of marketing in his office begging for something Jonah couldn't comprehend, much less deliver. *This day just gets better and better.*

The executive sighed. "Yes, okay. Sacha Ivanov has proved more effective than we could've possibly envisaged. The app is nearly ready, and the supporting infrastructure isn't far behind, thanks to his ability to perform several full time roles at once. It is the marketing team that isn't ready, and I'm coming to you for help."

"You don't have an advertising firm on retainer already?"

"We do. But they're at capacity. Like I said, no one was prepared for anything but failure."

"That's a sad base point for your company. Your staff meetings must be fun."

"Oh they are. Mr. Ivanov is quite...entertaining in his efforts to motivate."

"And effective too, it seems."

"Indeed." The executive leaned forwards, signalling that their casual back and forth was over. "Look, I know it's an audacious ask, but I'm aware that you didn't get the Lucozade contract you pitched for last month. That you have material in your arsenal for a sports-based campaign?"

"You want me to transfer a pitch for an energy drink to your half-baked fitness app?"

"Yes. I'd sugar-coat it, but frankly I don't have the time. If this conversation is about finances, rest assured we have the resources to cover your fees."

"I know you do. My mother represented your CEO in his divorce."

The Blutecc director winced, but kept his gaze fixed on Jonah. Begging. Pleading. All without words.

Jonah sighed and dropped into his desk chair. There was zero chance of him agreeing to recycle a concept from a failed pitch into something new, but as it happened, thanks to a delay in the La Glo campaign, there *was* wiggle room in his schedule. His design team were mostly tied up on other projects, but *he* could help if he wanted to.

"Fine," he said around a heavy sigh. "Gather everything you have and I'll put it to my creative team in the morning. Give us a day to pull a visual pitch together. If you like it, we'll roll. If not, you can find someone else. Or crash and burn. Whichever comes first. Does that sound fair?"

The executive nodded and extended his hand. "It does. I'll have Mr. Ivanov brief you before day's end."

Jonah closed his eyes. *Wonderful.*

The day was long. For most of it, Jonah remained convinced Sacha wouldn't show up. That Blutecc's marketing director had come to his senses before he'd approached Sacha and the ridiculous plan was off the table. But he briefed his team anyway, an entire day before he'd promised, and sent associates next door for more information.

They came back with a sketchy interface and graphics that looked like Jonah had drawn them in middle school. "What on earth?" He swiped through them. "Did they do these in Microsoft Paint?"

Winona shrugged. "I don't know. Sacha said they're all idiots. I don't think he was including himself or Helga in that, though."

"Helga?"

"The blonde. I think I love her."

Jonah pinched the bridge of his nose. "Okay. Let's start with what we know. This is a fitness app for women? It generates work-out sessions and meal plans, but it doesn't count calories or monitor weight loss?"

"I think so. No one seems to really know."

"Who pitched the app in the first place? Who developed the concept?"

"No idea. Blutecc bought it from a failed start-up. I don't think they even care what it's supposed to stand for."

"And what's that?"

Winona leaned over Jonah's shoulder and tapped the

work out sessions already uploaded to the prototype app. "That women are strong and sexy regardless of their weight and shape."

"Reality versus perception?"

"Confidence," Winona asserted. "And positivity. Fuck Instagram, basically. This is real."

Jonah grinned. "Okay. If you're swearing at me, I know it's important. I just don't understand why it's not important to anyone at Blutecc. How have they got this far into development without a clear picture of what they're doing?"

"I suppose because none of it mattered when they didn't have the infrastructure to support anything. You can't put pretty wallpaper on a house with no foundations, Jonah. You taught me that."

"That's kind, but I don't know squat about app development. This makes no sense to me."

"Does it need to?"

"Maybe."

"You're weird." Winona straightened up. "You never used to be. Is it Sacha? Are things not working out between you?"

"Things?"

"I saw you leave my apartment building together. He had his arm around you."

"He was probably holding me up. I drank a lot. Can we get back to work and not speculating about my private life?"

Winona flushed. "Sorry. I didn't mean to be rude."

"You're not being rude. Just remember where we are, okay? This isn't high school."

Winona took the hint and went back to analysing the scant information Blutecc had provided. It wasn't much, but in some ways it was a blessing. They had no ideas of their own to compete with whatever FG came up with. If nothing else, it lowered the possibility of creative conflict. "Pull together some logo designs," Jonah said absently. "The story boards can come later. For now we need to build an online presence that gets people excited."

"Excited about what, though? There isn't even a website to route it back to."

"Yes, but if we can create a profile for the app store, we can send their social media traffic to the app's pre-order link."

"They still need their website to function, though."

"It will." The voice came from the doorway.

Jonah glanced up and caught his first glimpse of Sacha since they'd parted ways that morning. His breath caught, but he tried to ignore it. The dark smudges beneath Sacha's eyes weren't his concern. They couldn't be if they weren't even friends.

He didn't deny you were sleeping together though. Present tense. He still wants that.

But Jonah didn't. Not without the friendship benefit. He hadn't realised it until Sacha had taken it away, or maybe not until Sacha had appeared *right now* in his office, but it was a hard fact.

I can't just sleep with him. I need more.

So does he.

Sacha cleared his throat.

Jonah caught himself staring and returned his gaze to his computer screen. "Your boss said you'd brief us, but unless you have more than we got from your development team there's probably no point."

"Who do you think is my boss?"

"The executive who came to see me this morning, maybe?"

"He is not my boss." Sacha ventured further into Jonah's office. "He is a marketing man with no brain."

"What brings you to that conclusion?"

"He cancelled space with the regular agency. He thought we'd never be ready before I even got here."

Jonah forced himself to look up again. "What about you? What do you think?"

Sacha shrugged, flickering his gaze over Winona as if he wished she wasn't there. "I think we can be ready if we do not waste time on other things. The website is built. It will hold if the app functions well enough to handle most traffic through the host platform."

"And will it?"

"Maybe. I need more time."

"How much?"

"Two weeks."

"From today?"

"If you say so, Jonah Gray."

Forgetting Winona's silent presence beside him, Jonah frowned. *Don't whole-name me if we're not friends. You don't get to do that.*

Sacha met his glare with blank eyes. "Blutecc shuts down the day before Christmas Eve. I will have a functioning app by then that we can soft launch and upload for pre-order through a product page."

"We can build that for you within a few days. We just need your boss—whoever that is—to sign off on the graphics. If we get you some concepts by the end of the week does that work for you?"

"Of course. We are not in a position to be difficult."

"I'm sure that wouldn't stop you," Jonah retorted, then regretted it. This wasn't about them—whatever that was—

and Sacha had the right to do his job in peace without passive aggressive smites. "Anyway, leave it with us. We'll do our best to create something that reflects what you've put into the project."

"Vodka and black coffee? Maybe not."

Sacha backed up and disappeared before Jonah could respond, hidden by the closed blinds of Jonah's office windows.

Jonah sighed, wishing he could track him across the floor and see where he went for no reason more than he wanted Sacha in view for as long as humanly possible.

He was wrong about me. I am greedy.

Greedy for him.

I can't get enough.

Considering how badly their day had begun, it was a scary thought.

13

Sacha received the email from Jonah's office at the same time as the rest of his team. It came through during their morning meeting, four hours earlier than they were expecting it.

A hush fell on the room as those with devices to hand scrolled through the content.

Sacha had an iPad. He retreated to the alcove with it, hiding away in the one place he was fairly sure Jonah couldn't see him from the FG side of the floor.

Not that he'd ever caught Jonah looking his way. No. It was only Sacha who spent all day staring at the glass like a fool.

He opened the email from Flash Gray. It was signed off by Winona. Jonah's name was nowhere in sight. But somehow Sacha heard his voice in every word he read, and saw his face in every crisp, polished design that filled his screen. Black and pink. Bold. Sexy. Strong. They were perfect. Scrolling through them reminded Sacha why he'd signed up with Blutecc in the first place: to preserve the earnest legacy of the start-up that hadn't survived.

This is how it was meant to be.

The meeting Sacha had walked away from was still going on. He returned to find Helga fighting for a budget increase to rebrand the entire operation using the concept FG had created. There was enough unique content there for the entire app, the website, *and* a social media campaign.

But the finance department shook their heads. "We can't throw more money at this project until we know it can deliver. We've covered the design fees. Until we have a proven interface, supported by a functioning website, we can't authorise any more funds."

Sacha had already been paid for his services. It had been a stipulation he'd insisted on before he'd arrived, to avoid meetings like this centring around his own renumeration. It shouldn't have mattered to him that the project was out of budget, he'd do his job regardless. But the notion of leaving unused artwork by the wayside felt so wrong he couldn't stomach it.

He met Helga's gaze across the conference table. "*Later*," he mouthed.

She glared.

Sacha looked away. He made his excuses and exited the meeting, craving coffee and his long overdue dose of Jonah Gray. Instead he found an empty break room and a coffee machine that hadn't been refilled since he'd done it himself at dawn.

There were no sweet treats to be found either. Sacha thought about ducking out to rectify it, but he had too much to do. If he was to justify the extra money Blutecc would be paying FG, there wasn't a moment to lose.

Sacha watched the water drip through the coffee machine, transfixed by the gurgling sounds as his mind strayed to the work he'd abandoned to attend a meeting that had ultimately gone nowhere. Helga's team had taken over the website, but the structure was still rickety enough that Sacha had to triple check them at every stage.

The app itself wasn't much better. Even thinking about it gave him a headache. The FG artwork had helped, though. For weeks, they'd worked without a vision that made them care. Now they had one.

"Hey."

Sacha blinked back to the present. Winona was beside him, helping herself to the coffee he'd neglected to notice had finished brewing. "Hello."

"Did you get my email?"

"I did. We were in a meeting when it came through so everyone who needed to saw it at the same time."

"And?"

Sacha reached around Winona and claimed the last clean mug. "We love what you've done. All of it. I did not expect so much."

Winona snorted. "That's what happens when Jonah gets involved with the creative team. He doesn't get to do it often, so he overproduces. I didn't even send you all of it. There's more."

"More? How can that be so?"

"He's a frustrated genius."

Sacha could believe that. In the rare moments he'd been lucky enough to glimpse Jonah across the shared office space, he was often hovering around his creative team, frowning at their screens, hands thrust into his pockets, lips pursed shut.

It was cute. "We will use as much as we can, even if I have to fund it myself."

"That's not good business practice, Sacha."

Winona's tone was teasing, but Sacha had left his jovial skin at home. He shot her a dark look. "Nothing about Blutecc is good business practice."

"So why do you work there? I've looked you up. You're, like, a head hunter's dream. You could work anywhere. Why here?"

Sacha shrugged. "I liked the app and what it stood for. I did not realise it was so decimated until I got here."

"But you can fix it, though, right? Helga told me you were smashing it out."

Sacha snorted. "Helga is kind, but she cannot possibly know that until we reach the end of the build. We have passed no quality control checks yet. We do not even know if the functionality we started with has survived the layers we've added."

Winona's eyes glazed over. She laughed. "I have no idea what any of that means. And you're wrong about Helga being kind. She's pretty mean, so I'd imagine she wouldn't say nice things about you that weren't true."

"She wasn't talking about me, she was talking about the app."

"Was she?"

Winona left her question hanging and left the room with her coffee mug. Sacha watched her float across the FG space and disappear into Jonah's office. She shut the door, and envy hit Sacha so hard his hand shook.

He set the empty coffee jug on the counter. Picked up his mug. Changed his mind and put it down again. Dropped it, actually, sending it clattering to the floor.

The handle splintered off.

Cursing, Sacha crouched to retrieve the pieces, frustration boiling over in his gut until he feared he might vomit. *You are a fool. If you were his friend, you could go in his office too, but you told him you weren't. That all you had was sex. And now this—a working relationship that's awkward as hell because you don't know how you're going to pay him.*

You're a fool, Ivanov.

"What are you doing down there?"

Sacha closed his eyes, bracing himself, then opened them again as he turned to face the new voice in the room. The smooth, gentle voice that belonged to the only person on earth who could rattle him so. "Tying my shoelace, Jonah Gray."

Jonah raised a brow. "You don't have any laces in those boots."

"Clearly. I don't have a full coffee cup in my hand either, it's in pieces on the floor, no? So what I'm doing is fucking obvious."

"Wow."

"What?"

"I heard you were in a bad mood."

"Who told you that?"

"Everyone in your office."

"What were you doing in this fictitious office of mine?"

"I meant the Blutecc office."

Sacha suppressed a heavy sigh and collected the fragments of his mug. Then he rose and dumped them into the bin. "I'm not in a bad mood. In fact, the email Winona sent me this morning made my day. I like your work. It is perfect for the project."

"Really? I wasn't sure if we'd hit the mark, given that no one on your team except Helga seemed to know what your app actually was."

"They do not care," Sacha admitted. "Blutecc is company

that harvests the bad fortune of others. The content is not important."

"How does that work?"

"You do not know? Flash Gray has shared office space with Blutecc for three years."

"And we've mostly ignored each other. It was a dynamic that worked until you came along. You're more social than you give yourself credit for, Ivanov."

"Not true."

"It is, but I don't want to waste time arguing with you about it."

"What *do* you want?"

"I want to know how a company can develop an app without having a vested interest in the content."

"Yes," Sacha countered. "But *why* do you want to know?"

"Because it's hard to create a brand without emotion."

"Well, it shouldn't be. It's corporate advertising. It is not meant to mean anything."

"Then you shouldn't have asked us to do it. FG doesn't—"

"It was not me that asked you."

Jonah blinked, and rocked backwards, as if Sacha's snap had physically hit him. "What are you saying? That you don't want to work with us? Because that's easily fixed."

"That is not what I said."

"Then what? You've had your head up your arse since Wednesday morning, and, frankly, I don't have time for it. My *team* doesn't have time for it."

Jonah spoke calmly, but anger spots reddened his pale, chiselled cheeks.

Sacha wanted to kiss them away.

He also wanted Jonah to shut the hell up and leave him alone. To walk out of the break room and disappear into a puff of smoke so Sacha could finish this goddamn app and put his brain back together again. He'd never lost his head over a project the way he was in danger of doing right now, and the only variable in his life was Jonah.

Leave me alone. Please.

Jonah stepped closer, narrowing the distance between them. "Look, I don't understand what I've done to piss you off so much in the last week, but whatever it is, I'm sorry, okay? I get that you don't want complications and I'll back off."

"It is—"

"I'm not finished."

Despite the sharp-edged negativity spiking Sacha's blood, a grin threatened to split his face in half. He stifled it, and gestured for Jonah to continue.

"We can't let our failed friendship affect our work," Jonah said. "If you don't want to deal with me directly, that's fine, but don't make things difficult for other people, my team or yours. If you can't do that, we need to draw a line under this right now."

Sacha wondered how they'd gone from pretending to be lovers for the sake of Jonah's mother to having tense conversations in a break room that smelt of old coffee and stale doughnuts. And why the words Jonah had chosen—*"failed friendship"*—hurt. Oh, the irony, when it had been him to stick a grenade under whatever they had become.

You are a fool.

A fool with an inner monologue stuck on repeat as Sacha drowned beneath the weight of Jonah's vexation. "We do not have a failed friendship," he said, then jammed his lips shut, as if he could stop any more nonsense piling out.

"How do you figure that?" Jonah's cheekbones sharpened.

"Is it because we were never truly friends to begin with? Is that where you're going with this?"

"I'm not going anywhere."

"Well, maybe you should."

"Are you speaking in metaphors now?"

Jonah pushed off the wall he was leaning against and shook his head. "No, Sacha. I'm not."

He walked out, leaving Sacha in a daze. He waited for the door to slam, but of course, it didn't. They were at work, not in a soap opera, and their strained exchange had already attracted enough attention.

Sacha turned his back on the curious stares of the FG employees who worked closest to the break room door. Jonah had spoken softly enough for them not to overhear, but Jonah's demeanour as he'd walked away would've been hard to miss from the moon. Sacha wondered if he'd find a mud pie in his coat pocket at the end of the day. That was the difference between FG and Blutecc—in fact, there were many—FG were a close-knit team who adored their leader.

Blutecc were as much of a fractured mess as Sacha was.

Minus the coffee he'd come for, Sacha left the break room and returned to his open laptop in the alcove. Helga was waiting for him. "Where did you disappear to?"

"The break room. If you'd moved your head slightly left, you'd have seen me."

"I thought you might've gone to see Jonah Gray."

Sacha bristled, irrationally annoyed at hearing Jonah's whole name fall from lips that weren't his own. "I did see him, actually."

"And?"

"And what?"

"Did you talk to him about funding? As in, we don't have any."

"No."

"Okay," Helga said. "How much of their content do they think we're buying then?"

"I told Winona we would take as much as we could use."

"We can't afford that with our budget."

"I know. I will pay for whatever we cannot from the company account."

Helga braced her fists on the table and loomed over Sacha. "That's ridiculous. It's not on you to fund this project, and even if it was, Flash Gray charge top-end rates for their services. We're talking silly money, Sacha."

"I have silly money. You forget that I do not do this shitty job for the same reasons you do."

"I can't forget something you've never told me. I don't know anything about you outside of this office."

"What do you want to know, Helga?"

Helga sighed. "I don't know. And thinking about it in any depth gives me a headache. *You* give me a headache, in actual fact. It would be easier to hate you."

"You don't hate me? That is sweet."

"Take that back. I am not sweet."

"I'll take it back if you will fetch me some coffee?"

"Why do you need me to do that? You literally just came from the break room."

Sacha didn't have the words to explain the disaster his excursion to the break room had become. He searched out his blandest smile and plastered it on his face in the hope it would sway Helga into satisfying his caffeine cravings without further need for flaying conversation.

Eventually, it worked. Or perhaps he creeped her out

enough to leave him alone. Regardless, she vanished, and returned with coffee and a Christmas turkey sandwich from who the hell knew where.

Sacha inhaled both, then spent the rest of the day hunched over his laptop.

It was dark when he came up for air. Quiet too. Even Helga had gone. A silent office was usually Sacha's idea of heaven, but as he glanced around, contentment was hard to find. It was eight o'clock and he'd coded his way to a place where perhaps they could start to breathe, but with no one around to share it with, it was a hollow victory.

You're getting soft. Since when have you needed a standing ovation to appreciate simple things?

Since never. It wasn't validation he craved, but company, and the devil on his shoulder could set itself on fire as far as he was concerned.

Sacha shut his laptop and reached for the bottle of painkillers he'd finally remembered to stash in the drawer. It was already half empty, only two doses left, but with the lion's share of his work now complete it worried him less.

He swallowed the pills and searched out his coffee cup to wash them down.

It was empty.

Sighing, he packed up his things and tried to remember where he'd left his coat. Though it was by far not the latest hour he'd found himself leaving the office in recent days, it seemed like a year had passed since he'd arrived that morning.

He rose with heavy legs and exited the alcove. Helga had left her computer on. He bent over it to shut it down, but found himself instantly absorbed in the graphics splashed across her screen. They'd been developed in the hours since Sacha had last seen them, streamlined to the top designs Blutecc had requested, and then expanded with more detail. Or less where required.

There was an email exchange open too, between Helga and Winona at first, then with Jonah copied in until the conversation had slimmed down to just him and Helga.

Helga: *Basically, we want as much of the concept as we can afford to licence, but we're limited by budget. Our finance department aren't going to budge on the final figure I sent to Winona this morning. Anything extra we'd have to crowdfund, or Sacha is threatening to pay for it himself.*

Jonah Gray: *Is that normal? For your team to fund your advertising campaigns out of pocket?*

Helga: *Not entirely. But it's often the case we don't have the budget to do what we want. We usually let it go, but that was before Sacha. He has some of us fired up enough about this app to want to move mountains.*

Jonah Gray: *I understand. And I don't believe those mountains should come at the expense of yourselves, so if it's any help at all, I am prepared to delay settlement of your account until a few months after your full launch date. By then, you should know if you have succeeded enough to draw more money from your superiors, and if you haven't been, we can talk again about crowdfunding.*

Helga: *Is that your way of telling me you won't let Sacha pay you?*

Jonah Gray: *It's my way of telling you how it is. Whatever Mr. Ivanov chooses to do is entirely up to him.*

There was nothing else. *Mr. Ivanov.* Sacha sucked in a breath. If not for the circumstances, he'd have found that kind of hot. As it was, the sight of Jonah's kindness interlaced with the cold courtesy Sacha deserved made his stomach roil. *I want him to call me Sacha.*

Sacha wanted a lot of things.

He shut down Helga's machine and left the office, turning off lights as he went. Darkness cloaked him, blanketing him in shadow, save a soft glow from beneath the door to Jonah's office.

Leave it.

And for once Sacha listened. He turned his back on Jonah's office, refilled the coffee machine, and left.

14

Winona: *Come for a drink. Nico promised he won't punch anyone this time.*

Jonah read the message and deleted it, still fixated on the storyboards he'd created for Blutecc's fragile fitness app. They were wholly unnecessary if Helga's budget prophecies proved accurate, but for some unknown and likely ludicrous reason, he couldn't leave them alone.

"Mr. Gray?"

Jonah glanced up. Curtis was in the doorway, clutching the coffee jug. Jonah nodded. "Help yourself, Curtis. It's fine. I'm not sure how old it is, though."

"It's not old. Mr. Ivanov made it before he left a few minutes ago. I thought he'd made it for you."

"Oh. Well. Okay, I suppose we'd better drink it then." Dazed, Jonah held out his mug.

Curtis filled it and disappeared, only to return with a slice of the Russian fruit bread Sacha had brought in for breakfast a few weeks back. "Where did you get that from? I didn't think anyone brought anything today."

"It was in the break room, Mr. Gray. By the coffee machine."

"Did Sacha—did Mr. Ivanov come back?"

"I don't know. I've had the hoover on. Do you want me to check?"

"No, no. It's fine."

Jonah waved Curtis away and took a slow sip of coffee. It was rocket fuel, he'd have known Sacha had brewed it even if Curtis hadn't told him. What he didn't know was *why*.

We aren't friends, remember?

Jonah remembered. As if he could forget. And he wasn't above admitting to himself that he didn't like it. Not one bit. Since the very first night they'd met, Sacha had become a bewitching constant in his life and their lack of communication now stung.

More than that. It hurt.

I miss him.

Jonah didn't like that either.

He drank his coffee, still poking at the designs for the fitness app, between scowling at the sweet-smelling pastry he couldn't bring himself to eat. It made no sense that Sacha had returned to the office to bring it to him, but at the same time, there was no other explanation. There was no one else here.

Maybe it's not for you. Maybe he brought it for Samson and Curtis. But if that was the case, surely he'd have left it downstairs with Samson, with clear indicator of who he wanted to eat it.

You're overthinking it. It's literally a piece of cake.

But it wasn't. It was Sacha. And nothing about him was ever *simple*. It was heavy stares and silence. Half smiles and shifting sands. Flinty eyes lit up by the smallest things, only to harden again moments later.

Sighing, Jonah pushed back from his desk, reaching for his phone as it vibrated for the dozenth time since his team had left for the night.

It was Winona again, reminding him they'd decamped to the nearest pub to the office, one Jonah would walk past if the car he was about to call waited in its usual spot across the road.

And wasn't that a scene he wanted to avoid? The last time he'd tried it on a Friday evening, his entire team had flooded out of the bar and corralled him as he'd opened the car door, alarming the driver enough for Jonah to pay him an enormous tip despite the fact he never made the journey home. *Stuff that.*

Resigned, Jonah found Curtis and told him to eat whatever Russian cakes he found lying around, then left the office.

The lift ride reminded him of Sacha, like every lift ride had since they'd met, but over the last few days, the memories had stopped making him smile. Now they irritated him as much as Sacha did, and Jonah gave up at the third floor and took the stairs the rest of the way down.

He emerged out of the building into howling rain. Somehow he'd missed it setting in, despite spending much of his day gazing out of the window. Dodging puddles, he crossed the street, and ducked into the nearest pub, an ale establishment with rough wooden floors and old school fixtures and fittings. Even with the gaudy Christmas decorations, it was a stark contrast to the wine bars it was sandwiched between, and Jonah had always liked it.

His team were in their usual place, taking up a long table at the back of the bar by the kitchen, shouting to each other, and singing along to Slade. They called out to him, hooting their appreciation that he'd finally shown his face.

Jonah rolled his eyes and went to the bar, knowing full well they enjoyed his wallet as much as his general presence. He ordered enough alcohol to keep them quiet for a while, then handed his credit card to the barman. "Keep it," he said. "I'll be back, I'm sure."

"I need a boss like you," the barman said. "Or one that buys up all the vodka like that one."

He jerked his head somewhere behind Jonah, then wandered off, taking Jonah's Amex with him.

Curious, Jonah turned and glanced over his shoulder. It shouldn't have surprised him to see the Blutecc team huddled around a couple of tables on the other side of the pub, but somehow it did. He noted the vodka bottles and shot glasses spread out around them. Helga's platinum hair, and the slumped shoulders of the executive who'd commandeered FG's services earlier in the week as she gave him a stern talking to. And then the amused attention of another man as he watched them, sipping from a vodka glass he held in his elegant hand, his golden gaze deep and addictive.

Sacha.

As if he'd heard his name light up Jonah's mind, he looked up, catching Jonah's stare before Jonah found the wherewithal to be elsewhere.

The world seemed to shift, and yet stop stock still, freezing Jonah in place. A body jostled him, sloshing beer on his arm, but Jonah barely felt it, caught in the snare of Sacha's endless gaze.

Sacha's lips twitched, as though fighting a smile. Jonah hated him for that, both because he yearned to see that smile, and for the notion that Sacha was laughing at him.

Fuck you.

Jonah's eyes burned, and the sudden fury in his gut

shocked him. He dropped his gaze and spun around, facing the bar again. The barman was on his way past with the weighted tray of drinks for his team. Jonah stopped him and helped himself to the whisky he'd ordered for himself. "Bring me another when you have a moment?"

The barman nodded, giving Jonah a fleeting once over that, in another life—one before moody, contradictory Russian computer nerds—might've excited him. That Jonah might've hung around the bar, scored the bloke's number, and perhaps taken him home for a friendly encounter without complication and heartache. But that version of Jonah was elsewhere, leaving him drinking whisky alone in a crowded pub.

He drained his glass and dropped it onto the bar, then he followed the raucous sounds coming from the FG table and found himself a seat among them. His back tingled, the nape of his neck alive with the knowledge that Sacha was somewhere behind him, but he forced himself to focus on the people around him. People who *wanted* him to be there. Nico was on one side of him, Winona the other. Carl was opposite, the only sign of his adventures a week ago a tiny wound dressing still glued to his temple.

His gaze was fixed on Winona. She smiled back at him, shyer than Jonah had ever seen her, and the proverbial penny dropped.

Beside him, Nico snorted into his pint. "No offence, boss, but you're staring at them like you just discovered sliced bread. Stop being weird."

"I'm not being weird," Jonah protested, but he snapped his stare from Carl all the same and helped himself to the nearest drink the hot barman had dumped on the table. It was vodka, of course. He'd ordered it for the accounts manager, but she was nowhere in sight. Perhaps she'd left. Jonah didn't much care. He drank her drink, and someone else's, and then the fresh whisky that appeared in front of him a few minutes later.

Nico eyed him. "Bad day?"

"Not especially. Long, but they all seem that way at this time of year."

"Because it gets dark early," Nico said. "And it's dark when you leave the house, or mansion, wherever it is you live."

"I don't live in a mansion." Though Jonah supposed a penthouse apartment in Chelsea wasn't much different. Nico lived in Hammersmith so he could be close to his ailing parents. He'd never told Jonah this, but Jonah had overheard enough pub gossip to know it. "What are you doing for Christmas?"

"The usual." Nico sank the rest of his beer. "Fighting with my sister while trying to stop my ma burning the place down because she's forgotten how the oven works. You?"

"The same, as in, the usual. I stay with my parents for a week or so, then I come back to the city for the New Year."

"Sounds like fun," Nico said, but Jonah could tell he wasn't all that interested.

And Jonah wasn't that interested either. Most years, by now, the anticipation of the festive season had usually got under his skin. The lights, the food, the crowds on Oxford Street as he battled through them to do his last-minute gift shopping, but it hadn't played out that way this year. Too busy to shop in person, he'd made most of his purchases online, and aside from the glitzy fir tree—the *yolka*—in his apartment, everything else had passed him by. And he couldn't even blame Sacha.

Why would you want to? Is it his fault you're obsessed with him?

No. It really wasn't.

"He's staring at you again," Carl said from across the table.

Jonah's booze-addled gaze sharpened enough to focus on him. "Who is?"

"The hungry Russian."

"Stop it," Jonah snapped. "He has a name, and I'm willing to bet this entire table of drinks that he's *not* staring at me."

Carl snorted. "Well, I guess there's no way of finding out unless you're willing to turn around and look for yourself. And if you're not, I can only assume it's because you know there's a distinct possibility I'm right and you don't want to get caught returning the favour."

"You're an arsehole."

"Never said I wasn't."

Carl went back to flirting with Winona across the table, sliding back into his conversation as if his exchange with Jonah hadn't happened, much less that his boss had called him an arsehole, and Jonah remembered why there was a tiny part of him that had always hated Carl. Or, perhaps, admired his ability to take things at surface value and move on, not like Jonah who was so stuck in his Sacha-themed brood that he could hardly think straight.

He turned back to Nico, who was shaking his head. "What?"

"Nothing, boss."

"Really? Because you look like you have something to say."

If Nico was affected by the uncharacteristic edge lacing

Jonah's tone, it didn't show. He shrugged and claimed another drink from the fast depleting tray. "Nope. Not me."

Jonah let out a sigh that seemed to come from the end of the world. Apologies danced on his lips, but he didn't voice them. Didn't need to. Nico wasn't listening anyway.

More drinks came Jonah's way. He drank them until he'd reached the limit on how inebriated he was prepared to be in front of his team, then he excused himself for some air.

He took his phone with him and stepped out of the fire exit. The night was still damp, and a bitter wind had struck up. Jonah enjoyed the chill, letting it sober him up. At some point, he'd have to call a car and go home, but he didn't feel like being alone just yet. His empty bed held little appeal, especially now he'd experienced the magic of having Sacha in it for an entire weekend.

But you are *alone. You're hiding outside by yourself and you don't even smoke.*

The irony made Jonah laugh out loud, startling an older gentleman who was having his own moment of peace with his pipe. Jonah raised his hands in apology and stepped back inside, hit immediately with a wall of noise that made his head spin all over again.

He ducked into the nearest bathroom. It was empty. Jonah leaned on the sink and studied his reflection in the mirror. He *really* needed that haircut, and beyond that, he was kind of a mess. The whisky had reddened his eyes, and there were shadows beneath them that rivalled Sacha's. Could he blame it on work?

Probably not.

As the thought completed, the bathroom door opened—Jonah had forgotten to lock it. He took a breath to tell whoever it was to wait a little longer, but the words died on his lips as the intruder made himself known. "It's you," Jonah said, astounding himself, as ever, with his powers of observation.

Sacha shut the door. Locked it, and leaned back against it. "It is."

"What do you want?"

"From this room, or from you?"

"Either. Both. Actually, I don't care." Jonah washed his hands and dried them on a paper towel. He fired the rubbish into a nearby bin and moved to the door, but Sacha was still there, slouching against it as if it was perfectly normal for them to be holed up in a grotty pub bathroom.

Not that the bathroom was all that grotty. The establishment was upmarket enough that the space was spotlessly clean and smelt of essential oils rather than bleach.

Regardless, Jonah had no desire to linger under the weight of Sacha's wordless stare. "Excuse me."

"Why?"

"Why do you think?" Jonah jerked his head at the door. "I want to leave."

Sacha didn't move.

And after a week of trying, and failing, not to stare at him without abandon, Jonah was abruptly lost in him—his stubbled jaw and strong shoulders. His hot, liquid gaze. "Move," he whispered.

Sacha shook his head. "I don't think you want me to."

"I do."

"You don't."

"What *do* I want then?"

"I don't know."

Jonah glowered.

Sacha's gaze remained steady and Jonah found himself struck by an overwhelming urge to shake him.

He kissed him instead, crashing their lips together, all the while steeling himself for Sacha to push him away.

Sacha didn't. He snatched a breath and kissed Jonah back, his arms coming around Jonah in a tight embrace that slammed their bodies together.

Jonah was instantly hard, his dick straining against his fitted suit trousers, but he fought Sacha's hold on him and reared back, tearing their lips apart as suddenly as they'd come together. "No. We're not doing this anymore."

"Since when?"

"Since you decided we weren't."

"When did I ever say that?"

Breathing hard, Jonah shook his head wildly. "You said we weren't friends. I took that to mean you didn't want to be."

"I never said I didn't want this."

"This? What is *this*?"

"It is what it is."

"Fuck off. That doesn't mean anything. What are you actually trying to say? That you don't want to be my friend, but you still want the benefits?"

Sacha frowned, gaze darting as he caught and processed Jonah's rushed speech. "I am...tired," he said. "And you speak too fast. Are you asking me I still want to sleep with you?"

"Yes. I suppose I am."

"Why do you ask me this?"

"Does it matter? Can't you just be clear on something for once so we don't have to talk in circles?"

"Why do we have to talk at all?"

"Fuck. You."

"I like it when you are angry. You are flushed and beautiful."

"Stop talking," Jonah growled.

"Make me, Jonah Gray."

Jonah was too drunk for this conversation, and he had a sneaking suspicion Sacha was too, if his flushed cheeks and hooded eyes were anything to go by. Perhaps that was why it made no sense. Why Sacha had followed him into the bathroom in the first place when a sober Sacha might've left Jonah alone. Like he'd left him alone all week, when their shared work had allowed him to, at least.

"You are thinking too much," Sacha said softly. "I do not mean to upset you. If you want to leave, I will stand aside."

"I don't want that," Jonah blurted before his brain engaged.

"What do you want?"

"Right now? Or in general?"

"Either. Both. You decide."

"I don't know the answer to the latter. If I did, telling you what I want right now would be easier."

Sacha licked his lips, a slow sweep of his tongue. "So tell me without words."

Jonah's body cried out for Sacha. To take whatever he was prepared to give. But there was something else, a fantasy that had played on his mind since the very first time they'd truly touched. Every encounter until now had been Sacha's call. He was dominant, rough, demanding, and Jonah had loved every minute, but right now, in this moment, he didn't want that.

He wanted Sacha to feel, even if he was halfway as intoxicated as Jonah.

Jonah pushed Sacha against the sink, crowding him, daring Sacha to stop him.

He didn't, and they kissed again, hot and heavy, before Jonah dropped to his knees and reached for Sacha's belt.

"Wait." Sacha stilled him, gazing down with half closed eyes. "How drunk are you?"

Jonah snorted. "That's sweet, Ivanov, but you don't need to worry about that."

"I am not worried."

"Liar." Jonah returned his attention to Sacha's belt, trying, and failing, to ignore the warmth in his chest at Sacha's concern. It didn't match the belligerence he'd arrived with, but Jonah was used to that. Sacha Ivanov was a contrary bastard.

And a horny bastard, given the fierceness of the erection straining his underwear.

Jonah's mouth watered. He worked fast to free Sacha's dick and swallowed him down before Sacha saw fit to stop him again. He opened his throat, taking Sacha deep, revelling in Sacha's rough gasp, and the taste of him. His scent. And the heightened moans as Jonah brought him quickly to the edge.

In his wildest dreams—and there'd been many since he'd met Sacha—he'd pictured this over and over, taking back the control he'd willingly handed Sacha that first night after the ball. He'd craved this for weeks, Sacha's gentle hands buried in his hair, his breathless murmurs of encouragement as he fucked Jonah's mouth.

"Yes, Jonah. Like that. You are so beautiful like this."

It was the second time Sacha had called him that. Jonah flushed and sucked him harder, enchanted by the sight and sensation of Sacha coming apart, eyes wild as he watched Jonah suck him dry.

Sacha groaned and flailed a hand free from Jonah's hair to

grip the sink behind him. "I'm going to come. If you do not want it in your mouth you need to stop."

Jonah didn't stop. He dug his fingers into Sacha's strong thighs and took it all as Sacha released, not letting go until he'd swallowed every drop.

He sat back on his heels as Sacha staggered against the sink, grinning. "Okay up there?"

Sacha steadied himself and glared down, though no real malice coloured his glittering gaze. "That was not in my plan."

"What plan?"

"The one where—I—*fuck*, I don't know. My English is—"

"Your English is fine when you want it to be," Jonah snapped. "Are you going to tell me what your grand plan was? Or are you going to show me?"

Sacha shook his head. "Neither."

He hooked his hands under Jonah's shoulders and tugged him upright, making short work of undoing Jonah's trousers and dragging his cock free of his underwear. His touch was rough as he flipped their positions, spinning Jonah to face the sink as he stood behind him, jacking him with a grip firm enough to roll Jonah's eyes. He gripped the counter in front of Jonah for support, and pressed his face between Jonah's shoulder blades, drawing pleasure from Jonah in short, sharp pumps, twisting his hand in just the right place.

Jonah shuddered, knowing he wouldn't last long. Blowing Sacha had worked Jonah up so much he'd been on a knife edge before Sacha had laid a hand on him. He bucked into Sacha's hand, groaning, and glad the noise of the crowds beyond the locked door drowned out the strangled yell that swiftly followed.

After, he came down with a shiver, and cleaned up with more paper towels. Behind him, Sacha was quiet.

Too quiet.

Jonah chanced a glance at him in the mirror and found him dressed again, and fixated with something on the ceiling, expression devoid of anything that mattered.

Nice.

Irritation returned to Jonah in droves. He zipped himself up and turned around.

Sacha slowly dropped his gaze. Jonah searched for something he recognised, anything to bind them together, then reality returned to him, and he remembered that things had changed. That he was searching for a connection that wasn't there.

You're not friends. He doesn't want that, remember?

In the cramped bathroom, it didn't seem to matter that Jonah *did* want that, very much. He wanted Sacha's grin, his embrace, and his dry humour. He wanted his kiss, and his arms around him in bed as they slept.

More than anything, he wanted Sacha to look at him.

But he didn't, and Jonah lacked the masochism for the endless wait. He tucked his shirt in, knocked his fist to Sacha's shoulder, and left.

15

Sacha rolled over in bed and stared at the ceiling. Unlike Jonah's penthouse bedroom with its panoramic cityscape on one side of the room, and his glittering *yolka* on the other, the bare hipster bricks and industrial pipes were all Sacha had.

And he was glad of it. The utilitarian view was all he deserved, aside from the headache that had nothing to do with overwork and everything to do with the eight shots of vodka he'd sunk last night.

You're an idiot.

It wasn't the first time the thought had crossed his mind since he'd woken with hazy memories of accosting Jonah in the pub bathroom. And on the fourth go-round, he didn't mean it any less. He pictured Jonah's face as he'd stormed out of the bathroom, and pulled a pillow over his head, muffling his groan. *It is your fault. You broke the rules.* Sacha liked rules, even if they were only for himself. But since he'd met Jonah Gray, he found himself breaking each and every boundary he'd ever set. No repeat hook-ups. No sleepovers. No drinking vodka and laying his hands on Jonah Gray.

Okay. That was a new rule, and one he'd broken way before he'd consciously put it in place, but still. Whichever way he looked at it, he'd fucked up. And all because he'd let his drunken horniness get the better of him when the actual reason he'd followed Jonah into that bathroom had been to check he was okay after he'd vanished from the FG table.

Jonah's kiss had caught him off guard. Then his anger. And his mouth on Sacha's cock. Sober Sacha might've seen the frustration behind Jonah's desire for him, but drunk Sacha had been too consumed by the pleasure of it. Too caught up in his spinning head and thundering heart. Even after, he'd lacked the brain power to string a coherent sentence together. Jonah had walked out before it returned to him, and he'd left the pub entirely by the time Sacha had pulled himself together enough to exit the bathroom.

Sacha had gone home after that, taking a cab to the Chelsea street that was a stone's throw from Jonah's penthouse apartment. He'd drunk more vodka, jacked himself under a cold shower with Jonah on his mind, then passed out face down on his bed, still wet from the frigid spray.

He'd woken up shivering.

He was still cold now. Lonely too, an emotion he couldn't make sense of. Being alone had never bothered him in that faraway place before Jonah.

So he is the barometer you measure yourself with now? The litmus test for your mental health?

You are a fool, Ivanov.

Sacha scowled. Even his own name no longer sounded right without Jonah's honeyed voice wrapped around it, and the sad fact irritated him enough to crawl out of bed and into the shower again.

The shock of cold water eased his headache, then

warmed enough for his limbs to feel like they belonged to him again. His thoughts remained stuck on Jonah, and his blood pumped south, but he ignored his dick, washed his hair, and scrubbed his skin clean of the scent of a late night in the city.

Back in his room, his phone was alive with texts from Helga.

Helga: *Where are you? Did you leave?*

Helga: *Your scarf is still on the table. I'll take it home.*

Helga: *Did you leave with Jonah? I can't see him either.*

If only. Sacha deleted the texts without reply, then changed his mind and thanked Helga for rescuing a scarf he didn't care about, confirming that he'd gone home alone. He didn't know about Jonah, but he could do without office gossip speculating about something that hadn't happened. It would annoy him too much, mainly because he wished it was true.

He threw his phone onto his unmade bed and retreated to the kitchen in search of coffee. While it brewed, he sat at his breakfast bar and opened his laptop. For once, he didn't have a great deal to do. A few hours at most before he reached a point where he could do no more without his team around him.

It was early afternoon when he hit the wall. He shut his laptop and glanced around his messy flat. He'd let things go in recent weeks, too caught up in work, and his obsession with a certain British red head. His fixation on Jonah remained, but with nothing to do with his hands, the disorder around him was abruptly infuriating.

He flew around his living space, gathering stray clothes, books, and newspapers. Filling the dishwasher, organising his barren fridge, loading laundry into the washing machine, and hanging suits that needed to go to the dry cleaners. It killed a few hours. Then he spent the evening on his couch. He ordered sushi and ignored a string of bad films while playing a game of chicken with his phone. Over and over, he opened the short message thread he shared with Jonah. Typed messages. Deleted them. All but one.

Sacha: *I am sorry about yesterday.*

He didn't hit send. He stared at it for a full half hour before he deleted that one too, admitted defeat, and went to bed.

Sunday morning dawned after the longest sleep he'd had in months. And for the first time in forever, he had nothing to do. He was free. It was a shame he had forgotten what to do with himself.

Boredom drove him out of the house and to the nearest shops. A Christmas market filled the street, alive with sparkly lights, and the scents of ginger, nutmeg, and cinnamon. Dozens of stalls were crammed into a small space, loaded with artisan foods and crafts, trading to the soundtrack of a brass band playing Christmas carols. Sacha had already bought his team gift vouchers to thank them for weeks and weeks of hard work, and he had no desire to buy presents for anyone else, but he wandered the market anyway, searching for something he couldn't quite name.

He trailed to a stop at a stall selling glass decorations for a *yolka* he didn't have. He picked up a green pyramid that was the same colour as Jonah's eyes. Held up to the sun it glittered like a prism. Sacha bought it without bothering to contemplate why.

A doughnut stall was doing brisk business at the end of the street. He'd passed it by on his way out, but the fresh air had awakened his appetite, and he drifted closer, poking at his phone, reading the messages Helga had sent him that morning.

None of them mattered. He replied anyway.

"You're going to crash into a lamppost if you walk around the city like that."

Sacha jerked his head up, his pulse already jumping before his brain caught up with the voice he'd been craving all weekend.

Jonah was right in front of him. Hardly surprising considering they lived in the same borough, but it took Sacha back all the same. He'd lived in his flat for three years, and he'd got impression Jonah wasn't new to his penthouse apartment either. How had they never bumped into each other before?

That's easy. You never leave the house in daylight. He's a daylight creature. Look at him with the sun in his face. Beautiful.

It wasn't a new conclusion, and in the time it had taken Sacha to think it, a protracted silence had stretched out between them.

Jonah sighed and made tracks to walk on by.

Sacha shot a hand out to stop him. "Wait."

"Why?"

"Because—" Because *what*? Sacha didn't want to be alone? Or was he finally going to admit that being alone had suited him just fine his entire adult life until Jonah had come along with his smiley, kind, perfect family and his damn fucking Christmas tree?

Sacha rocked back, startled by his own vitriol.

Jonah frowned and started to pull his arm away.

Sacha dug his fingers in. "Please," he said. "I am sorry I am difficult to understand. Will you please walk with me a while?"

For a long moment, he feared Jonah would refuse. That

the hardness in his emerald gaze was there to stay. Then it faded, revealing the gentleness Sacha adored so much. "Okay. I was walking past where I think you live anyway. I guess you could come too."

"Where do you think I live?"

"In the converted flats round the corner, the ones with the rose trees and grey hipster window frames."

Sacha snorted. "Okay, *luchik*. You might be right, but only because I give you directions to the bakery a few weeks ago. Not because you are clever."

"You don't think I'm clever?"

I think you are brilliant. "No."

Jonah started walking again, back the way he'd clearly come, and in the direction of Sacha's flat. He was carrying paper bags from the various market stalls.

"What did you buy?" Sacha asked.

"Gifts. For my parents, mainly. They'd never come somewhere like this, so it's a good place to buy them things they've never seen."

"What did you get them?"

"Candles. My mum loves them. And some honey for my dad. He's obsessed with bees at the moment. He has his own hives at their summer lodge."

"I dropped a honey jar once," Sacha said. "In my grandmother's house, on her favourite carpet. She told my mother I was a devil child."

"What did your mother say?"

"That I was an angel and my father's mother was too full of hate to see it."

"That's a strong statement."

Sacha smiled. "I am no angel now, and I wasn't then, but

the rest of it was true. My father's family are hateful people. I have told you this before, no?"

"A little. I think. I might've been drunk."

"I was drunk on Friday," Sacha said. "I did not mean to upset you."

"You didn't."

"Are you a liar, Jonah Gray?"

Jonah spared Sacha a sideways glance. "No. I was drunk too. I overreacted. After all, what's a bathroom hook-up between non-friends, eh?"

"You take me too seriously."

"Which part?"

"I don't know. All of me?"

Jonah shook his head. "I can't take you anyway whatsoever. You're a terrible communicator."

"I am sorry."

"Don't be. You are who you are. Maybe it's me that's the problem. You were always clear that you wanted an NSA arrangement. I pushed you for more."

Sacha stopped walking, computing the soulless Grindr phrase: *NSA: no strings attached*. "No, you did not. *I* said we could be friends who had sex with each other, and I thought we could, but I am not good at letting people into my life. It..." Sacha waved his hand, searching for the English words. "It scares me, maybe? I don't know. After my mother died, the people I was forced to be around were not nice people. I learned fast that it was better to be alone. I think I like being alone."

"You think?"

"Sometimes. And then there is you, Jonah Gray. You make me think strange things."

"Like what?"

"Like sharing your bed is what I want too, but I am scared to want it. It is a...contradiction, no? To everything I believe myself to be."

"What's wrong with contradiction?"

"If I knew the answer to that, this conversation would not happen."

Jonah frowned. "That makes no sense."

Sacha knew that. But it seemed no matter what he thought he knew, something different fell out of his mouth every time he was near Jonah. His sense of self altered to become a man who chased affection and friendship, all the while desperate for the high of the headiest sexual encounters he'd ever had.

They reached Sacha's building. His heart invited Jonah in to spend what was left of the weekend together, in Sacha's bed, on his couch, pressed up against his kitchen counters. He bought beer. Made dinner from the handful of ingredients he had in his cupboards. Watched films. Ate together, fucked together, slept together. But his head said no, a blunt refusal with no rhyme or reason, and he'd pushed Jonah away too much for him to fill the void Sacha's reticence left behind.

Sacha fished in his pocket for his keys. Jonah propped his shoulder on the wall, watching him.

"Can I ask you something?" he said suddenly.

Sacha nodded. "Of course."

"How did your mum die?"

"That is what you want to ask me?"

"Yes."

"Why?"

"I don't know."

Sacha let go of his keys and moved away from the door.

Jonah followed, until they were in the alleyway beside his building that led to the bin yard.

He'd had worse conversations in far nicer places. "My mother died in a car accident. It was icy. She came off the road on a Saturday afternoon and hit a tree."

"How old were you?"

"Nine."

"So you remember her, then?"

"Yes."

"And you don't like your dad?"

"No."

Jonah nodded slowly, like a man connecting dots Sacha couldn't see.

Stop. Please. But the words didn't solidify. They stayed inside, unsaid, like everything else.

Jonah straightened and moved his shopping bags from one hand to the other. He rummaged in one, and came up with a tiny, Christmas-patterned gift bag. "I got this for you. I don't know why, unless you want to call it a non-friendship bracelet. Or you can re-gift it to someone you actually like—"

"I do like you. That is—"

"Shh." Jonah silenced Sacha with a soft finger to his lips. "I saw it and thought of you. I don't care what you do with it or why. I'll see you tomorrow, at *work*, okay?"

Sacha opened his mouth, but Jonah left without waiting for an answer, ducking out of the alley and striding away, his auburn hair a beacon among the city crowds. Sacha drifted a few steps behind him, watching him disappear until he remembered the bag in his hand.

He took it inside and left his shoes and coat on the floor of the hallway, trashing the efforts he'd made to tidy the place up. On the couch, he set the bag on the coffee table and stared at it. Jonah had called it a non-friendship bracelet, but to Sacha, though he hadn't even set eyes on it yet, it seemed like a live landmine. As if the moment he saw it, everything would irrevocably change.

"I don't care what you do with it or why."

Jonah was no liar, but Sacha didn't believe him.

He didn't even want to.

With a shaky hand, he reached for the bag and opened it. Inside, he found a leather bracelet. It was charcoal grey, and a tiny silver charm in the shape of a *yolka* was woven into the simple braid.

Sacha held it up to the light, twisting it this way and that. The silver charm caught the light of the midday sun, like everything else he'd come across today had seemed to do. It was no match for Jonah's copper hair, but it enchanted Sacha all the same.

He'd never worn a bracelet. He stretched out his right arm and tied the leather around his wrist with his left hand and his teeth. The dark leather looked good against his skin.

It felt even better.

Jonah stared at the palm-sized ornament on his desk. The green glass had caught the winter sun, casting refractions on the dark carpet and fabric blinds, enchanting anyone and everyone who'd graced his office that day. But as beautiful as it was, it was the accompanying note that had enraptured Jonah more.

Jonah Gray. We will talk soon, I promise x

No signature, but Jonah didn't need one. Even without his full name spelled out, he recognised Sacha's spiky scrawl even though he'd never seen it before—it matched his personality. The delicate Christmas tree decoration? Not so much.

Or maybe it did, and Jonah didn't know Sacha Ivanov half as well as he'd thought.

You don't know him at all. The realist prancing on his shoulder was hard to ignore. Jonah dug deep for counterarguments, but all he could come up with was that Sacha liked to eat and be bossy about orgasms.

He wasn't bossy on Friday night.

There were exceptions to every rule, though, right?

Jonah hoped so, or he was destined to spend the rest of his days thoroughly confused.

We will talk soon... What did that even mean? Talk about what? As contradictory as the weekend had been, Sacha had made himself perfectly clear, and caught at the right moment, Jonah had accepted it. Mostly. Partially.

Actually, not at all, but he'd failed to figure out what that meant, so he'd left Sacha alone. Running into him at the market had been as unexpected as the gift he'd no plans of buying until he'd seen it on the hemp stall next to the coffee cart. And now here he was, eyeing up the glass pyramid that had mysteriously appeared on his desk that morning, when he had a million and one things he should've been doing instead.

It was lunchtime before he had a chance to venture out of his office. He didn't stop himself sweeping the floor for Sacha. Didn't even try. And for once, he didn't have to search far. Sacha was hunched over Helga's computer, frowning, as usual, his dark brows knotted, bottom lip caught in his teeth.

Why does he have to be so bloody sexy?

On cue, Sacha glanced up. Since the night of the ball, on the rare occasions they'd locked eyes across the office, it had become their habit to flit past each other as if the heat simmering between them wasn't there. Each time hurt progressively more than the last, even when it was Jonah who blinked first, as guilty of evasion as Sacha. But he couldn't look away now, and, neither, it seemed, could Sacha. His gold eyes blazed, and his lips turned up in a soft smile that warmed Jonah's blood.

He took a hesitant step forward, the note Sacha had left

playing on repeat: *We will talk soon, I promise.* "Soon" was a relative time construct. *How about now?*

"Mr. Gray?"

Jonah blinked. The engineer who'd finally come to fix the network issues was in his office doorway. "Sorry. What?"

"I just came to tell you I'm all done. I have some paperwork for you to sign."

Of course he did. Sometimes, Jonah feared that his signature was the only reason he'd been put on the earth.

He flipped through the half-dozen sheets on the engineer's clipboard, signing his name to who-the-hell-knew what. Sacha watched him, the half-smile still playing on his lips, until his phone distracted him, and his frown returned, deeper this time, as if it meant more.

Jonah frowned too, and the need to reach Sacha became abruptly more consuming. But the engineer wasn't done with him. Paperwork became a detailed explanation of the work he'd done. Then a guided tour, and a sales pitch for a permanent maintenance contract Jonah would've signed a thousand times just to make the conversation end already.

By the time he was done and the engineer had left, Sacha was no longer at Helga's desk. For reasons that made no sense, it felt like *Groundhog Day*—a series of tedious, predictable events that led absolutely nowhere. The day dragged on, and, of course, Sacha disappeared, taking the brief rush of hope he'd gifted Jonah with him.

As evening drew in, the office emptied out. Jonah was the last FG employee left standing. He tidied the break room for no other reason than to wait out Sacha's appearance from the alcove in the Blutecc office. Twenty minutes later, the coffee machine had never been so clean, but his only reward was looking up in time to see Helga turning the lights off in the alcove as she left.

She was alone. Jonah intercepted her at the exit. "Where's Sacha? Did he leave?"

Helga jumped, files slipping from her grasp and to the floor. "Shit. Sorry. Yes, he left hours ago. Didn't you see? You two seem to have eyes on each other every time I look up."

Jonah stooped to help gather the files. "I didn't see. I've been busy. He left this afternoon? Why? He's usually here until midnight."

Helga cocked a perfect brow as she stood. "I don't want to know how you know that, and I don't know why he left. He got a phone call that upset him then he was gone."

"A phone call? From who?

"I'm not sure, he was talking in Russian for most of it, but I *think* his father passed away."

"You think?"

"Yes. I'm Norwegian. I don't speak Russian, and he didn't stop to fill me in before he ran out. As it happens, I was on my way to ask *you* for more details. I figured he was more likely to tell you than anyone in our office."

"Why?"

"Because you're friends."

"No, we're—" The denial died on Jonah's lips. Whatever Sacha had said in the past, and whatever he'd planned to say before this, Jonah cared about him, goddammit. Whether Sacha liked it or not, they *were* friends. "He didn't tell me, but I've been in meetings all afternoon. He wouldn't have been able to reach me if he had to leave in a hurry."

"You should call him," Helga said. "I really don't speak Russian, but I could tell he was upset."

"He doesn't like his father," Jonah said absently, his phone already in his hand.

Helga sighed. "Yes, well, sometimes you reach a point where that doesn't matter anymore. Call him, Jonah. And let me know he's okay?"

"Of course."

Helga left, and Jonah trailed her too slowly to hitch the same lift. He drifted to the stairs and descended, tapping out a message as he went.

Jonah: *Are you okay? Helga said you got some bad news. Call me if you need anything x*

He sent the message on WhatsApp. It didn't deliver. Jonah took a car home before he tried calling, but the result was the same. Sacha's automated voicemail kicked in without ringing. Wherever Sacha was, either his phone wasn't connecting, or he'd turned it off.

Both options unsettled Jonah. He took a shower, ate toast for dinner, and spent the evening pacing his apartment. It was close to midnight when it occurred to him to take a walk to Sacha's building. He was on the doorstep before he recalled he had no idea which flat was Sacha's.

He hung around outside for a while, studying curtained windows for clues, but none were forthcoming. His gut told him Sacha would pick black linen over red velvet, but without knowing which flat the dark lined window belonged to, his instincts didn't help. He left before someone called the police.

At home, he left Sacha a voicemail.

"Hey, so...Helga thinks your father has passed away. If that's the case, I'm sorry. I know your relationship was diffi-cult, but that kind of news is never easy to hear. Call me if you need anything, even if it's a distraction. I'm here for you, Ivanov. Be safe."

He ended the call, shaking his head. *Be safe.* What was that supposed to mean? And how would it sound if and when Sacha picked up the message?

Don't think about it. Just go to bed and stop second guessing everything. He knows you're there. That's enough. It has to be.

Sighing, Jonah pocketed his phone and picked up the brown paper parcel he'd left on the coffee table when he'd come home from work. He unwrapped the green glass and took it to the Christmas tree in the hallway. Most years, he neglected to switch the lights on any evening when he didn't have company, but this year, alone or not, he couldn't think of a single evening since him and Lily had put it up that he'd forgotten.

He tied the gossamer thread of the ornament and hung it on an uppermost branch in front of a golden light. It glowed, ethereal and warm, shrouding the nearby angel in forest-green. He thought about snapping a picture and sending it to Sacha, but given the circumstances of his absence, it didn't seem appropriate, though considering it gave him a reason to check his phone again. Sacha still hadn't been online, and Jonah's earlier message remained undelivered. Logic reasoned he was away from home without means to charge his phone, but worry gnawed at Jonah's heart all the same. He stared at the green prism a moment longer, before he went to bed with one thought on his mind.

Please be okay.

17

Jonah woke with a gasp, pulse slamming. He brought a hand to his chest, as if he could press his thudding heart back in, and sucked in a long breath, searching his darkened bedroom for whatever had startled him awake. The Christmas tree twinkled from the hallway. Along with never forgetting to turn it on, it seemed he now neglected to turn it off at night.

Brilliant. Perhaps it was the green cast of Sacha's prism that had invaded his sleep. It made sense, as it was the only difference in his apartment in the three consecutive nights he'd woken in a cold sweat.

Three nights, and three long days since news from Russia seemed to have wiped Sacha from the face of the earth. No one had heard from him, not even Helga—unless she'd chosen not to tell Jonah, but given her concern for him a few days ago, that made no sense.

Unless he asked her not to.

Jonah rubbed his eyes, still breathing hard. Out of habit,

he checked his phone, bracing himself for the blank screen, and then the scratchy, sinking feeling as he scowled at the single grey tick on WhatsApp, letting him know the message he'd sent Sacha *three days* ago still hadn't delivered, but—

What the—? Jonah sat up sharply, bedsheets slipping down his bare torso. The screen wasn't blank. It was lit up with three missed calls, all within the last ten minutes. Sacha. Fuck.

How the hell did I sleep through that?

Frantic, Jonah jabbed the screen, calling Sacha straight back. It rang and rang and rang, and for a heart-stopping moment he feared he'd missed his chance. That it would go to voicemail like it had a dozen times over the last few days.

Then a rustling sound broke the deadlock, and a heavy sigh, like a weighted heart blowing smoke at the moon. "Jonah Gray."

Jonah sagged with relief. "Finally. I've been calling you for days. Are you okay? Where the hell are you?"

"That is lot of questions for the middle of the night."

"You weren't asleep," Jonah retorted. "You called me."

"I did."

"So?"

"So you told me to call you if I needed something."

"What did you need?"

"You, Jonah. Your voice. I needed to hear it, if only for a moment."

An emotion Jonah couldn't describe rushed over him. "It doesn't have to be a moment. I have time."

"No, you don't. It is late. You have to work tomorrow."

"I have to go to the office. I don't actually have much to do as we're about to shut down for Christmas. Besides, you haven't been concerned with me losing sleep every other time we've communicated in the middle of the night."

"We were naked?"

"Probably. Do I have to keep my clothes on to make you care about me?"

"I do care about you."

"Why? We're not friends, remember?"

Another weary sigh crackled the line. "And yet here we are," Sacha said. "You should not listen to me. Perhaps I am not a good judge of what we should define ourselves."

"You would leave it up to me?"

"Maybe. I was thinking of that before, but now my head is so full I cannot think of much at all."

"I'm sorry about your father."

Sacha inhaled a soft breath. Jonah wondered if he was smoking. He'd never seen it, but Sacha often tapped his fingers like a restless ex-smoker, and he seemed the type.

"Are you okay?" Jonah asked when Sacha didn't speak. "I know you weren't close, but—"

"We were not," Sacha said. "It is a relief that he is gone. I think I should feel bad about that, but I don't."

"Was he sick?"

"Yes. For long time. He drank a lot. Smoked a lot. Did not take care of himself."

"Do you have siblings?"

"Step-siblings. I am not close to them either, but I have to come to Moscow to sign things for them. I will not stay to put him in the ground."

"You're in Russia?"

"I am. Does that surprise you?"

"It shouldn't," Jonah said. "I can't explain why it does."

"You do not need to. You are a good person, Jonah Gray.

That is always enough for me, I am sorry if I ever made you feel like it wasn't."

Jonah slid out of his bed and to the window. The view made him feel somehow closer to Sacha, even in the silence that stretched between them. "You never *made* me feel anything. And for what it's worth, I'm sorry too."

"What on earth for?"

"For complicating things."

"Jonah." Sacha's voice was soft, chiding, almost. "It was complicated from the moment I stepped into that lift and saw you standing there. I *knew* I would not be able to forget you. That is not your fault. I just wish I was better at all the things you deserve."

"And what's that? And, actually, why do you get to decide? Maybe I'm happy enough with a grumpy Russian in my bed who won't talk to me or admit we really are friends?"

"Happy *enough*?" Sacha snorted. "That is not a thing. And I know we are friends. I am wearing your bracelet. I have not taken it off since you gave it to me."

Jonah blew out his own quiet breath. "I thought you'd give it away."

"To who? You think there is someone I would want to be friends with more than you?"

"I think we sound like twelve-year-olds having this conversation," Jonah countered. "Can't we just agree to agree and move on?"

"If you would like that."

"I would."

"Can I ask you something, though?" Sacha said. "Now that we are friends?"

In the darkness, Jonah almost smiled, but Sacha's serious tone gave him pause. "Of course. You can ask me anything."

"What did that man do to you?"

"Oh." It was the first time Sacha had referred to William Ratner without referencing his hair, but Jonah was in no doubt of who he meant. "Well, nothing, really, I suppose. He just makes me uncomfortable."

"He makes you uncomfortable because he did something to you. I saw it on that first night, and then shades of it later, even when he was not there anymore. You do not have to tell me, but do not ever say it was nothing."

Jonah thought back to every encounter he and Sacha had ever shared and tried to pin point moments where he could've given himself away, but it was all such a hazy blur, too many emotions to count. "I didn't mean it was nothing to *me*, more that it was a minor incident. I was sixteen. He backed me into a dark corner at the ball that year and shoved his hands down my pants. I fought him off and told him I'd stab him if he didn't leave me alone. The end." The words left Jonah in a rush. He thought he was done, but Sacha didn't speak, and he realised there was more. "I didn't tell anyone," he whispered. "Ratner's from a wealthy family—married with children. It would've embarrassed my parents if it had got out, and destroyed his wife, but you're right, it haunted me for a long time—still does when I have to face him every year and he tries to talk to me like we're fucking friends. Lily put a laxative in his drink one year just to get rid of him."

"I like her more and more."

"You'll meet her one day if you keep that bracelet on. How long are you going to be in Russia?"

"Until tomorrow," Sacha said. "Then I need to come back for work. There is a small problem with the app interface that only I can fix, and I did not bring my laptop with me. It is still at the office."

"Is there anything I can do to help?"

"Yes, Jonah Gray, but you are doing it already."

Sacha hated airports. Sometimes it seemed every flight he ever took was delayed, and his lunchtime flight from Moscow to London was no exception. It was late by the time he pushed his way out of Heathrow, and fell into a cab. Too late to visit the office, even for him.

Sacha: *I am home. Sleep. See you tomorrow?*

Jonah Gray: *I'll find you x*

Sacha pondered what that meant, and accepted the flutter in his chest. After long days spent with his step-siblings and Russian lawyers, he appreciated the warmth more than he ever had. Clung to it. Embraced it as he crawled into his bed and shut his eyes on a thundering headache.

Tired, but wired, it took a while for sleep to come. Jonah's voice kept him company. Last night, they'd talked until sunrise about everything and nothing, and standing on the balcony of his father's cold, empty home, Sacha had felt a true yearning to be somewhere else. Not *anywhere* else, but with Jonah.

So what? You are his friend, he is yours, and you still want to fuck him?

No. It was more than that now. Sacha wanted to wake up with him too. Eat with him. Decorate a *yolka* with him after a morning spent wandering the markets together. It scared him, but he liked the feeling. To be afraid of it was a thrill, and he didn't stop to wonder what had changed. It didn't matter. Sometimes the heart wasn't as complicated as people wanted it to be. Sacha wanted Jonah, and Jonah wanted him. It was enough, at least until Sacha fell asleep.

The next morning, he rose before dawn and took a car into the office. He didn't stop for breakfast, with the app launch looming, there was no time. Loaded with coffee, he hunkered down in the alcove and set to work fixing the teething problems the interface had thrown up in his absence. Time became the tap of his keyboard and the blue light of his computer screen.

"You'll go blind if you squint like that."

Despite the feminine voice, Sacha still glanced up looking for Jonah. Helga met his frown with a wry smile. "Nice to see you too. When did you last shave?"

Sacha's scowl deepened. "Why does that concern you?"

"It doesn't. I like the bearded look. I'm just wondering if you're okay. You didn't say much in your emails."

"You did not ask if I was okay. Why would I answer a question that wasn't there?"

"You couldn't read between the lines?"

Sacha shook his head. "I do not know what you want from me."

Helga sighed and produced a paper coffee cup from behind her back—the good stuff that bore no resemblance to the crap in the break room. "Never mind. How was Russia? Do you have to go back for your dad's funeral?"

"No. It is today."

"Today? Then why are you here?"

"Because I did not want to go. My father was a drunk asshole. I only go to give away all his money."

Helga blinked, caught off guard by Sacha's rare candour, and Sacha felt bad about that. He liked Helga. Her dry humour suited his own.

"I'm sorry," Sacha said. "It has been a long week, no? But do not worry about my father. It wasn't as important to me as it would be for someone else."

"Is that your way of telling me to mind my own business?"

"No. It is the truth."

Helga nodded. "Okay. Drink your coffee then. Do you want me to grab you some breakfast?"

"No."

"Sure? You get angry when you're hungry and we have a hell of a day ahead of us."

She wasn't wrong, but Sacha's head was still killing him, and nausea had started to roil in his belly. "Thanks, but I'm not hungry. Could you do something for me, though?"

"Of course."

"There's some medication in the desk by your computer. It's mine. Could you bring it to me?"

Helga frowned. "Do you mean the prescription bottle? If so, I threw it away yesterday. It was empty."

"Was it? Damn." Sacha sighed. "Never mind."

"Are you sure? I can send someone out to the pharmacy if you have your prescription?"

"No, no. It's okay. I will go at lunchtime."

"We have a meeting at midday, and another at two. You might not have time."

"Then I will be fine," Sacha said. "Do not worry. You said it yourself, we have a big day, yes? No time for headache. I will probably forget about it."

Helga seemed unconvinced, matching how Sacha felt, but he was right about one thing: there was no time.

She left him alone to get on with her own mammoth to-do list. Sacha soldiered on, putting out fires until the first of a dozen meetings came around.

It was the first time he'd left the alcove since he'd arrived. The Blutecc office was a frantic hive of activity, and the frenetic energy made Sacha's brain buzz. He winced and automatically looked for Jonah, but the FG side of the office was deserted.

"Christmas party," Helga supplied. "Their boss took them out for lunch. I don't think they're coming back."

"What? At all?"

"Not today. Are you ready?"

"For what?"

Helga nudged him. "For the meeting, Sacha. Jesus, you're on another planet today."

Sacha glared. "I am not that lucky."

"Whatever. Come on, we need you."

"That is sweet, but not true. You do not need me in this meeting."

"Then don't come. Go back and finish whatever you're doing. Regardless, stop blocking the door."

Dazed, Sacha stepped aside and let Helga pass. Then, unable to face his computer screen again just yet, he followed her into the meeting and took a seat at the end of the table.

He fished his phone from his pocket and typed out a message.

Sacha: *You are not here. Perhaps it is me who must find you?*

Jonah Gray: *You won't have to look far. I'll be bankrupting myself across the road for the rest of the day.*

Sacha: *Never ending lunch?*

Jonah Gray: *And then some. When will you be done?*

Sacha: *The app goes live at 5pm. I will watch and wait for a little while. Then I am finished until the new year and...I will find you.*

Jonah Gray: *Counting on it, Ivanov.*

So was Sacha. Hour by hour, minute by minute. His team was counting down for the launch, but Sacha had already checked out. The app was finished and it worked. He'd delivered, and now he was free, of more than just the bad days and late nights of a shoddy fitness app.

With his father gone, and Christmas looming, there was nothing in Sacha's heart but *yolkas* and Jonah Gray.

18

It was gone seven by the time the first Blutecc employees began to filter into the pub. Jonah watched, trying not to track them, and whip his head around every time the door opened.

Failed, naturally, much to Lily's amusement. "You're going to hurt yourself," she said.

Jonah sipped his glass of tonic water. "I don't know what you're talking about."

"That's because you're not listening. I don't think you've heard a word I've said since you came to sit with me under the pretence of keeping me company when actually you're using me as a convenient place to spy on the door."

"Am not."

"Are so. But let's not be children about it. I'm your friend, not your employee. You can be honest about the fact you're waiting on Sacha."

Jonah forced himself to look away from the door and sighed. "Is it that obvious?"

"Only to me," Lily said. "And maybe the dark-haired girl. What's her name again?"

"Winona."

"Yes, her. But I think she's more interested in Carl. What's going on there?"

Shamefully, Jonah had no idea. He was out of the loop with office gossip, and aside from checking on his general health and wellbeing, hadn't had a real conversation with Carl in weeks.

"You're rubbish," Lily chided. "And not for any reason that actually matters, so don't get all wounded."

"Wounded? Remind me why I invited you to my office Christmas party?"

"The same reason you do every year. So you could buy me Champagne all night while I insult you. Standard night out, dear boy, though I fear you're going to ditch me as soon as a certain Russian shows his face."

"Am not," Jonah said for the dozenth time since Lily had breezed into the pub, fresh from her early flight home. "He wants to meet you."

Lily snorted. "Nothing you've told me about him makes me believe that phrase has ever left his mouth."

"Well, not exactly. But he knows you're my best friend and meeting you is kind of non-negotiable."

"On what grounds? That's a little extreme for a fuck buddy, Jonah."

"I know."

"So...?"

"So what?"

"What's changed?" Lily refilled her glass from the bottle Jonah had dumped on the table to keep her quiet. "Last I heard you were angsting over the fact he probably only wanted to fuck you, not make a blood pact and exchange friendship bracelets."

She was joking, but her dry humour was close enough to reality that Jonah flushed. He ducked his head, glad of the dimly lit bar. "I was not angsting."

"You so were. And that's totally okay. It means you care, and there's nothing wrong with that. Besides, if what I hear about your Russian is accurate, he's definitely hot enough to warrant a bit of angst."

"What have you heard? And how have you heard it? You've only been here an hour."

"And you've spent most of it stalking the door, leaving me to eavesdrop, and word has it, your *friend*, is every bit as gorgeous as you said he was."

Jonah rolled his eyes. "He's more than gorgeous, Lil. You think I'd have got myself in this state over someone who was just a bit of eye candy?"

"Nope. And I know you wouldn't over someone who was just a good fuck, so I'm assuming you've done something ridiculous since I last saw you and fallen in love with him."

"I'm not in love with him. I don't know him well enough for that."

"Says who? Do you think all great love stories begin with a picture perfect set-up, spread over a formulaic space of time that leaves no room for doubt?"

"I—"

"Of course it doesn't. There *is* no formula. You don't have to know someone inside out to fall in love with them, boo. That bit is just the start."

Lily's words would've had more effect if Jonah had been paying her his full attention, but as she finished her rousing speech, Helga entered the pub. Jonah sat up straighter, waiting for Sacha to follow, but as she shook out her hair and draped her coat over her arm, it became clear she was alone.

Frowning, Jonah scanned the bar, counting the heads of the Blutecc employees he only knew by sight. There were probably some missing, but no one he'd ever seen Sacha with, even in the office, and doubt threatened the optimistic bubble he'd carried all day. *Did I get this wrong again? Has he gone home without me?*

No. That made no sense. After weeks of back and forth and mixed messages, over the past few days, something had shifted in Sacha. He'd made no promises, but he'd made his intentions clear. He *wanted* Jonah, in whatever way they could figure out together. *I'll find you.* Not even drunk Jonah could misinterpret that, and he wasn't drunk. Not even close. He hadn't touched a drop.

Lily was still talking. Jonah tuned her out and rose from his seat. He elbowed his way through the crowd to where Helga stood at the bar. "Where's Sacha?"

She turned, frowning. "What?"

"Where's Sacha?" Jonah repeated. "Didn't he come with you?"

"I thought he was here?"

"Nope. I thought he was still at the office with you."

"He was." Helga craned her neck and swept the bar. "Then he was gone. I thought he'd snuck out to be with you. I could tell he wasn't interested in the party once we were sure the app hadn't crashed in the first five minutes."

"It went well?"

"As far as we can tell. There's a bigger event going on at the launch venue downtown, and we've got people there, but for us grunts, it's over."

"You're not grunts."

"We are. We've rebuilt that app from scratch, and best case scenario, it succeeds well enough for Blutecc to sell it on to a bigger company. No one will remember what any of us did to save it. But that's life, I suppose. Sacha doesn't seem bothered, so I guess I'm not either."

"What will you do now? Is Sacha staying with the company?"

"Shouldn't you ask him that?"

She was right, obviously, but Sacha wasn't there. Jonah shrugged. "I'm just curious about Blutecc. I've never taken much notice in what you do, but this...project has fascinated me. It's made me wonder what will come next."

"More of the same, I'd imagine," Helga said. "Though I don't think they'll buy such a broken app again and try to develop it with no principles. Sacha ripped the board a new one this morning."

"He did, eh?"

"Of course. He's good at that. I think it's why they hired him, but it's days like today they sometimes wish they hadn't, especially when he waved your invoice in their faces and made them cough up to it."

Jonah laughed, picturing the scene. "Well, I suppose it's better than him paying it from his own pocket."

"He totally would've done that, you know."

"I know." It was probably the most in-depth conversation Jonah had ever shared with Helga. He absorbed it all, but his heart still called out for Sacha. "Where do you think he is? Did he go home?"

Helga shrugged. "Maybe. He's been under the weather all day, but I thought he was holding out to see you."

"Under the weather? In what way?"

"Headache. He gets them a lot—shoot, hang on." Helga dug her phone from her bag. It was flashing with an incoming call. "Sorry, I have to take this."

Jonah took the hint and left her to it. He went back to the table where Lily was talking animatedly to Nico. They were engaged enough for Jonah to subtly claim his coat from his chair and abandon them too.

He shouldered his way out of the pub and into the street. Smokers lined the pavements, but none were Sacha. *You don't even know he smokes, remember? That was a late night assumption you made based on your obsession with listening to him breathe.*

Jonah shook his head slightly, and walked away from the drinkers who'd spilled out of the pubs and bars, drifting across the road to the office on autopilot, his phone to his ear.

Sacha's voicemail kicked in. Again. As if he'd dropped off the earth for the second time in the space of a week. *Maybe he did go home. And he turned his phone off to get some peace.*

But as logical as the theory sounded, Jonah knew it wasn't true. There was nothing logical about Sacha Ivanov. Never had been.

Jonah swiped himself into the office building and strode to the elevator. Samson was at his post, for once wide awake. "Did you see Mr. Ivanov from Blutecc leave yet?" Jonah asked.

Samson shook his head. "Not that I remember. But everyone seemed to leave in a hurry today. Excited for Christmas, no doubt."

"No doubt." Jonah nodded and continued on his way to the elevator and up to the thirteenth floor.

He found it deserted, not even Curtis had reached there yet. Lights off, computers shut down. But instinct drew Jonah to the alcove that couldn't be seen unless you were in it, and he rounded the corner to the soft blue light of a laptop.

Sacha's laptop.

And Sacha was beside it, slumped on the floor, eyes closed, face pale.

He looked dead.

"Oh my god." Jonah closed the distance between them and dropped to a crouch beside Sacha. He put one hand to his forehead and clamped the other around his wrist, checking his pulse. "Sacha? What's wrong?"

Sacha's eyes flickered as Jonah counted his racing heartbeat. He groaned.

Jonah tightened his grip. "Hey. It's me. Jonah. Open your eyes, Sacha. Look at me."

Sacha took a deep, shuddery breath. One eye opened fully, the other stayed hooded, drooping slightly, unfocused and bloodshot.

"That's it." Jonah squeezed his hand. "Can you tell me what's wrong?"

"I'm fine," Sacha slurred.

"You're really not. Your heart is beating *really* fast."

"Is nothing. Too much caffeine. No food. It get better soon, now I finish."

"Finish what?"

"Work."

Jonah glanced at Sacha's open laptop and an overwhelming urge to throw it out of the window swept over him.

He settled for slamming it shut, cloaking them in darkness.

Sacha hummed and let his eyes fall closed again.

Jonah shook him. "Don't do that. You need to stay awake so I can get you some help, okay?"

He started to stand.

Sacha grabbed his arm. "No, I don't need help. Is just migraine, *luchik*. Please don't go."

"Sacha—"

"*No*." Sacha dug his fingers into Jonah's forearm. "Please. It will pass, I promise."

Jonah pried Sacha's grip loose and took his hand, squeezing it again, harder than before. "All right, all right. But you can't stay on the office floor. We need to go home, get you comfortable, okay?"

Sacha raised his head, slow, like it was weighted with concrete. He finally met Jonah's gaze with reddened eyes. "My home."

Jonah blinked his surprise. "You want me to come to your place?"

"Yes. For lots of reasons. But…" Sacha tapped his temple. "For medicine. I keep it at home."

"This has happened before?"

"Since I was young and car accident. There is problem in my brain."

Sacha's speech dragged as if he was drunk, and each word hit Jonah in slow motion, impacted him with brutal force. It bothered him more than he could say that he hadn't known this about Sacha. All this time they'd spent in each other's company, and he'd had no idea. "Okay. Let's get you home, then you can tell me more about it."

"Why?"

"Because I fucking care about you," Jonah snapped. "Stop fighting me."

Sacha smiled a little, but it didn't last. His colour was terrifying, and only the distant memory of Lily's premenstrual migraines kept Jonah's fear at bay. *He's not dying. Take him home. Get him his medicine.*

He found Sacha's coat and his bag, and helped him stand. "Your laptop is staying here."

"Is yours?"

"It's locked in my desk. I'm not looking at it until January 2nd."

"That is long time."

"Yes, well. I have my phone for emails and anything else can wait."

"You are a principled man."

"Not really. I just know what happens to me when I work myself into the ground." Jonah swiped his phone screen to summon a car to take them home.

Sacha was silent, leaning against the wall. Any other time Jonah would've felt his keen gaze on him, *raking* over him, studying him, the way only Sacha could. But not this time. Sacha could barely keep his eyes open.

Jonah took Sacha's laptop to his own desk drawer and locked it inside. He returned to Sacha's half smile.

"It is like you are taking me hostage."

"Not you. Just your laptop."

"Shame."

Jonah smirked and pulled Sacha's coat tighter around him, fastening the buttons. "Maybe next time. Come on. There should be a car downstairs any minute, my driver wasn't far away."

He took Sacha's arm and guided him to the lift. Inside, it lurched downwards, shuddering, as it had become prone to doing since the breakdown that had brought them together.

Jonah smiled, but when he looked at Sacha, he was deathly pale, shielding his eyes from the overhead lights with one hand, while his other arm was wrapped tight around himself, holding himself together.

"Hey." Jonah stepped into his personal space. "Lean on me."

Sacha shook his head. "I'm okay."

"Liar." Jonah pushed Sacha's hand away and guided his head down, pulling Sacha into an embrace that took some of his weight and allowed him to hide his face in Jonah's shoulder.

Sacha was tight, rigid with pain. Jonah massaged the nape of his neck. Sacha moaned.

"Shh. It won't take long to get home," Jonah murmured as if Sacha didn't know the distance between the office and his own flat. "It's okay."

The lift ride was over before Sacha could respond. Jonah slipped an arm around his waist and steered him out of the building into the waiting car. He gave the driver Sacha's address and the luxury vehicle slipped soundlessly into the evening traffic.

Sacha hunched forward, hiding his face again. Jonah rubbed his back and kept quiet, mind spinning as he replayed the day's events. While Blutecc had worked to the wire, it had been relatively serene on the FG side of the office. Deadlines were met, projects wrapped up, and they'd all been in the pub by lunchtime. Most of his team had been legless long before the Blutecc personnel had filtered in, but not Jonah. He'd stuck to tonic water, and he was thankful for it now. He'd never imagined the evening playing out quite like this, but he wasn't sure a drunk version of himself would've thought to go back for Sacha, and the notion of Sacha being alone right now made him feel slightly ill.

You feel ill? Imagine what it's like for him.

Jonah shivered, glad Sacha was paying him no heed. "*...I was young...car accident...problem in my brain.*" The only car accident Sacha had ever mentioned had been the one that had killed his mother. Never once had it occurred to Jonah that Sacha had been in that damn car with her, and he cursed himself for it now. Where else would he have been on a Saturday afternoon but with his mother? *Idiot.*

Maybe, and drunk Jonah might've let it run away with him, but with his head screwed on, Jonah knew it didn't matter. Sacha hadn't told him the details because he hadn't wanted to. Hook-ups. Friends. Lovers. Whatever they were to each other, it wasn't therapists.

The car pulled up outside Sacha's building. Jonah thanked the driver and roused Sacha, helping him out. "I don't know which flat is yours."

"Twenty-three, like today." Sacha found his keys and shuffled towards the entrance. "You can see my living room from the street."

"Black curtains, right?"

"Of course." Sacha opened the exterior door to the building. Another lift ride later, and they were outside his front door.

He slid his key into the lock with shaky hands. Jonah took over and let him inside. The door shut behind them and Sacha disappeared immediately into the bathroom, shutting Jonah out.

Giving him space, Jonah toed his shoes off and ventured further into Sacha's home.

It was exactly as he'd expected it to be—clean, masculine, devoid of much that gave anyone clues to who Sacha really was. For that Jonah had to rely on tangible moments in time that on their own sometimes weren't enough.

Added together, though, they were everything. Sacha was reticent, moody, and so contradictory Jonah could almost have hated him. But he was also fierce, kind, and funny, and there was nothing like his company.

Jonah moved around the flat, checking the fridge for food—there was none, the cupboards for coffee—there was plenty, and Sacha's bedroom for no reason other than bald curiosity.

The room was dark and cool, with black bedsheets and charcoal paint. There was a flat screen TV built into the bare brick wall, and lamps with soft, low-wattage bulbs. Jonah flicked one on and fetched water from the kitchen. He set it on the bedside table as Sacha returned from the bathroom minus his shirt.

"I'd say you looked better, but it would only be because you're half naked. You still look like shit."

Sacha grimaced. "I do not want to know."

"Did you take your medication?"

"Not yet."

"Where is it? I'll get it."

"It is in the drawer in front of you."

Jonah opened the drawer of the bedside table and found a brown prescription bottle tucked beside a bottle of lube and a strip of condoms. He forced himself not to speculate when the lube and condoms had last been of use to Sacha and grabbed the medication.

He shut the drawer with a louder slam than he'd planned, and turned to find Sacha behind him, sitting on the edge of the bed. "You seem angry," Sacha said. "Did I do something I can't remember? I am sorry I didn't find you at the bar, I—"

"You didn't do anything. I'm not angry, far from it." He rattled the pill bottle. "How many of these do you need?"

"Two, maybe more later if they do not work."

Jonah opened the bottle and tipped the pills into Sacha's palm. "Will they stay down?"

"I think so. Is usually only once if..." Sacha blanched and shook his head. "I do not know the words today."

"You don't need them. It's okay."

Sacha swallowed the pills and drank the water Jonah passed him. Jonah took the empty glass to the kitchen. When he returned, Sacha hadn't moved.

Jonah circled the bed, trailing a hand over Sacha's cool skin as he went, stopping to check his pulse. "You should sleep," he said, noting that Sacha's heart rate had slowed from the jackhammer pace it had been at the office. "Do you think you can?"

"Hmm?"

"Sleep," Jonah repeated. "As in, you should get into bed and try."

"What about you? Will you stay?"

Jonah snorted. "Of course. You'd have to call the police to get me to leave you right now."

"I don't want you to stay because I'm sick, Jonah. I want you in my bed."

"I know."

"Do you?" Sacha caught Jonah's hand as he backed up to unbutton his shirt. "I mean, really? Because I have been very bad at telling you what I want."

Jonah took his cufflinks off and placed them on the bedside table, then he knelt in front of Sacha, his hands on his knees, his gaze shifting from the bracelet tied around Sacha's wrist to his pain-stricken face. "You are bad at that, and if this is going anywhere, at some point, you really need to fucking stop, but I haven't been forthcoming with my feelings either, so I'm going to be now. Is that okay?"

Sacha nodded, the movement woozy. Heavy. Jonah wondered if he'd remember the conversation, but a dam had broken inside him. Everything he had to say was coming out whether Sacha remembered it or not.

"I like you a lot," he said. "Like, as in, I can't stop thinking about you. I care about you, and I think you care about me too."

"I do."

"Do you want to be more than friends who fuck?"

"Yes."

Relief made Jonah sway a little. He gripped Sacha's knees tighter. "So do I, and that's all that matters right now. We don't have to define it. But I need you to mean it, Sacha. I can't play this ridiculous game of back and forth with you while you figure out if your feelings are real. I don't have the energy for that, and I don't think you do either."

Sacha stared, for a moment so silent and still Jonah feared he'd made a terrible mistake. His blood roared in his ears, and Sacha's gloomy bedroom closed in on him. *Back off. You don't get to tell him how to behave. He's not a—*

Cool fingers tipped Jonah's chin, forcing his gaze up. Sacha blinked hard, and leaned forwards, pressing his forehead to Jonah's. "It's real. I promise. All of it. I think when my head is clear, I will tell you I am very close to falling in love with you, Jonah Gray."

It was Jonah's turn to stare, but Sacha was already gone. His head slipped from Jonah's, and he rocked forwards, saved from falling only by Jonah's presence in front of him. "Whoa." Jonah caught him. "Come on. Let's get you in bed."

He helped Sacha undress and eased him into bed. He

shed his own clothes, killed the light, and flicked the TV on, and by the time he slid under the covers, Sacha was barely awake.

Jonah lay down beside him, shifting around until Sacha was leaning against him, his head on Jonah's chest. He was still cold to the touch. Jonah tucked the sheets around them and ran his fingers through Sacha's hair.

Sacha sighed. "You are an angel."

Smiling, Jonah kissed his temple. "If you say so. Go to sleep, Ivanov. I've got you."

19

Jonah came awake still stroking Sacha's face. He had no idea how long he'd been asleep, just that the action movie he'd been watching on mute had made way for a documentary on Turkmenistan.

He switched it off and the haze of the early morning filtered through the window—they'd forgotten to shut the curtains. Jonah wondered if the light would bother Sacha when he woke and tried not to picture his red, pain-filled eyes from the night before. He focused on the last words Sacha had uttered before he'd passed out. "...*I am very close to falling in love with you...*" and his heart skipped a beat, for once, not because he doubted Sacha, but because he felt the same. A whirlwind had passed since Sacha had stepped into the lift all those weeks ago, but time could mean whatever they wanted it to, and Jonah's feelings were real.

I could love him. Maybe I already do.

His thumb passed over Sacha's cheekbone.

Sacha hummed.

Jonah stilled and stared down at him. "Are you awake?"

"A little. That is nice. Please don't stop."

Jonah resumed his ministrations. Sacha's breathing deepened as if he'd gone back to sleep, and Jonah let him be until Sacha hummed again, and pressed himself closer to Jonah. "How are you doing down there?"

"Better," Sacha said without opening his eyes. "I am sorry about that."

"Why?"

Sacha shrugged. "I sit on the floor for a moment. I never meant you to find me."

"I know. But I did. And it was okay. What would you have done if I hadn't?"

"I would have got up eventually. I always do."

Jonah slid his fingers through Sacha's hair again, grounding himself in the silky strands. "Can I ask you something?"

"Yes."

"Is your injury from the same accident that killed your mother?"

"Yes. I don't remember it, though. If I did not have the scars beneath my hair I would not know."

"You have scars?"

"On the left side and my neck. Have a look."

Jonah had already seen the scar on Sacha's neck. He reached for the lamp and bathed the room in a golden glow. Sacha sat up slightly, and parted his hair, revealing a curved scar on his scalp. Breath caught, Jonah traced it with his fingertip. "That's big. I can't believe you can't see it through your hair."

"It is old," Sacha said. "Long time ago, but my head hurts sometimes since then. If tired, if I do not eat enough. Sometimes if I come too hard as well, so it is always a danger with you."

"Has that happened? Has fucking me given you a migraine?"

"Once," Sacha said, his lips twisting in a smirk. "The second time we were together. I put my tongue in you, then I fucked you. I did not know it at the time, but it was...a lot for me."

Jonah searched his memories of that heady night, the long hours they'd spent hunched over their computers, and then the breath-taking orgasm Sacha had bestowed on him. He scoured every image that flashed through his mind but found none that clued him into Sacha's discomfort. "I wish I'd known you were in pain."

Sacha propped his head on his hand and stared at Jonah with his unblinking hazel eyes. "Why?"

Because I love you. Jonah shrugged, sidestepping the impact of the startling realisation that it was true—he really did love this infuriating man. "Because you shouldn't have gone through it alone."

"I wasn't alone. You were snoring beside me."

"I don't snore."

"How do you know?"

"Because you're smug enough to have told me a dozen times by now."

"That is maybe true, but why do you want to know I have a headache when you sleep?"

"Maybe the same reason you asked me to stay with you last night."

Comprehension dawned in Sacha's gaze. He reached out and cupped Jonah's cheek with a hand that was now warm, alive, because dear god he'd seemed half dead last night. "I think..."

"What?" Jonah whispered. "What do you think?"

"I think, perhaps, that you are right, Jonah Gray."

A smile split Jonah's face in half. He tried to contain it, but didn't care that he failed.

Sacha smiled too, droll and wry. "I do not know what amuses you so. You are not funny."

"I know. But *you* are."

"And how is that?"

"You don't like it when you lose control of anything...even something as wholesome as this?"

"Wholesome?"

"Yes. We can be good for each other, Sacha. You have to believe that."

"Oh, I do."

"Yeah?"

"Yes." Sacha pulled Jonah towards him. "But there is nothing *wholesome* about the way you make me feel right now, *luchik*."

Jonah let Sacha draw him closer until their bodies were pressed together, chest to chest, limbs entwined, hard lengths straining for release. "You still need to tell me what that means."

"What?"

"*Luchik*." Jonah cringed at his pronunciation. "You've been saying it since we met and I have no idea what it is."

Sacha's slight smirk softened. "I will tell you soon."

"Not now?"

"No. Not now."

"Why not?"

"Because there are other things I want to do." Sacha kissed Jonah's cheek.

It wasn't particularly sexual, but Jonah felt it in every nerve and sucked in a sharp breath. "Do that again."

Sacha kissed him again, then trailed his mouth to Jonah's, and their lips met in a kiss that was as fiery as it was sweet. Despite the frost clinging to the city outside, heat rose between them like a summer storm, familiar, and yet so different to the wildfires of before.

They kissed for unmeasured time, grinding a slow dance that found Sacha beneath Jonah, pulling him down on top of him.

Groaning, Jonah thrust against him, the friction almost unbearable. He wanted Sacha so badly he *ached*, but he moved with caution, watching Sacha for any signs of lingering discomfort.

Sacha caught his face in his hands. "Don't do that."

"What?"

"Hold back. I don't need it." Sacha wrapped his legs around Jonah's waist. His face was still lined with fatigue, but his gold-flecked eyes were bright and clear. He was present, right here, with Jonah. "I want something," he whispered.

Jonah bit his neck, then kissed the red mark he'd left behind. "You want me to ride you?"

"No. I mean, I do, very much. But not right now. Jonah, I want you to fuck me."

Jonah paused in his journey along Sacha's jaw, eyebrows rising in surprise before he caught himself. He'd be lying if he said he'd never thought about topping Sacha, but it was the stuff of fantasies he'd assumed would stay between him and the walls of his solitary showers. Not a reality whispered to him on a frosty winter's morning in Sacha's bed. "Are you sure? I didn't know you did that."

"You never asked."

"Touché. I guess it's never come up."

"Do you want to?"

Jonah fastened his lips to Sacha's in a fierce kiss. Then he broke away and reached for the drawer of the bedside table. "Yes, I want to. I want *you.*"

He found what he needed and sank back on his heels to roll a condom on, adding lube to slick himself. Then he loomed over Sacha again, enjoying the position of dominance while it lasted. "You've done this before, right? I don't want to hurt you."

Sacha rolled his eyes. "You won't hurt me. I have done this before."

"With who?"

"Boyfriend."

"You don't do relationships."

"It was a long time ago. Was young."

You're still young. We both are. But the moment for deep conversations had passed—for now. Jonah zeroed in on Sacha, tracking the rapid rise and fall of his chest, and the flush of his cheeks. A vulnerability that had never graced their physical chemistry before.

He gripped Sacha's leg, holding it to his chest as he lifted Sacha slightly, aligning their bodies. Breath caught, he bore down, blood roaring in his ears, and pressed in deep and slow, still keeping a watchful eye on Sacha's face as his features twisted, his discomfort clear. Sacha had spent enough of the last few days hurting. Jonah couldn't bear to cause him more pain, even if only temporary. He buried himself to the hilt and rubbed Sacha's chest. "Breathe."

"I am breathing."

"Deeper."

"No."

"Yes."

Sacha sucked in a slow breath and closed his eyes. Jonah felt robbed of his hypnotic gaze, but let it happen and kept rubbing Sacha's chest until he began to relax. "Okay?"

"Yes." Sacha smiled and found Jonah's hand. "You do not need to keep asking me that."

Fair enough. Jonah rocked his hips, back and forth, slow circles of maddening, eye-rolling pleasure. He groaned, floating away in the beauty of it. Sex with Sacha had always been a unique alchemy, but this, being inside him, was something else.

He built a rhythm that had Sacha's bed jumping against the wall, pressure coiling in his gut with every drive of his cock inside Sacha. Beneath him, Sacha arched and writhed, a layer of sweat coating his skin, jaw tight, eyes still screwed shut.

"Look at me," Jonah ground out. "I want to see you."

Sacha's eyes snapped open, hazy with need. "Harder. Fuck me harder."

Jonah obliged, ploughing deep with every slow pump of his hips.

Sacha groaned. "Yes. Like that."

His low growl went straight to Jonah's dick. Desperate energy consumed him. His body cried out to hammer into Sacha, but his heart wanted something else.

He kept his torturous pace, each drive a lesson in edging pleasure, until Sacha trembled beneath him, gasping as he started to come.

Jonah watched him, enthralled. Then his own climax caught up with him. He drove in hard, then stilled as pent-up pleasure overcame him, rushing out of him and into Sacha, a harsh, strangled cry his only sound.

It seemed to last forever. Jonah fought for breath, deafened by the heady rush of ecstasy. And then it was over, and he didn't know which way was up, only that he had to take care of Sacha.

He raised his head and began to pull back. Sacha tightened his arms around him. "No."

"I have to," Jonah whispered. "Just for a minute."

Sacha let him go.

Jonah moved fast to ditch the condom and clean up, then he hurried back to the bed.

Sacha hadn't moved.

Jonah found the rumpled bedsheets and tugged them up the bed and over them. "Come here."

"Hmm?"

"Here. I want to hold you."

Sacha sighed and shifted enough to curl under Jonah's arm, his head on Jonah's chest. His hair was damp with sweat and exertion. Jonah smoothed it back and kissed his temple. "Go back to sleep if you like. I'm not going anywhere."

"How did you know?"

"Know what?"

"That is what I was thinking."

"I didn't. I just wanted you to know."

Sacha sighed. "I do not need to sleep. I don't want to miss this with you."

"We can do it again, you know. It's not a one-time thing."

"It really is not, is it?"

"Not even close."

Sacha fell quiet, his gaze fixed on the window. It lacked the twinkly view of Jonah's penthouse apartment, but the brightening morning seemed to captivate him all the same.

It was as perfect as Jonah's wildest dreams. He didn't want

to blink, in case he missed a moment, and they lay in companionable silence until Jonah's phone invaded the bliss.

Jonah groaned. "I don't even know where it is."

"In your pocket?"

"Thanks, Sherlock. I'm naked."

Sacha chuckled and sat up to lean over the side of the bed. He found Jonah's abandoned trousers and retrieved his phone from the pocket. "It is your mother," he said.

The call rang out before he could straighten up and pass it over.

Jonah winced. "She wants to know if you're coming with me tomorrow. I never gave her a straight answer."

"Oh."

"I know. But she'll be fine."

"Fine? About what? I don't understand."

"Fine about you not coming. I'm sorry about that. When we went to the ball, I never factored in all this..." Jonah waved his hand. "Complication."

Sacha snorted. "There is nothing complicated about it. Give me your thumb."

"What?"

Sacha lunged and snatched Jonah's hand, pressing his thumb to the button on his phone in a smooth takedown a wrestler would've been proud of.

Jonah's phone flashed to life. Holding it out of Jonah's reach, Sacha tapped out a message with one hand, then dropped the phone on the bed with a satisfied smirk.

"There," he said.

"There what?" Jonah fumbled for the phone. "What did you just do?"

Sacha shrugged. "I tell her the truth."

"Which is?"

"That I will be there, Jonah Gray, wherever you are, because I do not want to be anywhere else."

20

Christmas Day

Sacha sat back in the aged chesterfield armchair, a wrapped present in one hand, a glass of something sweet and alcoholic in the other. At his feet, a small, red-headed child played with a carriage from the huge wooden train set Jonah had gifted his collection of nieces and nephews, butting it into Sacha's ankles.

"Sorry," Jonah whispered. "I warned you it was rowdy."

Sacha smiled. "Don't apologise. I like rowdy."

"Yes, but only in—"

"Dear god." Jonah's friend, Lily, silenced him with a dainty hand over his mouth. "Whatever you're about to say, don't. I don't need to hear that."

Jonah wriggled free of her grasp. "Since when? You only ever call to grill me about my sex life."

Lily tossed a mince pie at Jonah. It missed and landed in Sacha's lap. Sacha scooped it up and stuffed the whole thing in his mouth before Lily could claim it back. He'd never eaten them before, but since Eleanor had brought the first plate of them out yesterday, he hadn't been able to stop.

Jonah laughed. "You know you're making my mother's year right now, don't you? The amount of those you've put away? They're the only part of this spread she ever makes herself."

"They are good," Sacha said with his mouthful. "She has every right to be proud of them."

"Are you going to open your present?" Lily asked. "It's not much, and I only had Jonah's vague descriptions of you to go on when I chose it."

Sacha wiped his mouth and considered the small package Lily had presented him with after dinner. His only contribution to the pile of gifts under the tree had been the case of Dom Pérignon they'd picked up on the way here, and he felt bad that Lily had thought to buy him a gift. "You did not have to get me anything."

Lily slid over the smooth arm of the chair, landing square on top of Sacha, her small frame the perfect bundle of flesh and bone. "I actually didn't. It's something of mine I wanted you to have. Open it."

Curious, Sacha unwrapped the package. Beneath the gold and red paper, he found a fabric bag not unlike the one that had carried the leather bracelet Jonah had given him before Christmas. Inside was another bracelet made of gunmetal titanium.

"It's magnetic," Lily explained. "They help with my migraines."

Sacha held the bracelet up to the light. It was plain, and yet boldly beautiful. "How did you know they might help with mine?"

"I told her," Jonah said. "Yesterday, when you were in the

shower. Sorry. She asked me how you were and I'm not a good liar."

"I would not want you to be."

Jonah was pulled away before he could answer, yanked onto the floor to play with the pack of wild English children who adored him. He was the fun uncle, and Sacha could've watched him with them all day. Maybe he would, if Jonah could not escape the dog pile he was now beneath.

"You love him, don't you?"

Sacha blinked. Lost in watching Jonah, he'd almost forgotten Lily sitting in his lap as if they'd been friends their whole lives, like her and Jonah. "Why do you ask me that?"

"Because I'm nosy," she said. "I see how you look at him and it's so bloody lovely it almost makes me want a lover all of my own."

"Only almost?"

"Yes. Men are trash. Or maybe I'm just spoilt by having Jonah as my best friend. No one ever matches up to him."

"And they will not," Sacha said absently, slipping the bracelet onto his wrist beside the one from Jonah. "He is special."

"Yes, he is. You know, it's funny...this fake relationship you had. It never felt fake to me. I always knew you'd be here today."

"Did you?"

Lily nodded. "I think you did too."

"Hmm. I think you might be right."

Lily treated him to a megawatt smile, and lounged against him, her eyes drifting closed. Sacha's eyes were heavy too, but the tiredness hanging over him was the good kind, fuelled by twenty-four hours and counting of good food, nice people, and unlimited access to the only soul on earth Sacha had ever considered wanting forever.

It was as if he'd woken up in another world. One that made his bones warm and his face ache from smiling. Jonah lifted his smallest niece high above his head, spinning her around, and Sacha absorbed her exhilaration as though it was his own. At some point they'd go back to the city and to the lives that had brought them together. Sacha couldn't predict their future, but he was not afraid.

Jonah was joy, and Sacha wanted it all.

Later, after more food and alcohol, Jonah stole Sacha away from Lily and hustled him outside.

Sacha laughed. "This is the first time you have forced me to put clothes on, no?"

"It's cold." Jonah draped a scarf around Sacha's neck. "So shut up."

"You said that to me last night."

"I was talking to myself, actually. I'm not used to containing myself with your cock inside me."

Sacha let him have that one. Fucking quietly so someone's mother would not hear was new for him too, but he had no complaints. How could he?

They left the house and took a slow walk around the grounds of Jonah's parents' country estate. The house was huge, but without the ostentatiousness Sacha had expected. It was cosy, warm, and weathered enough that there was nothing grand or obnoxious about it. The grounds were wild too, punctuated by orchards and enormous oak trees.

Sacha loved it. "It is nice here. I don't know why your parents would ever come to the city."

"Work, mainly," Jonah said. "But they're doing less of that

these days. It won't be long before they only drive in for parties."

"I do not understand that either."

"Maybe they like canapés too."

"Maybe." Sacha kicked a pine cone. "I've never had a bad one from your mother."

Jonah laughed, like he had so many times since they'd woken up that morning, wrapped up in each other in a four-poster bed overlooking the mystical land they were walking now. "Tell her that and she'll start planning our wedding."

"There are worse things mothers can do, *luchik*."

"Okay, it's time." Jonah stopped walking, his hand in Sacha's forcing him to do the same. "You need to tell me what that means before I google it and misinterpret whatever it tells me."

"Google what?"

"*Luchik*. For all I know, you're calling me an idiot twelve times a day."

"I am not."

"So what are you calling me?"

Sacha found Jonah's hands and clasped them tight in his own. Despite the brisk chill in the frosty air, Jonah was warm, heating Sacha from the inside out. "It is not a direct translation, but to me it means sun ray, as in you are mine."

"Your sun ray?"

"Yes, or ray of sunshine, whichever, it does not matter. It is what you are to me, and you have always been, despite that we met under the moonlight, yes?"

"If you can call a broken-down lift moonlight, then yes." Jonah's grin was broad, and his eyes shone. "But whatever. I love it. And I'm glad I didn't know until now. You know you said it to me the night we met?"

"Did I?"

"Yes. When you rescued me from William Ratner."

Sacha bristled. That name would never cease to make him murderous. "Yes, well I meant it then, and I mean it now. I know I am not easy sometimes, but I will try to be better, I promise."

"You don't need to do that."

"Oh, I do, because I cannot promise that I will always succeed."

"No one's perfect, Ivanov."

"Is that what you would call me if you married me?"

"Maybe. It's not as kinky to call you by my own name."

"I would take your name. I have no attachment to my own."

"That's sweet." Jonah wound his arms tight around Sacha in a hug that pressed them together in all the right ways. Around them, it began to snow, light, English snowflakes that would not settle and yet still brought life to a standstill. They were fairy dust settling in Jonah's hair, and Sacha watched them pile on top of one another, spellbound, until Jonah nuzzled his neck. "What are you thinking so hard about?"

"I am not."

"Sure about that? You disappeared for a moment."

"I did not mean to. I am right here." Sacha found Jonah's lips and kissed him deeply. "You know you have been an angel for me, don't you?"

Jonah cupped Sacha's face, his thumb stroking Sacha's cheekbone. "You have for me too. I don't think I have ever felt more myself than I do with you."

"I do love you, Jonah Gray. I don't know what that means, or where it will take us, but I feel it here." Sacha brought

Jonah's other hand to his chest, pressing it tight so he could feel Sacha's stampeding heart.

Jonah's answering smile matched the sunshine he'd always been for Sacha. "It means everything, Sacha, because I love you too."

If you enjoyed Angels in the City, you'll probably love Hometown Christmas, Garrett's 2019 Christmas novel. You can find it here. Read on for a short excerpt after the back matter.

PATREON. Not ready to let go of Yani and Gavin? Or looking for sneak peeks at future books in the series? Alternative POVs, outtakes, and missing moments from all Garrett's books can be found on her Patreon site. Misfits, Slide, Strays...the works. Because you know what? Garrett wasn't ready to let her boys go either.

Pledges start from as little as $2, and all content is available at the lowest tier.

NEWSLETTER: Get free stories! **Including a missing moment from Angels In The City!**

For the most up to date news and free books, subscribe to my newsletter HERE.

This is a zero spam zone. Maximum number of emails you will receive is one per month.

EXCERPT: Hometown Christmas:

Yani sensed Gavin's gaze on him as he arranged the sausage rolls on the plate. He poked his tongue out. "Sometimes I do it for fun, okay? Stop eyeballing me."

Gavin popped the tab on a can of Fosters. It was the first time Yani had seen him drink since he'd confessed it was his favourite coping mechanism, and it was Yani's turn to stare. After a moment, Gavin rolled his eyes and shrugged. "Okay okay, I get it. If it's all right for me to drink when I'm happy, then you can play Jenga with meat and greasy pastry."

"You're obsessed with Jenga. Get some new jokes."

"Do something different then." Gavin swiped a sausage roll from the top of Yani's stack. It left an uneven number and Yani glared, but it was fleeting. OCD was losing the day to the sheer joy of seeing Gavin interact with his family—his parents Dawn and Nial, brothers, sisters, and a dozen nieces and nephews. The house was crowded, noisy, and full of life. Yani could tell Gavin didn't feel quite at home, but Yani did. For a moment, he missed his own rowdy family, but the pull to Gavin was too strong in his chest. *There's nowhere I'd rather be.*

He even understood why Gavin hadn't told him where they were going before they'd arrived. How many times had he done the same thing to Bex? Led her down the garden path so no one, not even her, would know he'd backed out at the last minute?

They took the sausage rolls into the living room. A toddler climbed up Gavin's legs and he swung her onto his shoulders. She wrapped her arms around his neck as though she did it every day, but her mother caught her. "Careful, Gracie. You know Uncle G has a bad neck."

Gavin scowled. "Hayley, it's fine. It was years ago."

The conversation moved on, and the toddler stood her ground, but curiosity started a slow, demanding tattoo in Yani's soul. He knew little about the accident that had ended Gavin's military career, or about Gavin's army life at all. For the longest time, he'd convinced himself that he was okay with that, but the deeper his feelings for Gavin grew, the harder it become to believe. *I want to know everything about him.*

At least, everything Gavin wanted to share.

The evening passed in a haze of sausage rolls, Doritos, and cheap lager. Gavin didn't drink much while Yani got quietly sozzled in the corner with a bloke who seemed to be known as "Uncle Giant" to everyone in the house, from the adults to the smallest children.

"He's all right, our Gavin is, you know," Uncle said, when he caught Yani staring. "Sometimes I forget he was ever gone."

"Gone?"

"Yeah. In the army and that. I never saw him for ten years when he was away, and then he didn't want us around when he was in the hospital. Can't say I blame him. We ain't a quiet crowd."

Yani smiled as he absorbed the revelations he knew would never come from Gavin. "Perhaps he doesn't need quiet anymore."

Uncle grunted and opened another can of Fosters. "Why would he? You can be quiet when you're dead."

Purchase or read on Kindle Unlimited HERE.

ABOUT THE AUTHOR

Bonus Material available for all books on Garrett's Patreon account. Includes short stories from Misfits, Slide, Strays, What Remains, Dream, and much more. Sign up here: https://www.patreon.com/garrettleigh

Facebook Fan Group, Garrett's Den... https://www.facebook.com/groups/garre...

BOOKBUB: https://www.bookbub.com/profile/garrett-leigh

Garrett Leigh is an award-winning British writer, cover artist, and book designer. Her debut novel, Slide, won Best Bisexual Debut at the 2014 Rainbow Book Awards, and her polyamorous novel, Misfits was a finalist in the 2016 LAMBDA awards, and was again a finalist in 2017 with Rented Heart.

In 2017, she won the EPIC award in contemporary romance with her military novel, Between Ghosts, and the contemporary romance category in the Bisexual Book Awards with her novel What Remains.

When not writing, Garrett can generally be found procrastinating on Twitter, cooking up a storm, or sitting on her behind doing as little as possible, all the while shouting at her menagerie of children and animals and attempting to tame her unruly and wonderful FOX.

Garrett is also an award winning cover artist, taking the silver medal at the Benjamin Franklin Book Awards in 2016. She designs for various publishing houses and independent authors at blackjazzdesign.com, and co-owns the specialist stock site moonstockphotography.com

Connect with Garrett
www.garrettleigh.com

ALSO BY GARRETT LEIGH

Find information about ALL of Garrett's books at www.garrettleigh.com

www.ingramcontent.com/pod-product-compliance
Lightning Source LLC
Chambersburg PA
CBHW020751190726
48285CB00006B/1985